Haskell Himself

a novel

by

Gary Seigel

FROM THE TINY ACORN...
GROWS THE MIGHTY OAK

HASKELL HIMSELF. Copyright © 2020 Gary Seigel. All rights reserved. Printed in the United States of America. For information, address Acorn Publishing, LLC, 3943 Irvine Blvd. Ste. 218, Irvine, CA 92602

www.acornpublishingllc.com

Cover art by Damonza
Interior design by Debra Cranfield Kennedy

ISBN-13: 978-1-947392-67-0 (hardcover)
ISBN-13: 978-1-947392-66-3 (paperback)

For Gordon

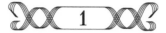

1

FRESH CARDS NEVER HURT

New York City, September 10, 1966

Miss Hogan told me to keep the gun aimed at her while she stared into the black hole of the gun's barrel.

"Perfect, Haskell," she said. Her thick Boston accent unintentionally gave her words a melodic kindness. "Smell the fear. You own that pistol. You're in charge, right?"

I nodded my head.

"Now, stick the gun back into the holster, and let's see it one more time. I'd like a little more firmness in the jaw and maybe more tension in the hips."

I straightened my spine and tightened my leg muscles.

"Remember, this guy does not value human life. He's a thug, and all he cares about is survival. You're not a sixteen-year-old in New York City anymore. You are a tall, thirty-seven-year-old Nevadan cowboy, an uncivilized killer and disruptor of order, surviving in the rough and tough 1840s. Got it?"

I am a tall cowboy, in his mid-thirties, who confronts the Sheriff who murdered his father. Miss Hogan plays the Lawman. Despite any personal qualms I may have about shooting someone in cold blood, I cannot let that interfere with my line reading. I am a vicious, amoral person who knows what he has to do.

I shoved the gun hard into the holster and closed my eyes. Don't worry about practicing the piano. You'll be ready by the December recital. Better not forget to stop at the drug store to pick up Mom's prescriptions and my zit cream. Oh, and with my senior year starting in one week, I better talk to Mom about paying my school fees and tuition. For some reason, we got another bill in the mail marked "late." The problem is, she comes home after midnight every night from work, and I leave so early in the morning. We're like ships in the night. Put all that aside! I must act in the moment. I'm not Haskell Hodge. I'm Killer Murphy.

I took some more deep breaths, feeling prickly all over. I can be this villain. I can inhabit this role. Almost miraculously, I felt a smirk fall across my face.

"All right! Excellent," shouted Miss Hogan. "Boys and girls, do you see that expression? Ah! He loves what he's doing. That's what separates a normal human being from a complete psychotic killer. Now, let me hear your speech."

When I was done, Miss Hogan raised her hands above her head and clapped. "Bravo! Excellent job!" She patted me on the back. This was our last exercise of the day, and I was relieved the two-hour session was over. I was exhausted. Being bad was not easy work. "I'll see all of you next Saturday. Have a glorious day!" She squeezed my arm. "Good job, Haskell. I'm very proud of you."

I don't know how I pulled it off. What made that scene particularly difficult was not only my lack of expertise with guns—I wasn't "feeling" the Old West. No farmhouse set. No props except for the revolver and the holster. We were in my acting teacher's studio. Just office furniture, blue countertop, an oven, a refrigerator, and a flashing Kit-Cat Klock complete with a swinging tail. John Wayne or Montgomery Cliff wouldn't work under such conditions, but that was the point. We were supposed to use our imagination and create our role out of nothing. Be the character. Inhabit his space. This was called Method Acting. I had been taking the workshop for six months, and I'd finally received some praise.

I used the bathroom to change my shirt. By the time I made it to the stairs, the rest of my group had zipped off somewhere, probably for pizza in the Village, without asking if I wanted to join them.

Miss Hogan must have seen the disappointment on my face because she put her arm around me.

"As time passes, they'll warm up," she said. "Don't let it bother you. You're talented. You really get into the roles. Today, I think you kind of frightened them. Who knew there was a psychopath lurking under those thick glasses? You're a delight to have in my class, and you'll be going places."

That was good enough for me. Miss Hogan was not one to dole out compliments freely, so by that afternoon, I decided not to allow myself to feel left out. It was their loss.

I nearly skipped down 14th Street, grabbing a sandwich at Nick's, stopping for a half hour to peruse the discount books at the Strand, then into the subway, up into Midtown, landing just outside the Waldorf Astoria where my mom was attending the annual Real Estate Conference of the Five Burroughs of New York City. She'd be there all afternoon, and I thought I'd surprise her.

Arriving at the end of lunch, I easily spotted her among the three dozen tables in the banquet room, the only woman wearing a bright red summer dress, her blonde hair wound into a tight chignon.

I wasn't sure what time she'd be home this evening—since she usually went out for dinner on Saturday nights with Bob, her boyfriend. I called him Old Bob because he was sixty-five years old, nearly twenty years older than Mom. I'd give her a kiss, say a hello, and maybe steal a crème brûlée off the table.

As I walked closer, I noticed half her lunch still on her plate. Balloons were strapped to her chair, and a big sign in the middle of a flower arrangement said, strangely, "Farewell, Miriam Hodge! We will miss you."

Was she transferring offices? Did someone give her a better offer? Why hadn't she said something? That was the problem; we were never home at the same time and didn't communicate much with each other.

I debated whether I should move closer and join them, say "hello," and, well, start a confrontation: Mom—what's this all about?

On second thought, I remembered Old Bob might have been awarded a contract to build a bridge in Antwerp. Mom had been hinting that if he landed the contract, she might join him for a few weeks and tour parts of Europe, maybe take off for a month. I could deal with that. She certainly had been talking about a European vacation for as long as I could remember.

Before I was born, Mom had been an actress, starring in mostly second-rate films people would watch on double bills at drive-ins. Her *Love* films took place in locations all over the world. *Love in Athens, Love in a Paris Post Office,* and *Love on the Panama Canal* were her better-known pictures. They were filmed, however, in Burbank, and Mom said she was eager to see the real Eiffel Tower and the real Parthenon, not half-baked replicas built on the back lot of a studio.

Was this a bon voyage send-off? I was glad she could put

aside her escrows, mountainous paper work, and late-night appointments to take a breather. Why not? I could easily live in the apartment by myself for a month. I was entering my senior year in the graduating class of 1967, and I might throw some parties. In a recent issue, *Time magazine* said the sexual revolution was in full swing, though you could have fooled me. Maybe having the apartment all to myself would prove advantageous. Once word got out, boys and girls from my academy, even from my theater class, might show up. We'd put on some rock and roll records, eat canapés, play charades, maybe open up a bottle of champagne, and who knows what that could lead to?

I decided I'd wait a bit until I spoke with Mom. She was jabbering away, and it seemed better not to interrupt her. Instead, I wandered past the dining area and through the enormous conference room. It was filled with separate booths. Inside each booth was a table draped with black cloth. A big banner announced the theme of the conference—"Finding Your Fortune in Real Estate." Apparently, instead of hiring a band or a comedian, the organizers had set up two dozen psychics, each with their own space.

In one booth, I saw an old man dressed up as bumbling Professor Marvel from *The Wizard of Oz,* hovering over a crystal ball. Someone else shouted, "Let me read your tea leaves!" and another chanted, "Come. Have your palms read. Experience the magic and the mystery."

I was one of only a few stragglers sauntering through the banquet room. I guess everyone else was finishing dessert. Strangely, no hotel employees stopped me. I mean, I was a teenage kid wearing hush puppies, brown corduroys, and an orange-striped shirt, while everyone else around me seemed much older and all dolled up in suits and ties. I didn't exactly blend in.

As I headed toward the exit doors, a woman dressed Arabian-style with dark pink silk scarves, a veil, even a fake beauty mark under her left eye, called my name. "Haskell? What are you doing here?"

I drew closer. Her booth said she was Madame Scheherazade from Persia, but I knew her as Mrs. Markowitz from the mail room at Mom's real estate office. She wore heavy rouge and blue eyeliner. The bracelets on her wrists jangled as she moved her thick, fleshy arms. If Aladdin had a Jewish grandmother, this is what she would look like.

"Good seeing you again. How's my Haskell doing?" she asked.

"I'm fine, Madame Scheherazade."

I thought I'd get into the spirit of this event, especially since she had created such a cozy environment. Her booth had an Indian rug on the floor, silks hanging from metal bars, and sitar music playing on a portable record player. The incense was a bit strong. I'd make this visit brief.

"You wishing your mom luck?"

"I think so."

"Very nice. You're such a good boy. And you're getting so tall and skinny. What does your mom feed you?"

"Not much. I live on sandwiches."

"Well, I bet they're delicious." Scheherazade laughed. "Has your mother told you anything about her trip?"

At first I thought maybe I should lie and say of course she had, I knew all about it. Instead, I stood there, shaking my head.

"She has not given me any specifics, though I assume Antwerp's a go?" I asked.

Madame Scheherazade swiveled in her seat, set her hands on the table, and looked up toward me. "Have you two not talked about it at all?"

"Not exactly."

"Sit, sit sit. Let's have a little chat."

When I didn't move, she stood up, put her hands on my shoulders and gently pushed me into the chair. Only a small mahogany table now separated the two of us.

"I could be right. I could be wrong. I don't know. Your mom's telling everyone she'll be on an extended leave from work."

"What does that mean?"

"Now don't get all agitated. Miriam doesn't always think things out carefully. She says a year in Belgium. "

"A year?"

"It could turn out to be one month, three months. Who knows? She might get bored. You know your mother. She can't sit for long. Right now, she's under such stress, she's tearing her hair out. Recently she had some very tough clients who cancelled their contract after your mom worked for months negotiating with their lawyers. It's also been a tough year selling real estate. Anyway, she wants a break."

I sat back and contemplated this news. If anyone deserved a break, it was my mother. She was always coming home after midnight, leaving before I went to school, staying gone most weekends for open houses and conferences. Still, it would have been nice if she had woken me up this morning and told me about her move before she announced it to the entire office.

"Mrs. Markowitz, I mean Madame Scheherazade. If she's gone for, let's say, an extended period of time"—a vague, maddening phrase Mom often used— "What will happen to me?"

As I pushed myself off my chair, ready for my quick escape, Madame Scheherazade interrupted. "Don't go yet. I know you're curious, and you'd like to speak with your mom. Perhaps this is not the best time."

"She's right in the other room!"

"Please, sit. Five minutes is all I ask."

She was right. Why confront her now? My heart was beating too fast for me to speak coherently.

"Everything will be fine. You have nothing to worry about." She shuffled a deck of cards and asked me to touch the deck with my fingers. "Let's look into the future. Let's see what the Universe says about all this, shall we?"

I figured, what do I have to lose? I slunk back into the folding chair. Yes, I was furious, but it would do me no good to run into the banquet room and make a scene. I probably needed a cool down.

"Do I get to stay in New York, or is she shipping me off somewhere?" I was now putting two and two together. She had been in touch with my father, whom I barely knew. Now I wondered if Mom were concocting some deal where I might live with him for a year. The last I'd heard, he was in India producing an expensive Cinerama version of Rudyard Kipling's *Gunga Din.*

"There is no way I'm moving to India, I'll tell you that right now. Mom doesn't expect me to follow her to Antwerp, does she?"

Madame Scheherazade shook her head and laughed as she split the deck in half and skillfully shuffled the cards several times.

"I will try to answer many important questions. Please, pull one card from the deck." She took my card and four others placing them faceup on the table. I had seen Tarot cards before in a number of movies, but this deck's graphic illustrations of grotesque animals and deformed human beings looked nothing like those.

She stared at the five cards on the table as if gripped with fear.

"What's wrong?" I asked.

"Let me shuffle them again and see what comes up."

"What was wrong with those cards?"

"Fresh cards never hurt."

"Didn't you like what you saw?"

She didn't answer. Once again, she shuffled them, had me pick a card from the deck, and lay all five facedown on the table.

"Let's do this one step at a time, shall we?" She turned the first card over: a skeleton carrying a scythe. I assumed this was the ominous "Death" card. Couldn't be good news.

"What is this?" I asked.

My hands were trembling. I could feel the blood flow through my veins into my head. My throat tightened and my ears burned. My mother would die in Europe. She'd board a ship that would hit icebergs and sink. Then she'd get eaten by a shark. Or she'd have one of her nervous breakdowns—the woman lives for work—and Old Bob would never know what to do for her. I was the only one capable of calming her down, leading her through breathing exercises, even talking her out of the second martini.

"It's bad, isn't it?" I asked. "This trip will ruin her. Selling real estate is her life. Even on those rare occasions when she and I might eat together at a restaurant, she'd inevitably make conversation with the husband and wife sitting across from us and end up handing them her business card, selling them on the merits of a new building going up on the East Side and speaking of it in such glowing terms, she'd have the couple begging for a brochure before we finished our salads."

Madame Scheherazade crinkled her nose and laughed. "You're a bit much, you know that? Your mother will not go crazy without work. It's quite the opposite. Work is what is driving her crazy. Situated upright, this card merely means the end of one situation and transitioning into something new. No big deal." She smiled, nodding her head, apparently quite satisfied with her explanation. "You're about to experience change."

"Like what?"

"Let's find out." She then turned over the next card, revealing a man hanging from a tree limb, upside down. I'm sure she could see the blood drain from my face as I stared at this card. Not only was the man hanging upside down, he was blindfolded, and his feet and hands were tied up.

"Now what?" I asked.

She waved her hand as if she were shooing away a fly. "Let me turn all your cards over before we draw any conclusions. The cards do not mean anything by themselves. It is the accumulation and coordination of cards that tell the story."

Madame Scheherazade turned over the third and fourth cards. One showed a coiled snake, and the other was entitled "The Fool," displaying a medieval jester with missing teeth.

"Now we're going places. These cards tell an important story. The coiled snake suggests you're asleep. Your mom has ignored you for the longest time. She's not shared with you what's been going on, and now is the time for you to uncoil yourself and face your future."

"Seriously?" Anyone could have come up with that explanation.

"And the 'Fool' card isn't as bad as it appears. He often pretends he's naïve, and yet he knows more than he lets on. In fact, he'll embrace whatever comes his way, careless of the hardships he will face because he knows the truth."

"And what is the truth?"

"You're going on a long journey, one in which you will

encounter great adventures." She folded her hands on the table, leaned slightly forward, and smiled. "Turn over the last card, why don't you?"

I turned it over and felt numb with fear. The card featured a man lying face-down with ten swords in his back. I wouldn't panic. I'd wait to hear the next nonsense she'd make up. A minute from now I'd be on my way.

"This card—the Ten of Swords. It may not mean something bad will happen. It may mean something bad has already happened."

"Like what?"

"Well, it makes perfect sense. The card could mean that the past is behind you and now is the time to forge ahead. It could mean your mother forced you into a situation that you feel is unfair. But the important thing? You'll make the best of it. The Universe is now inviting you to take that big leap into the unknown."

"I'm not a leaper, and I prefer the known over the unknown any day!"

"I'm not sure that's always possible. What these cards ultimately suggest, Haskell, is that you're heading somewhere, and you will hit snags and suffer some disappointments, suffer death-defying hardships or maybe even face enemies. Though this situation may at times grow bleak, you must resolutely carry on and never give up, keeping your chin up and your head high because ultimately you will discover your destiny."

Madame Scheherazade sat back, folded her hands on the table, and nodded her head. She looked thoroughly satisfied, as if she had just completed a marathon or, after years of archeological digging, had discovered the missing island of Atlantis.

"Sounds pretty good, no?" she asked.

I didn't even know how to respond. It seemed as if she was just making all this shit up as she went along, and I was too tired, and maybe too frustrated, to question her. I mean, why bother? She was obviously trying to make me feel better, but I wasn't convinced she knew what she was talking about.

"I should get going. Thank you for the reading."

Madame Scheherazade leaned forward. "Before you go, Haskell, give me your hands."

She placed both my hands inside hers, squeezed them gently as she closed her eyes. "If I may give you a word of advice, dear. I've known you your whole life. That piano recital you gave where you dressed up as Liberace? I was there. And when you landed that Sugar Flakes ad campaign, I bought a dozen of those cereal boxes with you on it, dancing with that animated tiger. I still have them in the closet. And when your mother dragged you into the office on Saturdays because you had no friends to play with, you often helped me with my crossword puzzles. I was so surprised at all the words you knew. You're a real darling, very different from the other boys your age. I've never met anyone quite like you. I know it hasn't always been easy for you, and sometimes kids can be cruel, but you know why, don't you?"

"They're idiots?"

She shook her head. "No, they're jealous of you. You are smart, talented, and unique. I have a strong sense that whatever you do, wherever you go, your only obligation in your lifetime is to be true to yourself. That's all that matters." She let go of my hands and pinched my cheek. "I hope that makes sense." Though she had a big smile on her face, her eyes became watery and she wiped a tear off her cheek. "You can go now, Haskell. May you have a safe and wondrous journey."

I can't say this reading gave me any relief. In fact, if anything, it made me more fearful and angry.

After I arrived home that afternoon, I sat for hours in the den forming the words in my head I would use when I confronted my mother. I was afraid I'd lose it and start yelling, which would make things worse. Eventually, I stretched out across the couch and shut my eyes. As much as I appreciated Madame Scheherazade's efforts to console me, I felt sick to my stomach, as if I had swallowed a stone.

What was to become of me? Would Mom let me finish my senior year at Bonvadine Academy and live in the apartment, alone, even if it's for a whole year? I didn't see her agreeing to that at all.

I hit the back of the sofa with my fists, hoping I could relieve my wrath before she arrived home.

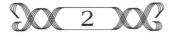
UNEXPECTED ADVENTURES

Three minutes after midnight, I heard the door unbolt.

"Haskell, you up?" Mom found me sitting straight up in a chair in the den, my feet resting on an ottoman. "Oh, Haskell! Sweetheart, why are you sitting in the dark?"

I did not mince words.

"Did the offer go through? Are you going to Antwerp with Old Bob?"

"I hate it when you refer to Bobby that way. He's not old."

"Well, answer me."

"Calm down."

"Don't tell me to calm down! I'm upset. This is terrible. Why would you do this to me? Where will I live?"

"Haskell, we discussed this briefly. I told you if Bob won this contract, I might go with him."

"You never said you'd go with him for twelve months. You said you might make it a vacation for a few weeks."

"Well, I changed my mind."

I buried my head in my hands. My mother was being so selfish, unreasonable, insensitive, and cruel.

"Let me use the bathroom, grab a glass of wine, and we'll talk.

All right? I've been closing escrows and finalizing contracts all night. I could use a libation."

She let out a big sigh as she moved into the bathroom. I heard the toilet flush and the faucet turn on and off. Mom sauntered out, grabbed a bottle of white wine from the fridge, and poured herself a glass.

"Do you want some, darling?"

I threw my arms in the air. She's asking me if I want alcohol? At twelve-thirty in the morning? What is the matter with this woman?

"No, Mom. I do not want a drink."

She pulled up a chair and sat across from me.

"I don't think there are any particular rules regarding when someone can enjoy a libation. You know how hard I've been working, and I know Dot spoke to you a bit. She said she read your Tarot. How did that go?"

"Not very well."

"You could have stopped by my table to say hello."

"I was too pissed off, and I was afraid I'd scream at you."

She sipped her chardonnay. "Just so you know, it's not been easy for me these last few months. I'm spent. Cancelled my date with Bob tonight because I had so much paperwork and so many loose ends. After selling homes and leasing apartments for fifteen years, you'd think I'd be a whiz at catching errors in contracts and knowing what to say and when to say it." She shook her head and put a heavy hand on my shoulder. "I told off a client. I've never done that before. Lost a huge contract I had been working on since January. Worried for the first time in years we wouldn't have the cash to cover all our expenses, so when Bob called me late last night and told me he'd won the contract and asked if I'd join him, believe me, I rolled it around in my head for hours. I knew this would have a big impact on both you and me."

She leaned forward and patted me on the knee.

"Wipe the frown off your face. It's not so bad. I know change is difficult for you. I wouldn't have even considered this, except my doctor's been encouraging me to take some time off. He says my blood pressure is high. My anxiety level has skyrocketed. I've been under such enormous stress."

"Well, reality can be crushing," I said, suddenly weary.

"And I am about to be crushed like a roach, so I've decided I'll take Bob up on his offer before I die of a heart attack." She pulled a cigarette out of her purse, slightly flattened, and lit it. "And this is a win-win situation. It really is, for you and for me."

"How do you figure that?"

"You, my dear, will spend your senior year in Southern California. I know this comes as a surprise, but you're going to love it. It's so exciting, I can't tell you how happy I am to get you out of New York."

"I love living here."

"Yes, but it's not the New York I remember. You can't walk through the park at night, and I'm always worrying that something will happen to you. Your Uncle Ted and Aunt Sheila invited you. You're in for the time of your life. You'll learn to play baseball, see shows at the Hollywood Bowl, and visit the brand-new, beautiful music center. And of course, Disneyland. Didn't you just tell me they opened up a train ride featuring dinosaurs?"

"I'm not ten years old."

Not just any dinosaurs. This train ride takes you across a volcanic mountain where you see the 100-million-year-old battle between Tyrannosaurus and Stegosaurus, the latter of which compensates for his smaller size with two brains, armor plates, and a death-dealing tail. As much as I wanted to see it firsthand, I could wait until after I graduated from the Class of 1967 at Bonvadine Academy.

"You know, Mom, you can travel as far as you want. Go on a moon landing for all I care, but let me stay here in New York and finish school."

"Sometimes in life, Haskell, adventures appear unexpectedly. You have so many surprises ahead of you. You will have the time of your life. My sister's house has its own swimming pool!"

"I don't know how to swim."

"Your uncle will teach you. In fact, he's so excited about having you join their family, he's already arranging a ski weekend."

I don't ski. I don't swim. I could watch baseball, though I had never played the game.

I felt a churning in my stomach. "I really want to stay here. I'm old enough to live by myself."

"I can't afford rent on top of my living expenses in Belgium. And I hate to break it to you, but I can't afford your private school if I'm not working."

I stared at her for a long minute before I ran into the bathroom. I had eaten some pizza earlier and thought I might throw it all up. I could manage a good dry heave, but my stomach still hurt, as if the dough had been laced with pebbles instead of pepperoni. I drifted into my bedroom, curled up on the bed, and buried my head in my hands. I took some deep breaths. Even with the coolness from my window air conditioner blowing directly on me, I felt as if my skin was on fire.

Mom trudged into my room and sat on the edge of the bed.

I lifted my head from my pillow and wailed. "This is one big bag of awful. Kill me now! I will not move to California. I won't know anybody. I'm so happy here. Miss Hogan gave us an exercise today where I had to play a psychopath from the 1840s. She said I did a terrific job. I can't stop my acting lessons when I'm having a major breakthrough. What if I moved in with Mary?"

"Your old babysitter? I don't think so."

"Well, why not? We could work out some financial arrangement. I'm sure she'd love the company, and we could rent a room from her."

The only downside of living with Mary? She collected tiny, delicate crystal figurines, and every time I stayed with her, I broke one. The first time, I snapped the fishing pole held by a little Dutch boy, and the second time, the ear of a dainty Victorian lady came clean off. Truly, my six-foot-two-inch frame made me like a bull in a crystal shop. I'd be extra careful. I'd take my shoes off before I entered her dining room. I'd keep my hands in my pockets and my elbows pointing inward at all times.

"I don't think that is an option. I already told your aunt and uncle you'll be moving in, and they're setting up a room for you."

"You did all this without discussing it with me first?"

"How many times do we have to go over this? I didn't know if Bob's job was one hundred percent approved until one in the morning. Frankly, I thought you'd be excited. In the winter, you won't be lacing up your galoshes or putting on layers of clothes, and in the summer, you can wear shorts all the time. Remember, I lived in L.A., so I know you'll have a wonderful time. You're only a couple of bus stops from the studios! You want to act in movies? Los Angeles is where you should live, not New York. You'll thank me for this some day. You really will."

She bent down and kissed me on my forehead, then inexplicably tiptoed out of the room. I wasn't asleep. Who was she afraid of waking up? Her conscience?

3

GO WEST, YOUNG MAN!

My mother seemed especially self-centered, even heartless. This just wasn't like her. The stress at work had caused internal damage, maybe eroded parts of her brain causing irrational decision making. I had no choice. I should take my fate into my own hands. Move near Hollywood? I'm sure there are worse places, I told myself. Still, I felt I'd be better off finishing my senior year at Bonvadine Academy.

Change could come later.

On Monday, I decided I'd visit my favorite teacher and probably my best friend, Mr. Varnish. We had finally connected via phone. I told him all about my mother's move to Antwerp and her determination to move me out west, where I'd live with the Teitlebaums. I even mentioned my encounter with Madame Scheherazade and her insistence that I jump into a new life, and he suggested I stop by the school around ten that morning for a chat.

I entered the hundred-year-old brick building on 58th Street and took the stairs until I reached the third floor. It was only one week before my senior year would begin, and I figured he was setting up his classroom, Room 301A. Sure enough, I caught him hanging posters. Upon seeing me, he shouted, his voice bellowing across the hallway with such unbridled enthusiasm it nearly made me dizzy: "Go West, young man!"

What a dumb joke! I thought.

"I'm not going west. I'm staying here. Any chance I could live with you and your wife?" I asked. "Rent a room? I wouldn't be any trouble. And what are the possibilities of applying for a scholarship? My mom can no longer afford my tuition."

Mr. Varnish wore a Yankee's baseball cap over his bald head, dirty jeans, and an old T-shirt, appearing as if he hadn't shaved in days. This was a bit of an adjustment. I was used to seeing him clean-cut and dapper, his socks almost always matching his colorful bow ties. I'd often sneak into his office after school, wondering if he'd be wearing the purple or the green ones. Boots or loafers? Suspenders? No suspenders? And always demanding ten minutes of his time so we could discuss challenging books.

He was, in many ways, my best friend, and perhaps my greatest fan. When I was thirteen, Varnish attended the student body talent show. I dressed up as Liberace—one of the most popular entertainers of our day and a real showman in flamboyant rhinestone jackets and elaborate boas and feathered hats. He was famous for his candelabras. In my parody of him, I wore a sequined jacket decorated with little candles, tux pants, and a bit of glitter on my face. Instead of playing a classical piece of music, I sat down, stretched my fingers as if I were about to conquer a concerto, and whipped out "How Much is that Doggie in the Window," boogie-woogie style. It was a sensation. Everyone in the audience clapped and cheered afterwards. I surprisingly did not get flak from any of my schoolmates—maybe because everybody loved Liberace, and there was a strict no bullying policy in our school.

My Social Studies teacher, an ex-war hero with a steel leg, had taken me aside and whispered, "Next time, you might want to imitate someone not so effeminate. Liberace is a closeted homosexual. There are better male pianists you can impersonate."

"Like who?" I asked. "What other famous pianists are there?" I made a big deal of it because Liberace was, as I said, hugely popular. He starred in his own movie. Even had his own TV show. His latest concerts at Radio City Musical Hall sold out every seat. What pianist was bigger than him?

I immediately sought solace from Mr. Varnish, and he said, "Don't give it another thought. Just be you."

"But being me," I told him, "doesn't always feel good."

"Get used to it, kiddo," he said. "Life is not easy for any of us. We must have perseverance and, above all, confidence in ourselves."

I don't know who he was quoting, but it made sense. I felt misunderstood, sometimes thoroughly ignored, but I always had Mr. Varnish as a sort of back up. And now I would not even have that. I'd live with a family I barely knew. No friends. No allies. No teachers familiar with my quirks.

Terrible things could happen out west. Mom thought New York City was dangerous? I heard about this area of the Valley where waste and toxic chemicals from a former nuclear and rocket-testing facility seeped into the soil, possibly affecting crops and all the food we would eat. After devouring a number of salads, I might become radioactive and turn into one of those green, hairy creatures I read about in my comic books.

And the beaches wouldn't be much safer. I heard about these shark attacks at Zuma Beach in Malibu. I might wade into the Pacific Ocean, and next thing you know, my aunt and uncle would be searching for me and all they'd find is my torso. No legs. No arms. No neck or head. I'd be shark bait for sure.

"Any chance I could get a scholarship?" I asked Varnish.

Mr. Varnish stroked his chin. "If anyone deserves a scholarship, it's you, Haskell. You're a straight-A student, right?"

"True."

"You study all the time."

"I do."

"Your papers are well-written and well-researched."

Yeah. Yeah. I know all that.

"I could write a letter of recommendation."

Yes!

"Would you?" I asked.

My heart beat faster.

"One essential problem remains. Where would you live? You can't stay with us."

"Why not? I could get a job on the weekends and pay some rent."

Varnish shook his head slightly as he continued sticking pushpins into the poster, a large portrait of Ernest Hemingway.

"First of all, we live in New Jersey. It's an hour commute each way into the city, and my wife's mother might be moving in with us in a few months. Also, sometimes Mrs. Varnish and I sleep in separate bedrooms because I snore, and we have this wolfhound who sheds hair all over the place."

"It's okay, Mr. Varnish," I said. "You had me at New Jersey."

I did not want a two-hour round-trip commute.

"Any ideas where else I could room for a year?"

"Here is my advice. Go to Los Angeles. If I were your age, I'd wake up every morning, put on my wet suit, and surf in the Pacific Ocean. I'd roller skate down the boardwalk in Venice Beach—a very exciting place with poets and writers and artists—

and put on a tie-dye shirt, a cowboy hat, and big boots. I'd play the guitar on Sunset Boulevard, an empty coffee can at my feet, and sing Kingston Trio songs, like 'Tom Dooley.'

"Most importantly? Take advantage of this great opportunity. Living with your aunt and uncle and your cousin will be a healthy change. With your mom working such long hours, you've spent a lot of time alone. Now you'll see what it is like interacting with a real family. If I were you, I'd jump at the chance."

I walked out of Varnish's office with my head bowed. Mom kept singing the praises of my aunt and uncle and how wonderful living with them would be, but my memories of my cousin, Hope, were not pleasant. On their last visit, Hope, who was six at the time, loved taking the elevator to the ninth floor of our apartment building because she'd press all the buttons on the panel, forcing us, and whoever else was in the elevator, to endure close personal proximity for far longer than most New Yorkers could bear. This didn't happen just once. It happened at least three times, and afterwards, we'd be standing in the hallway, in front of my apartment, and my aunt would sigh, massage her temples, pausing for the longest time until she'd finally spoken. "Hope? Please do not do that again. I find it very irritating."

That's it? That was all she was going to say? I mean, if she were my daughter, I would have spanked her, or better yet, made her sit in her room for a few hours. Maybe wear an "S" around her neck for Spoiled Child.

She also wouldn't get dressed on time. Made us late to a special dinner one night. Broke Mom's crystal lamp in the living room, and threw several tantrums when my uncle insisted she go to bed.

I thought about all this as I walked home from Bonvadine Academy, up and down the streets, mulling over what exactly

I'd tell my mother. That evening, she brought in meatballs, calzones, and a Caesar salad from Lombardi's. I waited until we had devoured all the food before I reminded Mom of Hope's ill-temper and childish behaviors.

"What bothers me is that Aunt Sheila hardly ever corrects her. Not even a slap on the wrist or a 'Go to your room.'"

"Aunt Sheila does what she has to do."

"No," I said, shaking my head. "If Al Capone had been Sheila's child, she would have sent him to bed early without his hot cocoa and biscotti and have come up with some lame excuse for his murder spree."

"Oh, Haskell, parents may treat their children a little differently in California, and she's not six any more. Hope is nearly nine years old. Wait and see. You've never had a sibling. It will be a healthy change."

My anxiety worsened. What did I know about living with a nine-year-old? I hadn't been with a nine-year-old since I was nine. And what would it be like living with an aunt and an uncle? I'd never lived with a "father" figure before. My dad called me periodically, like once a year, but I rarely ever saw him. Frankly, I wasn't sure I'd get along with Uncle Ted, since all he ever talked about was baseball. What would we have in common?

I felt a headache coming on.

And then Mom did what she often did in her real estate negotiations: she sweetened the deal.

"So, you were saying that you just did an exercise where you played a villainous cowboy? Is that right?"

"Yes, and it went well."

"I think I found you a screen test in Hollywood for a part in a TV Western."

"Really?"

"You'd be playing a pioneer kid in the Old West who has been living alone most of his life. The Cartwrights find him wandering in the fields, and they invite him in."

"Are we talking *Bonanza*?"

I was excited. This was TV's number-one show.

"Could this lead to a regular part?" I asked eagerly.

"No, I don't think so. Turns out the kid's a bit twisted. Gets in fights all the time, and he ends up drowning at the end of the episode. Still, what a great way to start your adventures in Los Angeles!"

My father, Tony Pawlikowski, whom I had met a half a dozen times, had connections with the company that produced *Bonanza*. It was a Western about a three-time widower and his three adult sons living on a big ranch called The Ponderosa, and every week they'd face numerous challenges. Sometimes they were silly stories, such as the time when one of the sons, Hoss Cartwright, fights a tribe of leprechauns. Most often, though, the episodes were more serious. In this one, I'd be playing a maniacal orphan who apparently can't swim.

My initial instincts? After six months in Miss Hogan's class, I could tackle this role.

The only problem was the kid was supposed to be short and rather tough and extremely handsome. I was none of those things. I was tall, weighing less than 150 pounds. A real beanpole. I wasn't exactly tough either, and with my big ears, I was certainly not handsome.

"Mom, I don't think this will work out. My physical appearance is all wrong." I pored over a description listed in the classified section of *Variety*. "He twirls a gun in the air?"

"We'll get you a gun tutor."

"There's no such thing. Come on!"

"They have gun tutors all over Los Angeles. We'll look them up in the Yellow Pages. An actor can transform himself into any role," my mom said, her face gleaming, mimicking my acting coach. "If they like you, they'll make adjustments."

"No one is going to take me seriously as a handsome, rugged boy in town. I'm too scrawny."

"Perfect! Your mom's dead, remember? So, she's not been around to feed you."

Maybe she's not dead. Maybe she just went to Antwerp, I thought.

"And I'd probably need to ride a horse, right? It even says here. 'Horse riding experience necessary.' You have to read the fine print, Mom. I've never ridden a horse. I've never even ridden a bike! I don't even roller skate!"

"They'd probably bring in a stunt double for those scenes," she said, dismissing my concern with a wave of her hand. "Well, if you don't want to try out for that part, that's fine. I have another great idea for you."

"What's that?"

"Sheila is good friends with the mother of a boy about your age who is also into acting. He attends the same high school you'll be attending, so he's someone you can hang around with when you arrive in Encino. He's quite the talent, apparently."

"What's his name?"

"Her last name is Stoneman." She grabbed a piece of paper from her purse. "And his name is Henry."

"I never heard of him."

Yes, I lied to my own mother. I had, in fact, seen his name mentioned in *Variety*. He had won a small part recently in a Disney film.

"We'll arrange for you boys to meet, and you can take it from there. You two have so much in common. It will be wonderful."

That night, I dug through my latest copies of *Screen Magazine* and spotted a photograph of Henry Stoneman. Quite handsome, wearing black jeans and black shirt with rhinestone buttons and a cowboy hat. He was in John Wayne's last movie, so he could probably ride a horse, use a gun, and speak fluent Apache. He had eighteen film and TV credits. Eighteen!

I fell into a deep, angry, solid funk, desperately hoping my mom might change her mind and this California nightmare would dissipate into dust.

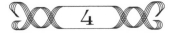

4

THE INFAMOUS PARTY

Three days before we were to fly west, I got a phone call from Debra Shapiro. Debra was my ice-skating friend from school, although I wouldn't skate with her. I'd sit on the bench and watch her do bunny hop jumps at the rink. I never skated because Mom followed the formula: Haskell + Skates = Memorial Hospital.

We also would occasionally study together. I tutored her in Algebra for free, but I hadn't seen her all summer. She had been a camp counselor in The Poconos while I stuck around the city, a volunteer at a performing arts camp in Central Park.

"I didn't realize you were moving to California." She sounded quite excited. "I wish I were going."

"I'll trade places," I said, and I told her the whole scoop. Mom's European excursion with Old Bob. My spoiled cousin. My fear of sharks and nuclear fall-out in the Valley. "In other words, Debra, I prefer staying in New York." I gave as strong a hint as possible that I was looking for a room to rent.

"Well, we'll miss you. Can we see you before you go?"

"Probably not."

"Come to my birthday party this Saturday. Remember where I live?"

I had not been invited to any of her previous parties, not even her Bat Mitzvah, but I had occasionally joined study groups at her house. Her parents were very rich, and she lived in a three-story brownstone near the Hudson River.

"How did you find out I was leaving town? Did you bump into Mr. Varnish?" I asked.

"Your mom saw my mom at Bloomingdale's. You're leaving Sunday?"

"That's the plan."

This phone call felt like a conspiracy engineered by two moms—a backhanded invitation or a pity offer.

I told her I didn't think I could go. I'd be too busy packing.

"Come for an hour. We'll all wish you farewell. You'd see everybody from our class."

Now I felt even more miserable. Was I the only kid in the class not invited already? "Debra, this seems very last minute."

"Don't feel that way. You just weren't around. I'm not pulling your leg. Honestly, I can't imagine not seeing you before you're three thousand miles away. Please come."

How could I turn that down? She seemed genuinely excited. Though most of my clothes had been shipped, I still had a pair of corduroy slacks, a clean white cotton shirt, and my new Keds. Mom said I should be fashionably late, after the crowd shows up. Even though I was a stickler for promptness, my mom knew a thing or two about party etiquette, so I deliberately showed up an hour late. As I took the steps up to her front door, I could see through the windows. A big banner read, "Happy Birthday, Debra." The living room, nearly the size of our whole apartment, was empty. Where was everyone? I rang the doorbell, waited almost a whole minute before Ellen, one of the girls in last semester's biology lab, let me in.

"Guess who's here?" she shouted. "What took you so long?" She grabbed my hand and led me down a long hallway into the den, a wood-paneled room with floor-to-ceiling bookshelves, filled with titles I didn't recognize. Law books, maybe, on legal procedures, contracts, torts.

Debra, who had been sitting in a circle with a dozen other students from class, stood and gave me a hug. "I'm so glad you came. You're just in time. Let's make room for Haskell."

At first, no one moved, until finally Sheldon stood up, gave me his spot, and squeezed between Janice and Marcia.

"So, it's time for the game," Debra announced proudly. She placed an empty Coca-Cola bottle in the center. We would each have a turn at spinning the bottle and, whoever it pointed to, could either kiss the person or take a drink.

"We did this years ago!" someone complained.

"Come on, Debra. Think of something better!"

Debra raised the Coke bottle in one hand and a rare bottle of Scotch in the other. "We'll give it a new twist," she announced, waving the whisky above her head. I saw several kids raise an eyebrow, but it sounded quite exciting. I had never drunk Scotch before, and what better way to get your first kiss than as a bit of inebriated fun?

Soon it was my turn. I spun the bottle, and when it stopped spinning, it pointed directly at Debra. I knew what my choices were, and I boldly chose the kiss. I fell onto my knees and leaned toward the lovely, beautiful Debra with her long hair and sweet perfume. As I kissed her, she quickly pulled back, wiping my saliva off her lips and laughing.

"Oooo. That was so wet. It was like kissing bathroom tile." Everyone joined in on the laughs, and I rolled my eyes and threw my hands in the air.

Sheldon, who was sitting on my left, whispered, "You'll do better next time. Don't worry about it."

The next time came too quickly. Sally Adler, a girl in last semester's English class, spun the bottle, and when it landed on me, she chose the kiss. I was quite flattered. This time I prepared myself, hoping my kiss would be more luscious than wet. I swallowed and dried my mouth with the palm of my hand.

"Oh, Haskell! Kissing you is as erotic as kissing a concrete slab." Everyone got another big chuckle out of that one, too. Of course, she should brag. With the pimples all over her face, she was lucky I kissed her at all. I was so embarrassed. I walked out into the hallway, searching for the room with all the jackets, when someone grabbed my arm and pulled me into the bathroom. He locked the door and pushed me against the wall.

"Don't say anything," said the boy. He put his index finger over my lips. I could hardly breathe. I had no idea what would happen next. "I'm Tom, Debra's brother."

I had never met him before. I thought he attended film school in Los Angeles, where I was heading.

"That was awful what they said to you. It's not your fault."

We were standing inches apart. Our noses nearly touched. I glanced down at his freshly ironed shirt through which I could see his muscles. My heart was beating so fast, I thought it might fly out of my chest and roll around on the floor in delirious circles. All I could do was swallow a few times, I was so nervous.

"You just have to kiss the right sex, and you'll be fine," he said, leaning in and kissing me. Though his breath smelled of alcohol, we made out for ages. Okay, maybe only a minute, but it felt like hours, until someone wanting the bathroom knocked on the door and wouldn't leave.

Tom told the intruder: "This house has six bathrooms, you moron."

And before I knew it, he was pulling down my zipper. I immediately panicked and threw open the door. My friends were standing right there, staring at me. At my open zipper. Maybe at the bulge in my pants. Who knows? They saw Tom. They saw me. It doesn't take an A in calculus to piece it together. They discovered a secret even I wasn't quite sure existed.

Within minutes I found myself running out of the brownstone, heading toward my apartment building, tears streaming down my cheeks. Once I made it inside the lobby, instead of waiting for the elevator—it seemed stuck on the sixth floor—I took the stairs up all nine flights. Breathless, I unlocked the bolts on our front door, flew down the hallway and into my room, slamming the door behind me. Soon, I heard my mom's door squeak open. She appeared wide-eyed, wearing fuzzy slippers and a pink housecoat. "You're home so soon. What happened?"

"I don't want to talk about it."

"You sure? I'm all ears."

"I DON'T WANT TO TALK ABOUT IT!"

I had vowed I'd keep my cool before Mom left. Obviously, I was violating my promise.

I lay in bed kicking my feet and hitting my head against the pillow, so frustrated by the humiliation. How could I ever face my friends again? But then I remembered—I may never have to because I was moving. What am I worrying about?

The next morning, I announced I was now glad we were leaving New York City, and I looked forward to living on the West Coast. "I can't wait. The sooner we leave the better. California, here I come. Haskell Hodge Goes West!"

My mom shook her head as she buttered some toast. "Something really awful must have happened last night. Are you sure you won't share?"

"I'm very sure! Now, drop it."

It was not something I would ever share. I would bury that evening's events deep inside my brain, sequestered from oxygen, hidden from view, and never unearth them. It would be like one of those time capsules, left untouched for fifty years, maybe longer, and I would be dead before my secret ever got divulged.

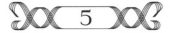

5

THE FLIGHT WEST

Of course, a few days later, I changed my mind.

Mom and I were flying together for two reasons:

Reason One: Bob had a home in L.A. Also, one of his sons lived in Reseda, near where my Aunt lived. After a short visit, he and Mom would rent a car, drive up the coast of California, stop in Big Sur to visit another one of his kids—Bob had five sons—and who knows, while making their way up toward San Francisco where they'd catch a Paris flight, they might tour the Hearst Castle. As if there weren't enough castles in Antwerp.

Reason Two: Mom agreed she'd fly with me because I had a serious flying phobia. I had never flown on an airplane before. All I knew about airplanes was either from John Wayne's *The High and the Mighty*—a nail-biting, edge-of-your-seat film about a plane with serious engine trouble—or from a much more recent and scary TV episode of *The Twilight Zone* featuring William Shatner as a nervous passenger who spies a hairy monster standing on a wing, pilfering wires and motor parts. The plane lands safely, but had the monster enjoyed a bit more time, who knows what might have happened?

I knew full well this was supernatural fantasy. Still, I was paranoid, and I did not want to sit anywhere near the wing. I wouldn't have it any other way, and I was grateful Mom was holding my hand as the plane took off. She was still holding it as we left the Eastern Seaboard, and our old life, in the jet stream.

"There is something I must share," I said, pitching my voice so it was just audible above the noise of the plane. This would be the last chance for a face-to-face chat in a while, so I figured, what the heck?

"Sure, honey. What's bothering you? Is it about Debra's party? You seemed so upset."

Despite my determination to bury the memory, I felt I had to let it out, and Mom was the only person I could tell. She was my mother; she was biologically wired to love me no matter what, right?

When I finished my tale, I let out a deep breath. After an excruciating few seconds of silence, during which I squeezed my eyes shut so I couldn't see the horror on her face, I asked, "Mom? Am I a big fat homo?"

"Oh, come on, Haskell, you're not fat."

I turned in my seat and looked at her incredulously. "Mom, you're missing the point! I've never felt what I felt when I kissed Tom. It was incredible." Tears streamed down my cheeks. "I am in such big trouble."

My mom looked around to see if anyone was taking notice of our conversation, then she turned toward me. "You're blowing the whole thing out of proportion," she said in a stage whisper. "Here, wipe your face." She handed me a handkerchief. "Your first kiss was terrific. Just be happy with that accomplishment."

"If we're counting, it was my third kiss, and it was far better than the first two. It doesn't take an Einstein to figure out why.

I kissed a boy, and I liked it. And that makes me a homo."

"Stop calling yourself a homo, for God's sake." My mom let go of my hand and leaned back against the head rest. "All that happened was a kiss. No big deal. I've kissed a girl once or twice."

"No, you didn't."

"I did. I even had a dalliance with a fairly famous movie star. I can't tell you her name, but the initials are BS."

"Barbara Stanwyck?"

"I'm not telling you. We met at a cocktail party, and she took me on a private yacht. Whisked me off to Catalina."

"Now I know you're making this up. You hate Catalina."

"The affair didn't last long, but I'm not sure I would have objected if it had."

"I think there's something seriously wrong with me. I really do."

"What a bunch of nonsense! This is the sixties. Anything goes these days. Take a trip up to San Francisco—you'll see."

"I don't know, Mom. I wished I could have been one of those cartoon characters whose head and neck sink into their bodies. I even prayed the homo part of me would disappear. Also, I would have liked it had Debra called me afterwards and said, 'It's fine, Haskell, don't worry about it.' Of course, she hadn't. She and all the others were probably relieved the queer wasn't coming back to school. Thank God Haskell Hodge has gone west! is what they're probably saying."

My mom reached over and held my hand again. "Oh, Haskell, what will I do with you? I wish you hadn't shared all this with me right now. I've been going through so much. I would appreciate some time without any bombshells. No hassles. No sordid problems. I am so ready for a long vacation." She grabbed her purse from under the seat and retrieved another handkerchief. She handed it to me, and I wiped away the tears from my cheeks and the snot from my nose.

"Bob was making such a big deal about what hotels we'd stay at on our way up the coast. I said we should just drive up the entire way, check into the St. Francis, and call it a day. What do you think? My mouth's been watering for some good sourdough bread, a bowl of clam chowder, and a hot dish of yummy fried clams."

I didn't know what to say. I had never seen her so happy.

Mom squeezed both my hands inside hers. "If you love me, as I know you do, you'll figure it all out and not make a big deal of it. I could use some peace of mind. Your mother is exhausted."

I quickly loosened my hands from hers, sat back, and tried to blink this nightmare out of my head.

Maybe I'd be better off if the monster on the wing would crash through my window, grab me by the neck, and whisk me off to his polar planet. I imagined I'd find it populated with human beings who were exactly like me. No mothers. No Teitlebaums. They'd even call it Planet Haskell, where fitting in was easy because all Haskells think and act exactly the same.

Mom lit a cigarette, and though she angled herself so she faced the aisle, puffing the smoke toward the door of the pilot's cabin, the smell stuck in the back of my throat.

6

BRUNCH AT THE QUEEN'S ARMS— ENCINO, CALIFORNIA

After my mom took off with Old Bob, I spent a day or two adjusting to the new time zone, so I slept quite a bit. I also enjoyed settling into my new room—putting up posters, arranging my books, comics, and records. By the fifth day in Encino, after an unpleasant encounter with my cousin Hope, I noticed the little minx was ignoring me. I'd walk down the hallway and say "Hi," but she wouldn't answer, her face stiff, like a tough piece of beef jerky. In fact, during Friday night's dinner—the Teitlebaums celebrated *Shabbat* with candles, a *challah*, and a takeout brisket from Gelson's with carrots and potatoes—Hope insisted on taking food to her room. When my aunt asked why, she announced: "I am not in the mood for a family dinner tonight."

Not surprisingly, my Aunt did not argue. She merely put a plate together and placed it on a tray. We waited until Hope meandered down the hallway toward her bedroom before the three of us—Uncle, Aunt, and I—gobbled down the delicious food and chatted about my mother's bold decision to leave her real estate empire behind and live with Old Bob.

"Will Miriam survive a month, let alone a year, playing

housewife and not working?" my aunt asked. "Domesticity seems so outside your mother's field of knowledge."

I didn't argue.

"Beside the fact, Bob is hardly monogamous. Your mother said she knows he sleeps around a bit and has women in different ports. Plus, he's married. His wife won't give him a divorce, and you know what my sister tells me? She says, 'Good grief, Sheila. It's the '60s, not the nineteenth century. I've not been exactly the Virgin of the East.'"

Generally, I turned a deaf ear on my mother's sex life. Occasionally, if it were a tale from her past, involving some off-the-set romance with one of her co-stars, I might listen. If, however, she had a meal with an escrow officer and it led to more than dinner and a movie, I'd tune the story out completely.

I'm sure she shared all her stories with her sister during their extensive Monday morning phone calls, and Aunt Sheila listened enrapt and enthralled. She, who married Uncle Ted at eighteen, probably lived vicariously through Mom's sordid stories, including her midnight swim with the young actress Angie Dickinson, a late night romp with a bellhop at The Beverly Hills Hotel, and twenty-four hours with Frank (as in Sinatra) in his private cave at the Sands Hotel. These are the ones I remember. That last one, especially, I found quite outlandish. I think Mom made it up since, according to my research, Miriam Hodge and Frank Sinatra were not even in the same city at the same time that weekend. But as I said, Mom loved telling these tales, and my aunt soaked it all in.

It was probably best that Hope was not at the table. I also figured that over time the rift between Hope and me would mend. Whatever had upset her, she wouldn't hold on to it forever.

The next morning, my Aunt Sheila suggested we all go out

for a lovely Saturday brunch and reacquaint. "This will be a wonderful way for us to kibitz and overcome any animosities or difficulties we may have experienced so far," she said. "What do you say?"

Once again, Hope resisted. "I will stay home. You guys go and enjoy yourselves." Hope ran down the hallway, and I heard a door slam. I had been sitting across from my aunt and uncle at the breakfast table, poring over the Calendar section of the *L.A. Times*. As soon as my aunt and uncle heard their daughter slam her door shut, they gave each other a stare, stood up at the same time and marched down the hallway toward Hope's bedroom. Both parents raised their voices several decibels. Uncle yelled, "You're going with us. If you stay home, we're removing the TV from your room, and you'll lose TV privileges for the entire weekend!"

Well, the threat of a catastrophic punishment must have done the trick. By eleven-thirty, my little cousin, dressed in a sweet pink-checkered pleated skirt and a white blouse, crawled into the back of the station wagon, her arms firmly folded across her chest, wearing a scowl the size of Montana.

As we approached The Queen's Arms, a fancy restaurant smack in the center of Encino, I was struck by its architecture. Located on Ventura Boulevard, next to a car dealership on one side and a Piggly Wiggly market on the other, this building resembled a medieval castle complete with turrets, flags, a slated roof, and stained glass windows.

Inside was a maze of dark corridors guarded by suits of armor. Dragons were everywhere—on the goblets, engraved in the wooden legs of the round tables, and painted on the walls. Even the maître d' had a fire-breathing dragon emblazoned on his vest. I thought it was a fair attempt at imitating the thirteenth century, or whatever century they had in mind.

We sat in a booth shaped like a crescent moon. I was on one end, then my uncle, my aunt, and finally Hope on the far side.

"Hope, why don't you put down your pencil for a little bit, and let's order," my aunt said. "You know, I don't think it's the time to do some elaborate art project. And besides, aren't you hungry?"

Hope leaned over her sketch pad and, with pencil in hand, drew an impressive rendering of a fire-breathing dragon facing a tall, skinny boy who had long curly hair and ears protruding from his head. Unfortunately, he looked discernibly like me.

"I'm not hungry," Hope said firmly.

"Well, you didn't have much breakfast. You must be hungry. Put your pencils away. You'll pick them up again after we order."

"I don't want to."

Hope feverishly used red and orange pencils to draw the flames emanating from the dragon's mouth.

I figured she was taking her frustrations out through art. She was upset with me because our basketball game yesterday hadn't gone the way she planned. She expected a cousin to have fine athletic skill, someone who would not lose seven games in a row of H-O-R-S-E. Perhaps someone who knew how to make a basket. I thought I tried my best at being a friend. I even offered to take her down the street for the Saturday matinée at the Encino Theatre—prizes, popcorn, candy, even an acrobat performed during intermission, and she said, quite irritatedly, "I really don't enjoy spending a beautiful day in a dark theater watching stupid movies." My idea? We'd hit the second half of the kiddie matinée—*Gay Purr-ee*, an animated movie about Paris in the 1890s featuring the voice of Judy Garland—and stay for the four p.m. reissue of *Quo Vadis*, a historical epic featuring a hilarious performance by Peter Ustinov as the depraved and manic Nero. I knew right then, when Hope snubbed her nose at this double bill, that things would not improve between the two of us.

I was counting on our smiling server Maid Marian to change Hope's mood.

"We are so utterly delighted you are back, Mistress Sheila, Mistress Hope. Ah, Sir Ted! Good to see you all again. And this must be Sir Haskell?" She reached down and shook both my hands. "I'm Lady Marian, I'll be your server."

I hardly think New Yorkers would put up with such phoniness, though most boys my age would appreciate her slinky outfit. Her boobs practically popped out of the frilly, lacy blouse. As she poured water from a silver tankard into our empty goblets, Lady Marian caught me staring, winked, and obligingly angled herself toward me.

My aunt lightly slapped my hand and shoved the menu in front of me.

"Ted and I will have daiquiris. Haskell, what do you want?"

"A daiquiri," I answered. At sixteen, I could usually pass for eighteen, which was the legal drinking age in New York.

Of course, this wasn't New York.

"He'll have a Roy Rogers," my aunt said. "And a Shirley Temple for my daughter."

"I want a daiquiri, too!" Hope shouted.

"You will have nothing of the sort. Read the menu and decide what you want."

Thank God we got the drinks out of the way, although I believed they should have at least made a stab at creating medieval concoctions—maybe called the cocktails The Black Plague or Bloody Typhoid Mary.

"You know what you want to eat, Haskell?" My aunt once again tapped my arm. I ordered the Sir Beef-a-Lot double patty burger, and Hope asked for an Earl of Turkey and Bacon Sandwich.

I tried to ignore Hope's drawing, though it seemed, as she drew, the flames were getting closer and closer to the boy's face, eventually engulfing the poor kid in fire until we could no longer see his eyes or nose.

"Hope? What are you doing?" my aunt gasped.

"What does it look like?" Hope had a gleam in her eye.

"I really don't know. It seems as if you scratched out the boy's eyes and nose!"

She incinerated me.

"Hope, sit up."

My cousin now sat up straight. If she didn't insist on being such a sourpuss, she would be rather cute. Hope had dark curly hair and a tanned complexion, the result of a summer of swimming and outdoor sports. She was not as attractive as her mother, but my mom always said daughters were never as attractive as their mothers.

"Hope Jasmine, put your pencils down and join the conversation. It's the last time I'm going to ask you."

"I really don't feel like it."

Was this girl really eight and three quarters? Or was she two-and-a-half and only looked nearly nine? I suppose I should not have been surprised. When she visited New York a few years earlier, she had been a holy terror.

My aunt confiscated some of the colored pencils, but somehow Hope uncovered a new batch from a mysterious pocket in her jacket.

"What did I just tell you? You've been acting strange ever

since we arrived here. Is this how you want to behave at our first lunch out with Haskell? We wanted this as a sort of celebration. Let's put on our best attitude, shall we?"

Hope continued eviscerating the portrait of me.

"Did you hear me?"

"I'm not talking right now, Mother. I'm busy. Can't you see?"

Finally, Aunt Sheila confiscated all the colored pencils and all the crayons and stuck them in her purse, deep enough where Hope couldn't easily reach them. "Haskell is part of our family now, for at least a year."

Hope sat stone-faced.

"While Aunty Miriam takes a much-needed break, Haskell is going to do his senior year in high school here. It will be lovely." She paused a moment. "Look at me." My aunt cupped Hope's chin in her hand and waited until Hope's eyes met hers. "It will be lovely, particularly for you. After school, Haskell will be around to help you with your homework. It will be like having an older brother. You've always wanted an older brother, right?"

Hope nodded her head.

"Good, then you just have to give it some time. Haskell has only been here a few days. Before you know it, you'll be great buddies."

Soon the food arrived, and Hope lifted up the top slice of bread and studied the sandwich carefully as if she expected something to fly out of it.

"I didn't want mayonnaise on the bread."

"Why didn't you say something when you ordered it?" My uncle finally spoke. He had been listening to the Dodgers game, holding a transistor radio up against one ear even as he fielded Aunt Sheila's sneers and dirty looks. Now he set the radio on the table.

"Daddy, I thought they'd know how I like my sandwich. We eat here enough times."

Now my Aunt intervened. "They might remember our names, but they can't keep track of what condiments their guests put on their sandwiches. The chef and his staff are not mind readers."

My uncle lifted his daughter's plate off the table. "I'll scrape the mayonnaise off the bread, dumpling."

"It's still going to be there, Dad. I don't want even a smudge on the bread, and they put too much turkey. I can't even hold it in my hands."

"Do you want me to order you something else?" my uncle asked.

Hope sat back and let out a big deep sigh, as if the world and all its horrible troubles had fallen on her thin shoulders.

"No, I'll eat around it." She scraped the white milky mayonnaise off the toast, pieced the sandwich together with just one slice of turkey and several pieces of bacon, and finally, after much preparation, munched away.

I was glad the sandwich situation was resolved without her throwing a tantrum. I figured I could get used to this. She was a finicky eater, as many children are. I was also determined to be open-minded and optimistic. This was only my fifth day. She was a kid who had been an only child all her life. It couldn't be easy having me here, taking some of the attention away from a set of parents who apparently, for at least these past nine years, had been solely devoted to her. Perhaps she saw my presence as an intrusion, maybe even a rivalry.

I'd better assure her I do not mean to take her place.

I waited until she was done eating all the bacon, leaving the two pieces of bread and most of the turkey.

"You know, Hope, I want to be your friend," I said in a

gentle, soothing voice. "I want to be as helpful to you as possible. I certainly don't want you to feel as if I'm taking over."

Hope busily attacked her coleslaw with her fork.

"The good news is, I've already been in third grade, so I'll help you with your math problems or really anything you need. I'm very good at word problems. And as far as basketball goes? You know, after you won those games, I practiced all by myself. The ball kept hitting the rim, but I finally figured out the correct trajectory to aim it properly, and wouldn't you know? I started making baskets. I got pretty good at it, too. Practice makes perfect, right?"

Hope didn't say a word as she shook the ketchup bottle, pounding it with the palm of her hand until ketchup poured out of the spout too fast, dousing her French fries with a thick blanket of red sauce.

"Hope? That's very wasteful," my aunt lightly slapped her daughter's arm. "Next time be a little more judicious with how much ketchup you use."

"I'm using most of it. I love ketchup."

"It looks like you're using the whole bottle, and when someone is talking to you, you should answer them, or at least acknowledge what they're saying to you."

"What do you want me to say, Mother?"

"Haskell just said he spent hours yesterday practicing his basketball so he can be better at it the next time you want to play with him. All you have to do is say, 'Thank you.' It's not that difficult."

"Thank you," she mumbled.

"And talk to him a little bit. Tell him something about your friends."

"Since you ask, my friends saw Has-skull practicing basketball."

She pronounced my name as if I were a forty-foot ape who lived on some island besieged by a super race of primitive people.

"And he may have practiced for an hour, who knows? But he kept missing the backboard and the rim. And when he'd miss the ball, he'd run down the street with his feet sticking out. Even Vanessa's brother—Lucky?—was laughing so hard. He said, 'Is that your cousin out there? What's his problem? He's such a fairy!' We looked out the window, and not only did he keep missing the basket, but while he chased the ball down the street, he sang, 'Somewhere Over the Rainbow.' Lucky asked me, 'When's your cousin Judy singing at Carnegie Hall?' I was so embarrassed, you have no idea."

"I wasn't singing. I was humming!" I said firmly.

"You were singing like Dorothy in *The Wizard of Oz!* And now all my friends heard you, and they all think you're a dork. You run like a dork. You talk like a dork. You dribble a basketball like a dork, and you definitely sing like a dork."

My aunt banged her fist on the table. "That's just about enough. You apologize right now."

"You asked me to have a conversation. I'm having one, Mom. He's an embarrassment. Vanessa feels sorry for me. 'Your cousin buttons the top button of his shirt? And he can't skate or play basketball or even ride a bike?' She says he's not just a dork, he's the Duke of Dorkdom!"

"Hope, that is enough!" Uncle rubbed his face and squeezed his temples. "I can't believe you let your friends talk about Haskell that way. They don't even know him."

"Daddy, did you hear the music coming out of his room last night? I'm sure the whole neighborhood heard it. Some lady screaming at the top of her lungs, 'You Can't Get a Man with a

Gun!' Has-skull was singing along with her. You're right. I would love a big brother, but I don't want that one." She, of course, pointed directly at me. "I would prefer he pack up all his comic books and record albums and go back to New York where he came from."

Without wasting a moment, I stood up, threw down my napkin, and said, "Fine! You don't want me living here? I'd hate to see you or your brilliant friends feel so unhappy. I'll leave. And by the way, the lady screaming at the top of her lungs happens to be Ethel Merman, whose distinctive voice makes her the undisputed First Lady of the musical comedy stage!"

I wanted to grab Hope by the throat and shake her like a maraca, but instead, I grabbed the portrait Hope made of me and skewered it to one of the silver candlestick holders, turning it into paper shish kabob.

"That's what I think of your lousy picture."

Then I don't know what came over me. I threw a glass of ice water in her face. Some of the ice unfortunately landed on my aunt's blouse.

Poor Aunt Sheila shrieked as the ice cubes slid down her bra. Truly, Hope had unleashed a maniac inside me.

And then, I figured I had gone this far, why not go all the way? "You want another cousin to take my place? I'm not good enough for you? Well, be my guest. Find another one!"

I shoved her plate forward and, though most of the food landed on her lap, some of the ketchup, coleslaw, and mayonnaise splattered onto her face and into her hair.

Hope slid out of the booth and stood in the aisle, arms dangling, sopping wet, shaking like a cocker spaniel after a bath, her skin spotted with specks of ketchup as if she had come down with a sudden case of measles.

I did not wait around long enough to hear what my aunt or uncle had to say.

Instead, I flew down the corridors, whirled past Sir Lancelot and Lady Marian, out the exit doors and into the parking lot. Is this the dumbest, stupidest, lamest thing I've ever done? My intestines ached. I felt like I would throw up. I was so angry, I could hardly breathe. I ran down the sidewalk until I found a bus stop. What would I do? Where would I go? I had no money. My suitcases weren't with me. Even if I figured out a way to get back to New York, where would I live? How would I support myself?

I sat on a bus bench, my pulse beating in my throat.

What bothered me the most? I had been found out.

Hope had uncovered in a very short period of time what I had been hiding most of my life.

I was a dork. I was a complete and total dork, and I didn't need Hope reminding me of this fact. I certainly knew I was different, but I didn't know what kind of different I was. Yes, I didn't listen to the same music as everyone else. I dressed a bit differently. I wasn't particularly coordinated. All that could be adjusted in time. Why draw such rapid conclusions based on a couple of days in the Valley? As Madame Scheherazade warned me, I'd have my ups, my downs, my enemies, and my friends. Never give up, she said, and then some nonsense about being true to myself.

I finally stood up and sprinted down Ventura Boulevard. I may not have played basketball. I may not have known any sports. I may have even been uncoordinated. But, with my long spindly legs, I could run like hell.

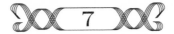

UNCLE TED MAKES ME WORK

I stopped running when I heard my uncle shouting my name. "Haskell!"

He had been driving his shark-finned Cadillac up and down the boulevard. I had seen him earlier and dodged him by zigzagging in and behind stores and through parking lots until he finally caught me staring in the window of a hobby shop.

I loved battery-powered airplanes. Never owned one, but I would watch other kids in Central Park soar their planes high in the air and carefully land them without crashing into a tree or a duck pond.

"Please get in the car, Hask!"

I had the feeling I could outrun my uncle. I don't know why I stood there. Maybe I wanted to get caught.

He climbed out of the car and ambled toward me, stopping a few feet away. "Please get inside the car."

I shook my head. "I can't go home with you."

"It will all work out just fine." He reached out and placed his hands on my shoulders. "I'm not angry at you. You got a little carried away today and so did Hope. We'll get this all resolved. I promise you. Now get into the car."

I shook my head. "Aunt Sheila probably thinks I'm some sadistic ice-thrower. Hope hates me. She's always hated me. I can't live with you, Uncle Ted. It is impossible. We'll have to figure out some alternative."

I took a few steps back. I felt so emotional, nearly dizzy, my mind turning and turning as though a wildness had overtaken me.

My uncle shook his head. "Nothing's impossible. You know, things may not seem so bright right now. But they will only get better."

He winked at me, as if a wink would make it all better. A wink meant: Don't be an idiot—get in the car . . . It could be a lot worse.

I finally dragged myself into the front seat, crossing my arms against my chest. My stomach was doing somersaults. I felt so agitated and confused.

What is wrong with me? I hated myself for what I'd done at the restaurant. I would never live down my tantrum. Why would I throw water in her face and food on her lap? And why would Hope make such a big deal out of my clumsiness? After all, I practiced basketball for nearly two hours, and I improved. I made baskets. What did she expect? I'd miraculously become Sandy Koufax?

Actually, I think he was a baseball player, not a basketball player.

Here was another problem. Not only was I no athlete, I knew nothing about sports. I had won a ping-pong championship playing against kids half my age at camp last summer— my single moment of athletic greatness.

No, I was a total dork. A dweeb. A real yo-yo. I didn't belong here. These were not my people. This was not a family who would understand me.

I wished I could snap my fingers and instantly relocate to New York City. In the Classics Illustrated comic version of *Captains Courageous*, this kid is washed overboard from a transatlantic steamship and rescued by fishermen off the Grand Banks of Newfoundland.

Yes, I needed some sea captain or fishermen rescuing me.

Of course, I get carsick when I sit in the backseat for too long. How would I possibly stomach a month at sea? I'd spend most of the time heaving over the deck railing.

"You're awfully quiet," my uncle said as we drove down Ventura Boulevard, one of the longest streets in the world. We could be on this boulevard forever.

I plopped my hands hard on the dashboard, figuring I better say something.

"I hate my mom for dumping me here. I really do. This is not what I wanted. I had my life in New York. A recital, a graduation, and a wonderful acting class. Now I'm stuck in a place where I don't belong. She's eating Belgian chocolates and sleeping late in Antwerp, and where am I? In the Valley of Ten Thousand Swimming Pools, and I don't even know how to swim. Uncle Ted, I cannot live here."

Uncle Ted tapped his fingers on the steering wheel.

"When I was a kid, I was very challenged by my mom."

Here it comes. The pep talk.

"She drove me crazy. I resented her."

He trudged through the snow and sleet.

Guess Uncle Ted was trying to make me feel better.

Be a good listener, Haskell.

"My father worked two jobs, leaving every morning before five and sometimes not coming home until nine or ten at night, just in time to read me a book."

"What would he read?" I asked.

"I loved anything by Jules Verne. One night when we were in the middle of *Twenty Thousand Leagues*, my mother tore into my room and yelled at my dad. 'When are you fixing the pipe under the sink?' she asked my dad in a shrill voice. He replied, 'When I'm done reading Teddy his story.' 'Fine. Teddy gets his story. I get water under the sink.' Inevitably, my dad would fix whatever was broken. Still, Mom nagged almost every night. Something was always in need of repair, and it couldn't wait until the weekend. One night, Dad kissed my forehead, told me he wouldn't return home until the end of the week, and walked out of the house."

"What did that mean?" I asked.

"He walked out on us. It was horrible. My mother cried and pounded her fists against the wall and tore up every photograph that had my father's picture in it. It was 1931. Cleveland. Winter. Freezing cold. I begged my mom. 'Please make up with Dad and bring him home.'" Uncle Ted pulled onto the freeway at Laurel Canyon. We headed south.

"So, what happened?"

"She never spoke to him again. On Friday nights, he'd bring a wonderful brisket over for Shabbat dinner, but my mother pretended he was not in the room. Instead, she'd use us kids as messengers. 'Ask the *gonef* how he could afford this brisket?' 'Tell the *gonef* I need an extra two dollars for the plumber.' 'Tell your father, the *gonef*, he should take his shoes off when he enters the house. What a mess he makes!'"

"Why was she so angry at him?" I asked.

Uncle shrugged. "She was humiliated. She knew she had driven him out of our home, and she never could admit it."

"Did she ever give in and talk with your dad?"

"Hold on a second." Uncle Ted pulled off at Sunset Boulevard into the parking lot of KHJ, the local television station he worked for, but he kept the motor running so we could enjoy the air conditioning. "Never missed a Friday night, always brought my mother money in a green envelope, and not once in all those years did she acknowledge him."

"You'd think this would eventually run its course," I said.

Uncle shook his head. "Seven years later, at my Bar Mitzvah, I'm walking down the aisle, carrying the Torah, when my mom reaches out, clutches my arm, and whispers, 'Tell the *gonef* his lady friend is not wanted at the luncheon.' She pointed at Hermione Goldenblatt, one of the seamstresses at the factory. Nice woman. My father would eventually marry her. A bright spirit who taught me card games, endured Saturday triple features at our Rialto, always showering me with kisses and hugs. But my mother? Sourpuss Fanny? 'Tell the *gonef* if she shows up at the luncheon, I will leave the temple. *Iz az farshtanen?*' So here I was, holding the Torah tight against my chest, a line of men forming behind me. I stopped. I bent over, cleared my throat, and said softly, 'Mom, today I am a man. Therefore, I am no longer your messenger boy. If you have a message for dad, he's right behind me.'"

"What did she say when you said that?" I asked.

Uncle laughed. "Nothing. She stormed out and made a scene, slamming the door so ferociously the wind knocked the yarmulkas off all the men sitting in the back row of the synagogue."

"Wow. That's awful."

Uncle Ted squeezed my shoulder. "Only my mother and my father could have changed their situation. I had no say in the matter." He leaned over and pinched my cheek. His voice was calm, deep, and safe. "I wish your mother had asked you rather than told you about this move. I'm sure it's very difficult to leave all your friends, especially at the start of your senior year. Sometimes parents can be rather self-centered. Your mom may have been under a great deal of pressure and thought it best to take some time for herself, but she should have discussed this with you ahead of time."

"I'm glad you understand."

"Most definitely. I'll give Miriam credit for one thing. Want to hear it?"

"No, not really."

"I'm telling you anyway. Sheila said her sister complained that she had no time for you. The moment she'd come home from work, she'd have to go to sleep, and then, sometimes she'd leave for work before you got up. She knew she was not in any way capable of being the best mom, and so she asked your Aunt Sheila and me if we could pinch hit for her."

"What does that mean?"

"In baseball, pinch hitters often replace a starting player when the pinch hitter is thought to have a better chance of reaching base or helping other runners score. Your mom thought, for this short period of time, Sheila and I could be substitute parents. And we're thrilled!" He reached over and squeezed my hand. "I am excited you're in the family."

"Don't you hate me after what I did?"

"You lost your temper. In the future, take some deep breaths when you get angry. Count to ten. I'm sure your aunt is giving Hope the same lecture. We can talk about this later." My Uncle Ted now signaled for me to follow him. "I have a surprise for you."

He pointed toward the cement building ahead. Four stories. Windows lined with metal bars. A big gated entrance. On the flat roof were all sorts of instruments and wires. The strange machine above was called a satellite receiver.

"How would you like to do some work for me today?"

"Doing what?" I asked. As punishment for my crimes against Hope, would I be cleaning toilets? Filing papers? Vacuuming? These were all tasks I did occasionally at my mom's office when she'd bring me in on weekends.

"I'm programming the movies for November and December, and I could use your help. I'm in charge of the *Million Dollar Movie*. Have you heard of this program?"

I shook my head. I knew Uncle was head of programming for the local TV station. I didn't know exactly what he did.

"We play the same film at eight p.m. every night for five nights in a row, with limited commercials, and we customize the commercials to fit the film. For example, last week Planters sponsored *The Greatest Show on Earth*, a circus movie. We brought in an elephant and fed him a bag of Planters peanuts."

"Did he eat the whole bag?"

"Of course." Uncle sang this little jingle: "Jumbo loves our nuts as much as people do."

"What a great line! Did you come up with it?"

"No. We hired a composer and lyricist for that one. And the week before we got the president of Dreyfus Air Conditioning to introduce our movie of the week, *The Big Heat*, while pouring water over his head . . . Get it? Cool himself down. Quite clever, don't you think? We're only a local TV station, so we have to compete creatively with the big networks."

I was perking up.

My uncle looked at his watch. "A Saturday afternoon is the perfect time for this. Fewer interruptions. I could use some help picking out films to match each advertiser."

"What about Aunt Sheila and Hope? I'm sure they expect an apology from me."

"I dropped them off at home before I went hunting for you. Your aunt and Hope will be thrilled to have the rest of the day to themselves, and you and I can spend some quality time together. You'll apologize later. What do you say?"

Was Uncle Ted inviting me to be the guest programmer? Choose from hundreds of movies? Watch one film after another? Spend a whole afternoon alone with him? Slap my face. Call me Ishmael. From the depths of despair to the heights of bliss in less than a minute, a kid could get the bends coming up so fast.

"Let's do it."

My uncle smiled and patted me on the back.

We took a stairway up, turned right on the second floor and entered a sound booth. Reels of movies lined the shelves of this narrow room. "Here's our list of advertisers. Why don't you look over the films in our library, see what's appropriate, and choose a few."

I had seen many of these films before and did not need to rewatch them. For example, the first film I picked was *The Good Earth*. It had an incredible scene where locusts eat an entire crop, nearly destroying the lives of Chinese peasants. This would fit perfectly for Terminix, a popular advertiser specializing in destroying termites, bugs, and mosquitoes. I picked *The Big Sleep* for a mattress company, chose *The Pajama Game* for the JCPenney store, and, in an odd choice, selected the *The Murders in the Rue Morgue* for the Los Angeles Zoo, since the film featured a gorilla.

I examined rating sheets. I pored over background infor-mation about each advertiser and studied charts showing demographics and audience preferences. Uncle suggested I also choose a Western. "The president of Fritos loves cowboy movies," Uncle said. I selected *Westward* with Jimmy Stewart, which I had never seen. After watching the entire film, I noticed Henry Stoneman's name in the credits. He played the little kid at the end of the movie who cries his heart out when his dog is shot by the villain. Maybe he has two minutes of screen time.

How on earth did he land this role?

I asked my uncle about this, and he repeated what my mother had told me when she was selling me on the idea of living near the various Hollywood studios. "He's local. If the part calls for only a few minutes of screen time, the studio saves money by hiring actors who live nearby. Producers hate spending money flying actors out and putting them up for days or weeks at a time, especially for small, somewhat insignificant roles. Sheila knows this boy's mother, right?"

"I think so."

"Well, that's even better. We'll set you guys up, and he'll teach you the ropes."

This made sense. At first, I wondered if he'd see me as a rival, but then we were such different types. I was not nearly as handsome or muscular as he was, and if the part required a more oddball, goofy kid, I might have a better chance at landing it.

We ended up watching *Goodbye, Mr. Chips*, featuring an Academy Award-winning performance by Robert Donat—an amazing feat, since it was the same year as *Gone with the Wind,* and everyone in the universe had expected Clark Gable to nab the Best Actor award.

This film made me miss Mr. Varnish so much, especially when Chips retires and all his students from years past visit him to say goodbye. "Well, remember me sometimes," Chips says. "I shall always remember you. *Haec olim meminisse iuvabit*," he tells them. Translated from the Latin, it means: "In the future, it will be pleasing to remember these things."

I could not imagine any film better than this one. It left me exhausted, my face red and damp and worn from crying. I told my uncle he should definitely broadcast this film and see if a tissue company would sponsor it. He liked the idea a lot. We finished our movie marathon, and it was time we drove home.

"Follow the leader!" Uncle Ted said, as he signaled for me to descend the stairs toward the car. I sat in the front seat with a heavy knot in my stomach.

"I don't want to go home and face everyone."

"Well, if it makes you feel any better, neither do I. So, before we go home, I have an idea that might make our homecoming easier. You game?"

8

MONEY BUYS ME LOVE

Uncle Ted started the ignition, pulled back onto the freeway, turned off at Vine Street, and drove into the Tower Records parking lot. The store's sign lit up in glittering neon.

"What's this about?" I asked. "Why are we going shopping now?"

"So, here's my idea." Uncle Ted grinned. "We don't usually buy albums for Hope because she doesn't put them back into their covers after she plays them, and they get all scratched."

"That's appalling."

"But she's been wanting the latest Beatles album. I think it's called 'Yesterday' or 'The Next Day.' I can't remember. This may be way out in left field, but I think if you offered her a kind of peace offering, it would begin the process of reconciliation."

"You mean bribe her?"

"It's not so much a bribe. It's more of a—how do I put it—a let's-start-over-again gift. If it came from you, she'd appreciate you more."

"This is like what the cowboys would bring the Indian chief in order to avoid a war."

"Nah. You're watching too many movies. It's just a gift, for

God's sake. Hope will be excited. Who doesn't appreciate the music of the Beatles, right?"

Not such a bad idea. I liked some of the songs the Beatles sang on the radio. "And I Love Her" was probably my favorite. "Devil in Her Heart" was probably Hope's.

"If they have a copy of this new album, we should purchase it. What do you say?"

I say I trust my Uncle.

I wandered into the store, took the escalator to the second floor, and picked up a copy of the new Beatles album, *Yesterday and Today,* featuring cover art of the four handsome mop heads. Well, three of them were good-looking. I never found Ringo very attractive. I'd buy the minx this album, and I'd buy myself *It's a Bird... It's a Plane... It's Superman,* a new musical comedy revolving around Superman's efforts to defeat a ten-time Nobel Prize-losing scientist who seeks revenge on the World. Two albums. Five bucks. I had the money. Bingo!

When I brought the albums to the register, the clerk stood silently staring at my purchase. His light curls quivered as he shook his head.

"You know, I'll just mention this, but I have a rare find: the original cover of this album. I have one left. You interested?"

I told him I didn't know anything about it.

The clerk bent down and removed from under the desk an album cover showing the four mop heads clad in white butcher coats, sniggering like naughty schoolboys while covered in pieces of raw meat and broken doll parts. "This rare Butcher Cover is only one of 500 printed, and I've sold three. I have one left. If you're a Beatles fan, don't pass on this special opportunity. This will be worth something someday."

"Well, how much is it?"

"Nine dollars," he said.

More than four times the cost originally.

Nine dollars? Baby parts? Bloody animal flesh? A plastic baby's severed head on Ringo's lap? I mean, was this up Hope's alley, or what? I had the feeling she'd do backflips.

Price aside, I wondered if this were a big mistake, especially since the gory cover might be an inappropriate gift for an eight-and-three-quarter-year-old.

I asked my uncle, and he said Hope loved everything about the Beatles. If this was as rare as the clerk made it seem, we should buy it.

He handed me ten dollars.

"It will be worth it if it will buy me some love," I said. I was making a joke, a play on some lyrics I remembered from a recent Beatles song.

"It's actually '*Can't* buy me some love,'" the clerk said, and handed me the *A Hard Day's Night* album from the 1964 movie.

"Or is it 'Money Can't Buy Me Love'?" a customer asked, twirling the love beads around his neck.

The clerk then grabbed a guitar from behind the counter and sang the whole song while customers waited in line. New Yorkers wouldn't stand for such an interruption. The crowd would have yelled, "Shut up and use the cash register, dummy!" Here in Hollywood, though, the dozen or so in line not only stood patiently and listened. They whistled and applauded when he completed the song.

"All right. I'll buy all three," I told him.

"You owe me only $15.20." Oh, what the hell? What was money for? And if it wouldn't buy me love, they were returnable as long as the plastic remained on the albums. I walked out with one record for me and two for Hope.

"A very nice thing you did," my uncle said, "and I think you'll find it will reap big rewards."

We drove the congested 101, heading for Ventura. "You two got off on the wrong foot. Hopefully, this will cheer her up. Create some camaraderie. Prove that it is possible you can be good friends."

I wasn't going to hold my breath. Still, I figured the sooner I made Hope happy, the easier life would be for me.

● ● ●

When we arrived home that evening, my uncle disappeared down the hall and into his bedroom. I had the feeling he was preparing my aunt so she wouldn't be too upset by the gifts we purchased or the butcher cover art.

I strolled into the kitchen and caught Hope, sitting alone, eating a bowl of Sugar Flakes.

Her mouth full, she placed her finger on the photograph of the red-haired kid leaping in the air alongside a cartoon tiger on the cereal box. "That's not you, is it?" she asked.

"This kid is not me. I scored the Sugar Flakes print ad account when was I five, when I was adorable."

"Oh, you're definitely not adorable now."

"Thanks for the reminder."

I sat down across from her and rested my arms on the formica tabletop.

"Just so you know, Has-SKULL, one of those ice cubes almost chipped my tooth."

"I'm sorry."

"It almost chipped my tooth. It *didn't* chip my tooth. But it almost did."

"Apologies."

"And my skirt is permanently stained from the ketchup."

"I'm really sorry. I'll buy you another one."

"I snap out of things very easily. I'm not angry at you anymore. My mom's kind of angry at both of us. I have a high pain tolerance."

I hadn't believed she'd take any responsibility for her tirade, and I was right.

"Maybe tomorrow—Sunday?—you'll help me with some math homework?" she asked. "That would make up for your dork-a-thon."

"You mean, you want me to do the homework for you?"

"You sound just like my mom."

"I will not do it for you, but I will help you."

"Mom always says the same thing, but she ends up doing the homework."

"I'll teach you the concept, and you'll answer all the questions. You'll do fine."

Hope smiled. "That's what you think. Math is my worst subject."

"I'll make it easy for you. I'll turn you into a math whiz. I'll help you improve your grades, so you don't lose privileges from bringing back a bad report card. I'll even throw in a couple of record albums."

I had set the Tower Records bag on the empty chair beside me.

Her eyes lit up. "Oh, let me see,"

"I bought you two albums. There's just one caveat."

She glanced up at the ceiling and rolled her eyes. "Now what?"

"I'm warning you, it's a rule. A commandment. Thou shalt keep the albums on two conditions. One: You take proper care of them, which I'll help you do. Dorks are particularly adept at caring for LPs. And two: You'll work on being more understanding. We're stuck here together, and I promised your dad I'll work harder at fitting in. I expect you to act as an ally, not an enemy."

My uncle and I had discussed this in some detail. I wished he were here explaining it, but I think I did a good job synthesizing what we had talked about.

Hope resumed eating cereal.

"Don't do me any favors, Has-skull. You make absolutely no sense. You're really weird."

"Fine. Have it your way . . ."

I stood up, bag in hand, and started toward the hallway.

"Don't I get to see the albums, at least?"

"Raise your right hand and make a promise. Then they're yours."

"What if I don't want the albums?"

"You can return them and get whatever you want."

"Really?"

"Really."

"They're not stupid albums?"

"I don't know. They might be stupid. They're both very popular. Judge for yourself."

"They're not by Ethel whatever-her-name-is?"

"No, you made it quite clear you do not like that kind of music."

"And if it's Petula Clark singing 'Downtown?'" She stuck her finger down her throat.

"No, these are rock and roll albums by the world's greatest group of musicians."

"Herman's Hermits?"

"No."

"The Animals?"

"Absolutely not. They're even more famous than any of those groups."

"Oh, let me see!"

"Raise your right hand and swear you'll be my ally, not my enemy. And you'll do your homework without any arguments."

Hope gave a lopsided grin.

"Forget about it! You're asking far too much."

My uncle warned me she'd give me a hard time. He said don't relent. Be consistent. Be firm. This felt clumsy and silly, but hopefully we were on the right track toward a successful relationship.

"Okay. I'll keep these for myself."

I pulled out *A Hard Day's Night*, showed her the cover, then placed it back into the bag.

She dropped the spoon on the floor. "The Beatles! Oh, my golly! You got me *A Hard Day's Night?*"

"No, it's *my* album. I need a commitment from you if you want this as *your* album."

She sucked on her lower lip.

"Raise your right hand and swear you'll be my friend, and you'll do your homework every day without argument . . ." Uncle said make it specific and clear. "For two weeks until October tenth. I'll keep track. Swear?"

"All right, already. I swear! Now can I have my albums?"

I handed her the movie soundtrack first.

"This is fantastic. I love this."

"You do?"

"Yes. Yes Yes Yes Yes Yes. Even though the movie is in black and white, I loved it anyway. I hear these songs on the radio.

I've been wanting this album so badly. Thank you, Has-skull Bas-skull."

She reached over and gave me a big hug.

"Wait. There's more. I saved the best for last. We need a binding agreement through Halloween. No, let's say Thanksgiving."

For a quick second, I thought, why give her the second album now? Or better yet, why don't I save it for when I need another bribe? The chances of her staying consistently obedient for a day, let alone a month, seemed impossible.

Unfortunately, I waited too long. I had already said I had two albums.

"What else is in the bag? Let me see."

I slowly pulled out the butcher shop cover of the Beatles album.

Hope's jaw dropped.

Pulling her chair back, she launched herself straight up like a rocket ship and began jumping up and down. "How did you find it? How did you find this? Where did you find this?"

"I wouldn't get so excited. I'm not sure I made the wisest decision. Your mom may not approve."

Hope raised the album cover over her head.

"Oh, Mommy, you won't believe this! Look what Haskell found!" Hope ran down the hallway toward her mother's room.

I heard Aunt Sheila scream. "What a disgusting photograph! Ted? You didn't tell me about this. TED! My God, this makes me sick. Why would you let our nephew buy a record cover like this? Haskell, come here a minute."

I didn't move. The plan was that my uncle would give my aunt some sociological and historical background for the album cover, fluffing up its importance.

My aunt stomped down the hallway toward me, stood near

the stove, a cigarette dangling on the edge of her mouth.

"I was talking to you."

"I didn't hear you."

"Why would you buy Hope an album like this? Didn't you make enough trouble today?"

"I didn't mean to make trouble today. I bought the album because—"

Before I could finish the sentence, Hope interrupted. "Mom, this album cover alone will be worth a lot of money someday."

"Go to your room, young lady!"

"You don't understand. This is the greatest album in the whole universe! You have no idea. All my friends have talked about it. We couldn't find it anywhere. It's nowhere in any of the record shops, and Haskell Benaskel found it! Oh my God, Oh MY GOLLY! Wait until I tell Vanessa!"

"I don't care if it's worth a hundred dollars. What's with all this blood? The baby parts?"

Ignoring her mother's protests, Hope scrambled out the front door, crossed the street and vanished into Vanessa's house. I wondered if my purchase would permanently change my reputation, and I'd no longer be the Duke of Dorkdom or the "fairy" cousin. Instead, maybe I'd be dubbed the cool, amazing, wondrous music-minded kid from New York.

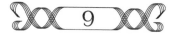

9

ENTERING THE VALLEY OF
THE THUNDERING ECHO

That Sunday morning, Vanessa's brother—the neighbor who called me a fairy—knocked on our front door.

"I heard you found the butcher album cover," he said. "Groovy! Where did you get it? Unbelievable, man. Do they have any other copies? I'm Lucky, by the way. "

Lucky wore a tank top with Encino High School Swim stamped on the front, showing off his muscular physique. He had short blond hair, blue eyes, a thick chin, and chiseled cheek bones. I wished I had his looks and my brain.

Initially, I was angry at him for making fun of me. So, he called me Judy and referred to me as a fairy. Still, this was only hearsay. Hope had been angry when she told me about it. I figured I should be open-minded and give the guy the benefit of the doubt, so I told him about my adventure at Tower Records.

"Bitchin'!"

"Yeah, yeah, it was good. I had a fun night with my uncle."

"Bitchin', man! How did you even know about this cover?"

"I enjoy the Beatles. Who doesn't?"

"Groovy! Out of sight!"

"I love their music," I said. "I'm also fond of The Rolling

Stones, Janis Joplin, and The Mamas and the Papas."

I thought I'd throw that out there. The song "California Dreamin'" was a favorite of mine.

"They're all right. Led Zeppelin, now there's a band. I also think Jimi Hendrix is by far so fucking brilliant."

I nodded, though I wasn't as familiar with these musicians.

"So, I wanna ask you something. We're playing some touch football outside. Wanna join us?"

I would not ask what touch football was. The dork in me thought I should take five minutes, look up 'touch football' in the *World Book Encyclopedia*. Otherwise, I might misunderstand the rules of the game. On second thought, I figured, I'd imitate whatever the other boys were doing.

I told him I'd be happy to join them. When I walked out of the house, Lucky introduced me to his two buddies.

"This is Winston." I shook hands with a shorter kid, maybe a year older than me, with spiky straight hair, wearing a Ram's football T-shirt. "And here's Nate." Nate's lean frame, long legs, and crew cut made him seem even taller than me, though he was probably about my size. "He's our drama nerd, aren't you, Nate?"

"I build sets. I'm not in drama. I'm on the construction crew and—"

"No one wants to hear your dumb shit." Lucky shook his head. "So, we're scrimmaging. Wanna join us?" Lucky asked, grabbing the football out of Nate's hands.

A scrimmage? I figured if they'd teach me, why not? Seize this opportunity! No sense harboring bad feelings. If the doofus makes an effort, be cordial and open. It was a great opportunity to make some friends.

"Let's do it," I answered.

The Teitlebaums lived on a cul-de-sac. Their home, like many of the others on the street, was Tudor-style and had a steeply pitched roof of varying heights. Though most of the exterior was brown stucco, the walls were accented with brick and stones and diamond-shaped windows, some lined with leaded glass. Other homes on the street were either of a Hawaiian flavor with fake lava rock and wood-shingled roofs or Spanish-style with tiled roofs and stucco exteriors.

Strangely, at the end of the street, in the middle of the cul-de-sac, was a Southern-style mansion with huge white pillars, a balcony running along the whole outside edge of the house, and a finely trimmed rose garden leading up to the front door. All the other homes were fairly new, maybe built in the mid-fifties, and situated on tiny lots, separated from each other by cinder-block walls, but this home seemed much older with full-grown trees, set on property two or three times larger than all the others.

I asked Winston, who was tossing the football back and forth in his hands, why this home appeared so different from the others. He stared at me, scratched his spiky hair, and wiggled his head slightly, like one of those Hawaiian bobblehead dolls people place on their dashboards.

"Just stop Lucky from catching the ball, dumbass," he told me.

"How am I going to do that?"

He changed the tone of his voice so he sounded as if he were speaking down to a three year old. "I'm going to toss the ball to you, and you're going to run with it and try to make a touchdown, without anyone stopping you. Got it, fuck-face?"

So, there were four of us. Winston and I stood at the end of the cul-de-sac with our backs toward the Southern plantation-style home, and Lucky and Nate were a few yards in front of us. Nate tossed the ball to Lucky, but I caught it, not really certain what I should do next.

"Run, Teitlebaum!" Winston shouted.

The idiot thought I had the same last name as Hope? I guessed I should run. Nate was on my right, attempting to stop me, and I managed to get around him, as well as Lucky, and, for the first time in my life, I played football, consciously running with my feet straight, not turned out, sprinting as fast as I could with the ball tucked under my arm, like Burt Lancaster in *Jim Thorpe—All-American.*

"You can stop already!" Winston shouted, shaking his head. I was about a dozen houses down the street.

"My name is Haskell *Hodge*," I shouted.

"Well, dumb-fuck Hodge, don't run all the way to Van Nuys. The goal is right there, at the Gittelson house."

I had no idea where that was.

"What's the matter with you, four eyes? Do I need to draw you a map?"

Nate interrupted. "Winston, no one told him where the goal line was."

"Everybody knows where the goal line is."

"He's new. He just got here from New York. He'll get the hang of it. Leave him alone."

"If I hadn't said anything, he'd be all the way in Northridge. Who does that?"

I finally made my way back into the cul-de-sac and Nate, who had been standing on the opposite side of the street, ambled over to me, bent down, resting his hands on his knees.

"Look, you did great. You're a fast runner. Don't listen to that jerk. Generally, your end zone is there." He pointed at the tan house with the roadster in the driveway. "Our end zone, on the other hand, is that mailbox."

A black colonial-style mailbox sitting on a fancy podium

stood at the edge of a lawn bordering the plantation house.

"You do just what you did. Catch the ball and run. Just be careful not to go onto the lawn there. You know that house is a replica of Tara, Scarlett's house in *Gone with the Wind*."

I had never seen the film, but the home matched the photographs showcasing the movie in various magazines.

"The guy who lives there bought the estate a few years ago, and he signed some contract saying he'd never tear it down, even though it doesn't match the architecture of these other homes."

"It's weird."

"The guy's even weirder. He hates anyone trespassing on his property. He once told us the next person who tramples on his grass will get his head blown off."

Nate lightly punched me in the chest with his fist.

"We're not going to let that happen, are we, Pilgrim?" Nate said the line as if he were impersonating John Wayne.

We played for a good half hour. We did a lot of running back and forth. Not once did Lucky call me Judy or make fun of me when I fumbled the ball. And Nate, who had been kind enough to explain to me the rules and boundaries of the game, ended up at one point being on my team. "This time I'm going to run, and you're going to pass me the ball."

"What if you don't catch it?"

"Throw it toward me so I will catch it."

"So the point is to aim it carefully and high enough so that Lucky or Winston don't grab it instead."

"Exactly. You're getting the hang of it."

I aimed it carefully, contemplating where Nate would be by the time the ball reached him, and I certainly didn't want Winston or Lucky nabbing it, so I held it high above my head, as I contemplated how far and in what direction and at what speed I should toss the ball.

"What's the fucking matter with you? Toss it already!" Winston screamed.

"Nothing wrong with thinking things out first before making the move," Nate shouted back. "If you don't think, you can't toss."

Not only did I appreciate Nate's support, but I noticed he was probably as familiar with movies as I was. That line came loosely from one of my favorite Disney films, *Alice in Wonderland*, where the March Hare says, "If you don't think, then you shouldn't talk."

After awhile, we all got tired of running back and forth. Winston said he had a date that night with Kimberly Jackson, as if everyone should know who Kimberly Jackson was. Nate's parents were taking him to Tiny Naylor's for the early bird special. And Lucky?

"You got something to do tonight?" Lucky asked.

Was he talking to me?

"Wanna hang out?"

I looked at him blankly. Hang out?

"We're neighbors, right?" he said. "It makes sense to be buds."

Maybe people out west were cooler than people back east.

"Sure, fine with me," I said.

"Your cousin said you have a thousand comic books in your room. Can I see them?" he asked.

I didn't have a thousand. I owned four hundred and twenty-seven, but who's counting? I also had my record albums all organized alphabetically in boxes and my comic books stored on shelves, each box categorized and numbered.

He followed me into the house. Just as we were about to climb the stairs, my aunt stopped us. She was wearing thick oven mitts as she prepared dinner in the kitchen. Lucky gave her a big hug.

"Hello, Mrs. Teitlebaum. It's a pleasure to see you again. How has your day turned out?" he asked.

He almost sounded too polite, like Eddie Haskell, the conniving neighbor on *Leave It to Beaver*, who became well-mannered only in the presence of adults.

"What's for dinner? It smells *so* delicious."

"I'm baking a Stouffer's lasagna, Lucky. Stay, why don't you?"

"Wow. I've never smelled anything so delicious in my life. I'll think about it."

We ran up the stairs to my bedroom, and I warned him, "My aunt's an assembler, not a cook. She buys already-made food, bakes it, and then places it on plates. It's good. I don't want to discourage you from staying for dinner. I just didn't want you expecting something from Naples or Florence or Milan when it's from the frozen section of Piggly Wiggly."

Lucky lifted an eyebrow.

Sometimes I talk too much. Maybe I'm too honest. Anyway, he spotted the dozen or so boxes of comic books, stacked high on several bookshelves, and asked if he could look inside one of them.

"Be my guest!" I said.

After flipping through a dozen or so—I also had some very valuable early Superman and Spider-Man double issues—he glanced over to the wall beside my bed, where I had scotch-taped one massive movie poster of *The King and I*, showing Yul Brynner barefoot, his red embroidered shirt wide open, showing off his muscular chest, and Deborah Kerr wearing a magnificent green silk dress, dancing elegantly.

He cocked his head as he stared at the poster, and I steadied myself for some snide comment.

This was not a typical boy's room, I'll admit, and I never expected any visitors.

"I saw that movie with my mom, and I slept through it," he said.

"It is long. I can see why someone might sleep through it." Keep it brief, Haskell.

"And it made no sense. All of a sudden the king dies?"

"Well, in real life, I don't think they fell in love. The film suggests his heart was broken when Anna, his children's schoolteacher, insisted on returning to England."

"His heart was broken? I didn't get that. He just suddenly gets sick. What did he catch, a cold or something?"

"Heart failure, I suppose."

"They wanted to end the movie."

"Exactly. Of course, it was a stage musical first, and before that I think it was a serious dramatic film with Rex Harrison, and even before that a novel by Margaret Landon based on a true story."

"Did you read the novel?"

"I did. Yeah. It's very good. I have a copy of it, if you're interested."

"No, no, no, no, no, no. That's all right."

Lucky's eyes now veered toward the bookshelves jam-packed with novels. I had brought only certain favorites from New York, such as *The Great Gatsby* and all of H. G. Wells. A lot of Twain and Dickens. The rest we sold or donated to the New York Public Library.

"You like books, don't you?" he asked.

"I love reading."

"I have a hard time concentrating. Books bore me. I've never read a whole book."

"Sure you have."

"Nope, never. I have a book report due on Wednesday, and I haven't even started reading it. Reading makes me so sleepy, I can't concentrate."

"Try reading in the morning when you're more awake. I have the same problem at night."

"It doesn't matter when I read. I can't concentrate. And I'm in a pickle. I'm almost nineteen and I have to graduate this year."

"Well, what's stopping you?"

"I flunk my classes. That's what's stopping me. My parents got me into this special reading class where I wouldn't have to read too many books, but this teacher—Mr. Donaldson—got drafted and his replacement, Miss Harrison, got these big ideas and wants us to actually read a book."

"Well, there's nothing wrong with that."

"I know, but the book is really boring, and I swear I have no idea what it's about. I can't get past the first chapter."

I asked him what book he was assigned, and he said *Great Expectations*, one of my favorite Dickens novels.

"And after we read the book, I'm supposed to write a book report."

He pulled out a mimeograph paper, all crumpled up, out of his pants pocket and showed it to me. Simple questions: What does the main character want? Who is the antagonist? What's the theme of the novel? Describe the setting of the book. What do you like best about this book?

The instructions were to write a paragraph for each of the five questions. How difficult could that be?

"Would you help me write this?" he asked.

My heart leapt at the idea. I could use a friend, and tutoring a neighbor might be the perfect connection. So far, this Saturday had turned into an almost complete reversal of my bad fortunes. I wanted him as a pal. He was a swim champion who was enormously popular. I figured it couldn't hurt my chances at fitting into my new high school.

"Why don't you write a draft, and I'll correct it!" I suggested. This excited me. I could feel included in his group even if I weren't part of it. I was doing exactly what Madame Scheherazade suggested: Embracing the change. Going with the flow. Those weren't her exact words, but I think that is what she meant.

"Actually, let me explain. I haven't read the book. I have no idea what it's about. I need the report written, typed up, and finished by . . ." He counted the days on his fingers. "It's due in three days. Wednesday." Today was Sunday, so actually it was four days. I would not correct him.

I decided I'd make a proposal. "I'll tell you the story. I'll even read parts of the book out loud. We can discuss exactly what you want in the book report, and you'll sit down and write it. That way it will be in your words, not mine," I told him.

"I have a simpler idea. Just pretend you're me."

"I'm not sure I could do that."

"Dumb it down. I don't care." He laughed. "You can figure it out. How long would it take you? An hour? Two? I'll pay you if you want, or we can exchange services. I heard you can't swim. I'll teach you. I'm a very good swim instructor. Last summer I lifeguarded at the YMCA and taught classes as well."

This was a predicament. As much as I would love good swim instruction and Lucky as an ally, I did not feel comfortable cheating. I was about to say "No" when I experienced a stroke of genius. A thunderbolt sparked my imagination.

"I'll tell you what," I said. "I have the Classics comic version of *Great Expectations*. It's an easy read. Beautifully illustrated. The whole plot is there for the most part. After you read it, you and I can talk it out and then write a report. Your teacher will never know you didn't read the novel."

I dipped into my sacred box of Classics literary comics—the *Aeneid. Barchester Towers. Bleak House. Crime and Punishment. David Copperfield.* Normally, I would never let anyone borrow these because they were old and worth more than the ten cents I paid for them. For Lucky? To earn his friendship? I would make an exception.

"Here!" I removed the plastic cover and handed him the beautifully illustrated Classics comic version of *Great Expectations.* "You can borrow this. Enjoy!"

He shook his head again. "I'm not interested in reading the comic book. I know I'm asking a big favor, Haskell. And I promise I'll repay it. You start school tomorrow, right?"

"I think so."

"Well, I'll tell you what. Besides giving you swim lessons, I'll always be there for you. If any kids make fun of you or attack you, I'll back you up."

"You'd be my bodyguard."

"Sort of."

"Why would I need that?" I asked.

"You never know." He moved closer and lowered his voice to a whisper. "I'm just being honest with you here. Once there was a kid—we'll call him Tom—I think he was from New York like you. Also wore glasses, and he was a bit of a sissy, if you know what I mean. Kids made fun of him all the time, but he was damned smart. Whenever the teachers asked questions, he always raised his hand. Stayed after class and helped put stuff away. He was what you might call an ass-kisser."

"A teacher's pet? They're pretty irritating."

"Right? Exactly. You know what I'm talking about. Yeah, well, this would drive Mark Remshaw and his buddies crazy. They asked Tom if he'd write a couple of term papers for them, and he refused. Got all huffy about it. One afternoon, they followed Tom home and they beat the crap out of him. I think they bruised him up pretty badly. "

"Was Tom, okay?"

Lucky shook his head. "No. I'm afraid not. Our boy Tom never showed up at home that night. His parents got very worried and called the police. A neighbor walking his dog later that night found Tom's body."

"They killed him?"

Lucky nodded his head. "Yep. Left him in a ditch, right behind Du-par's coffee shop."

"And then what happened?"

"His family buried him a few days later. Some say his ghost haunts the dirt hill just behind Du-par's. Although that rest-aurant doesn't appear to be hurting for business, I personally would never eat there at night, even though the pie and pancakes are excellent." Lucky smiled and clasped his hands together. "So, I don't know why I told you this story. I really don't."

I sat back and scratched my head. Was this kid seriously threatening my life? If I didn't help him with his book report, was he suggesting I might be killed?

This put me in a serious predicament. I was supposed to start school tomorrow, and I figured I not only needed swim lessons,

I wanted to stay alive. At the same time, I had the feeling that the story was made up. This was what I called a scare tactic. I was not so easily duped. I mean, I wasn't an idiot. Besides, I had seen this happen before at Bonvadine. Someone didn't read the assignment, turned in a report someone else wrote, and both students got brought into the headmaster's office and expelled. I was sure if I asked my aunt's opinion on this dilemma, she'd say, "Do it! I'd hate to find you in a ditch!" My level-headed uncle, on the other hand, would agree with me. Cheating was wrong, and if I got caught, it might stain my record and prevent me from getting into a fine college. It was the stain that wouldn't go away. Certainly, I didn't want us to be plunged into a plagiarism scandal the moment I started school. But at the same time, I didn't want to turn Lucky Miller into a dire enemy. The two of us must be able to come up with some compromise.

"I can't write the entire paper for you," I finally said. "Plain out cheating, and I'm not a cheater, and I'm sure you're not either."

"You're either going to help me or you're not. Which one is it?"

"I will help you, Lucky. We'll collaborate. I'll read a summary of the novel out loud, I'll make some suggestions, and you can dictate the answers. It won't be labeled plagiarism. I'll proof-read and edit your work. I'll even add some ideas. What I won't do is write the entire book report from scratch without your input. If we were discovered, it could ruin us. You'd be thrown out of school, and who knows? You're eighteen, right? You could get drafted and sent to Vietnam. I might never get into college with plagiarism on my school record. I'm looking out for both of us." I took in a deep breath. "So, do we have a deal? We could start right now if you want."

I thought this was a very reasonable compromise. I went in for the close, as my mom would put it. "When should we get started?" I put my hand out to shake his.

He briskly headed toward the door. "I'm not interested in your plan. Vietnam? The draft? We're talking about a stupid two-page book report. You either write it or you don't. Which will it be?"

I paused maybe a few seconds too long.

"Don't do me any favors. I'll find someone else who will write the damned thing."

Before I could open my mouth and try another solution, Lucky dashed out of my room, racing down the stairs into the kitchen.

I thought my offer very fair, a real compromise. I couldn't take the risk of getting caught in a plagiarism scam. Should I throw my ethics to the wind? I felt a sinking in my stomach. Wasn't my compromise enough? Had I made a huge mistake?

I took another deep breath and cupped my hands over my nose and mouth. I counted to ten.

I think I better just go along with this plan. Otherwise, I'll be found in a ditch.

I darted down the stairs, and my aunt stopped me.

"Haskell? Everything all right?" She still had those frog-green oven mitts on. "Lucky whirled out of here like his pants were on fire. I thought he'd stay for dinner."

I ran out of the house, determined to change my fate. I'd write the paper. After all, it wasn't in his best interest to tattle on me. No one would find out, and I'd have someone protecting me. As I descended the steps toward the sidewalk, Lucky jumped into his Chevy and revved up the engine.

I called his name as he pulled away from the curb.

"Lucky, I'm sorry. Let's figure this out," I shouted. "I'm just scared of getting caught."

He rolled down his window and stuck out his thick head. "Well, we wouldn't want that to happen, would we?" He yelled back and gave me the middle finger. "No worries, Judy. I'll find someone else."

The car dashed down the street sputtering huge gusts of black engine smoke. I stood there for the longest time mourning my fate before trudging back into the house and up the stairs and falling across my bed.

By some miracle, could I make myself disappear into a land of enchantment? I remembered a chant Hercules used in one of his Italian movies, transporting himself from a terribly sticky situation—surrounded by ogres, sixteen-foot pythons, and the three-headed dog, Cerberus—to a place of safety and calm. He simply closed his eyes and recited: "*Per favore, o gli dei respirano la vita in lui.*" Voilà! He disappeared and landed in the Valley of the Thundering Echo. Don't ask me how I could accurately recall those words—in Italian, mind you—but I thought, as crazy as it may sound, maybe by reciting those words I could calm myself down and transport myself out of Encino and into some faraway desert. Dasht-e Kavir? Kalahari? Lompoul? Or anywhere for that matter—free of Lucky Miller and his band of hooligans, and anyone else I couldn't stand. I closed my eyes, hoping that when I woke up, I might be somewhere else.

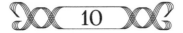

10

WELCOME TO ENCINO HIGH

Aunt Sheila clucked her tongue like a chicken. "Rise and shine! It's six-thirty and time for school!" Cluck. Cluck. Cluck.

I don't think I had ever been up this early before.

"This school has been ranked high on a list of best academic schools in California. You'll enjoy it there. Honestly, you will. Now get dressed. I'll have some breakfast on the table! Want some eggs? I'll answer my own question. Of course you do. A good breakfast in the morning on your first day of school is vitally important!"

I put on a pair of brown slacks, a long-sleeved orange-striped shirt that I left unbuttoned at the top, and a pair of Hush Puppies. I also grabbed the same backpack I had used at my academy.

My aunt shook her head as I entered the kitchen. "This backpack has seen its day."

"It's quite functional."

"It says Bonvadine Academy on it."

"It will hold my books."

She handed me some dollar bills. "Buy something at the student store. I'm sure they have backpacks, hats, and T-shirts with the school's insignia. Remember, it's all about fitting in. And didn't you wear this same outfit the other day?"

"I like this shirt."

"Okay, I'm going to buy you some new clothes. Please eat something. I made you hard-boiled eggs."

"Yummy."

"You haven't even tasted them yet."

"You can't ruin hard boiled eggs, can you?"

Aunt Sheila nearly accomplished just that. Some of the shell was still on the eggs, and they hadn't been cooked quite long enough, so they were slightly runny. I ate both anyway, spit out the shell, and did not utter a word of complaint.

"So, the plan is this." She hovered over me while I still sat at the table. "Since it's your first day in school, we're going early. First, you'll meet the principal, go on a grand tour, chat a bit, and then you'll plop yourself in your Period One classroom and start the day. I'm sure everything will go swimmingly."

I didn't answer her. I buttered my white toast, drank a glass of orange juice, and sipped on what Aunt Sheila called a cup of coffee. "What is this?" I asked.

"It's actually instant Sanka," she said. "It's easy. Just a spoonful in a cup of boiling water. Ted always drinks his coffee at work, so I'm satisfied with this."

"It's terrible."

"Next time, you make your own coffee. Hurry up. Eat and drink. Let's go."

I'd either make it myself in the future or teach my aunt how to use a percolator.

"I know you're worried, this being your first day at school. You'll be fine. Four thousand kids. No one will notice you."

"Four thousand?"

"I don't know. It's a big school. I can't keep track of enrollment statistics."

She pulled out a chair and sat, folding her arms on the table.

"What's bothering you, Haskell? You look worried."

"I'm okay."

"I'm proud of you for doing your best at fixing whatever rift you had with Hope. She's not easy, and the gifts you gave her made all the difference in the world."

"You're not still mad at me for buying the butcher album cover?"

She lifted her chin and closed her eyes for a moment. "I don't love that kind of grotesque artwork. But I know the photograph is probably making some statement about the condition of our world."

"It's a reaction to the meaninglessness and absurdity of our existence."

"Really? What do you even know about the absurdity of existence, Haskell? You're only sixteen years old."

"I'm learning about it pretty quickly."

She set both her hands on top of mine.

"Take the frown off your face. You will have a lovely day."

I decided I wouldn't tell my aunt about my encounter with Lucky and how horribly it ended.

"If you're worried about being the new kid in town, a stranger on campus, don't give it another thought. You'll blend in just fine. And guess what? Dick Van Dyke? His kids go there."

"They do?"

"Yep."

"Do Jerry Van Dyke's kid go there, too?"

"I don't know who that person is, Haskell."

"He was in a TV show where his mother dies and is

reincarnated as a car." Whoever came up with that idea deserved a Pulitzer.

"You know, I'm not sure this is the kind of snarky conversation I want first thing in the morning."

"I'm telling you the truth. It is called *My Mother the Car*. It's still on TV in reruns."

"I never know when you're making stuff up. Do me a favor? Eat up so we can get going. Come on. Let me show you something before we take off for school."

As we made our way out of the house toward the car, my aunt signaled for me to follow her onto the sidewalk.

"Let's hurry. I don't feel safe leaving Hope alone in the house while she's still sleeping. When I get home, I'll get her ready for school. I'll drive you, since it's your first day. Normally, you'll catch the bus at the bottom of the street." She pointed north. I couldn't see the end of the street, so it was a good quarter of a mile. The walk didn't scare me. "Now, if you look in the other direction, you'll see the famous *Gone with the Wind* movie house."

"This guy, Nate, told me about it."

"Did he mention the little animal graveyard? The original owner buried his dogs there and when he sold the property in 1962, our whole neighborhood chipped in and bought this small piece of land so we could bury our dogs there, as well."

"A communal dog burial ground?" I asked.

"Yes, it's all fenced off for us. Lovely, no?"

"Did you ever have a dog?"

"Yes, Poochy, our toy poodle, is buried here. Lots of our friends have taken advantage of this plot of land. The other day I attended a small service for June Stoneman's poor Pekingese. Got run over by a mail truck a few days ago. Very tragic. I know

June through the docent program, and we do a lot of things together. She's a very vibrant, intelligent woman, born in Tunisia, married a Jewish man named Harris Stoneman. He's a lawyer." My aunt smiled faintly and then slightly shook her head.

"What's the matter?" I asked.

"Henry Stoneman! He's June's son, and I promised your mom I'd arrange for the two of you to meet. It completely escaped me until now. Memory! He's an actor. I'm sure you'll bump into him."

"Not with four thousand students."

"You'll probably be in one of his classes. The odds are in your favor. He's smart. You're smart. You're both actors. His mom says he's also a very good pianist. On the other hand, you may never bump into each other, so we'll call him. As I said, I know his mother."

Fine with me. I could use a friend. A real friend.

"If you take this road over the hill, you'll be at a nunnery and then at the elementary school where Hope attends. I prefer she not take this route, but I can't always supervise. Anyway, should you need some quiet time, this graveyard has a very special sense of solitude."

We walked back, and I sat in the front seat of her station wagon, paying close attention as I watched her make a number of turns until we landed in an asphalt parking lot badly in need of repair. On one side were a dozen bungalows, their walls covered with graffiti, and on the other side, a series of recently built stucco buildings.

"Hang on. Do I go toward the new building or the dilapidated bunkers?" I asked.

"It used to be an army hospital, but the L.A. school system transformed the barracks into lovely, air conditioned classrooms. And the crematorium, the morgue, even the surgery rooms, were converted into multipurpose rooms and administration offices. They might appear nasty on the outside. Inside they're quite comfortable. Dr. Freed's office is in Bungalow Four."

"How do you know all this?" I asked.

"From my docent program! We spent a full hour discussing the transformation of the Army Hospital into this school. You have your bus pass?"

I checked my wallet, and I did.

"Dr. Freed will give you your schedule, and anything else you need, you just ask Freed's secretary, Miss Ito. I know you will do fine."

She leaned over and kissed me on the forehead.

"Go and have a wonderful day!"

I pretended I was excited to start school, though I was petrified. My armpits were already damp, and I felt light-headed and near-dizzy, as I headed toward The Morgue, better known as the Vice Principal's office. Several boys sat on a cement retaining wall, chatting away. They were not dressed like the hoodlums in *Rebel Without a Cause*, thank goodness, with thin, white T-shirts, the sleeves rolled up to show off bulging biceps. In fact, one of the boys wore a nice paisley shirt tucked into a pair of cotton black trousers and the other had on an orange-striped shirt nearly an exact duplicate of the one I was wearing. Under his arm was a copy of *Silas Marner*, one of my least favorite novels. I'm not sure what gave me the deep sense of dread. Fear of bumping into Lucky or rereading George Eliot? Or just the plain unknown. New books. New teachers. New students. And this dilapidated, creepy school with the barbed wire fencing. Buildings that still resembled barracks. Graffiti. I felt as if I were not entering a school but a detention center.

In the distance, I could hear the sound of a marching band

attempting a terrible rendition of a stereotypical Native American war chant.

I stopped, bent down, and gave myself some positive reinforcement my acting coach had taught me. Breathing deeply in and out brings you power and inspiration. No matter what happens, never give up. You can do anything you put your mind to. Still, since I arrived a week ago, it seemed I faced one hurdle after another. By some miracle, could the day go smoothly?

11

AN ENCOUNTER WITH THE HOOLIGANS

"We are the Encino Braves. And last year, we came in tenth!" Vice Principal Freed told me proudly. I had no idea if this was a good or a bad thing. "We have a couple of players who probably need some extra coaching, don't we? Hardison is out with an injury! Franklin? Fumbled the ball and we lost ten yards. We conceded far too many goals in the last few minutes of the game while having a poor scoring record ourselves."

Why would any of this interest me?

"We only played ten games, but you know, it's not how you win, it's how hard you play the game, right?" A big bald-headed man with a ruddy complexion, Dr. Freed shook my hand and welcomed me before giving me a quick tour. "Let's see. You're ten days into the semester so you'll have some catching up to do, but that shouldn't be a problem." He lowered his voice to a whisper. "I have your academic records." He raised his eyebrows. "You'll do fine."

He showed me my homeroom located in a bungalow once used as housing for soldiers. We swung around and landed in the multipurpose room, the original army mess hall. The gymnasium was housed in the old surgical center. "Soon it will receive a hundred-thousand-dollar face lift. Yes, indeedy!" he boasted. We ended up once again in his office, where he handed me my schedule of classes.

Freed claimed Encino High had the highest academic scores in the Valley, and eighty percent of the students eventually attend two- or four-year colleges. These statistics were just a bunch of random numbers to me. He told me, since it was a month into the semester, he would place me in regular classes, not advanced sections, since those required instructor permission. Once I acclimated to the school, I could request a transfer into certain advanced sections.

I didn't have a problem with this. It seemed quite fair.

After our conference, Freed delivered me to Bungalow 2B103. First period, Calculus. Mr. Frost, wearing a vest and a sweater buttoned to the chin—even though it was nearly ninety degrees outside—explained the problems clearly, and I found the material perfectly in line with what I had studied last year at Bonvadine. The hour went fast. If the rest of the day was any-thing like this, it would be a cinch.

Second period was English, taught by a sexy, beautiful Mrs. Green, recent graduate of Cal State Dominguez Hills. She had her diploma hanging on the wall. We spoke for a few minutes before class, and she warned me this was a "standard English class," not advanced by any means. "If you decide this section is too easy, let me know." The discussion today was on tragic sacrifice in *Of Mice and Men*, a book I had read before. I had no problem rejoining George and Lennie, Candy, Slim, Curley, and Curley's wife. I knew the book well, but I decided not to raise my hand or make any effort at sounding as if I were a know-it-all. Even if Lucky's story of the boy in the ditch was merely a scare tactic, I would heed the warning.

Don't come off as arrogant or conceited or too knowledgeable, I told myself.

So far, I had not bumped into a single hooligan. I had not even seen Lucky once, so the day had gone well. I laughed at my ridiculous paranoia. What a waste of time! Several girls asked me questions about New York, and when one of them recognized me as the grown-up version of the freckled big-eared kid on the Sugar Flakes cereal box, she ended up telling all her friends. As I walked toward my third period class, a group of girls followed me.

My third-period American Government class was taught by Mr. Pottle, and as I approached the room, I spotted Lucky and a bunch of his hooligans tossing paper airplanes and laughing uproariously.

"We have a genuine Judy Garland impersonator in the room!" Lucky shouted when he spotted me. He was his old self again. "Judy! How's the voice? You'll sing for us?" Fortunately or unfortunately, the room was so noisy, Pottle didn't hear Lucky's clever joke. Girls combed their hair, boys threw spit wads at each other, and the hooligans busily wagged their tongues, constructing paper airplanes and shooting them across the room. It was a mess. The noise level was much worse than my other two classes. Clearly, either Mr. Pottle could not control his class, or he enjoyed the commotion while he finished eating his sweet roll and coffee.

"Mr. Hodge? I want you sitting right over here." Pottle pointed to a chair on the aisle opposite Lucky Miller. "I have a brand-new book for you. Please cover it by tomorrow's class. You can buy book covers at the student store."

Pottle, a tall Lincoln-like man wearing a full suit and a bow tie, began circling the room, dropping quizzes on students' desks.

Lucky stared blankly at the quiz in front of him.

"Oh my! I got the same score!" oozed the girl who sat behind him. She proudly showed Lucky her test paper. A thirty-seven out of a hundred, which was a fail, wasn't it? If I failed a quiz, I would start seeing stars and darkness. My throat would close up. I'd choke on my own saliva. What normal person would be excited or show even a hint of delight at failing a test?

After Pottle strolled up and down the aisles handing back the tests, he stood at the front of the room, shook his head, and tittered. "You will all take this again on Friday. The questions will remain almost the same. Study chapters three and four. No reason why each of you can't get a passing grade."

Shaking his head in disgust, Pottle then approached the blackboard, grabbed a piece of chalk, and wrote out the question:

What happened at the Constitutional Convention?

"This will be one of the possible essay questions. Can anyone answer it now?"

I did not volunteer. I must feign ignorance, I told myself.

"Miller?"

"Yes, sir."

"Answer my question. What happened at the Constitutional Convention?"

"Which one?" Lucky asked.

Yikes. He was dumber than I thought.

Pottle hovered over Lucky's desk, grabbed the piece of paper Lucky had doodled on, rolled it into a ball, and tossed it across the room. Bull's-eye! It landed directly into a trash can. Even Mr. Pottle excelled at sports.

"The Constitutional Convention. 1787. Your assignment last night? Share one thing you learned. One thing, Miller! I'm not asking for much!" Several girls raised their hands, hoping they might rescue their hero. Pottle insisted only Lucky answer. "You have your book? Open it up and see what it says. I don't have any problem with you reading from the textbook."

Quite fair. I couldn't believe I was actually rooting for Lucky.

"Read us what it says!" Pottle repeated, growing impatient.

The room was silent as we waited.

"Miller?"

"Yes, sir." The blond doofus sat up straight.

"Answer my question. Last time. What happened at the Constitutional Convention?"

Dead silence.

"Do you even have your book?" Pottle took in a sharp breath.

The girl sitting on his right handed Lucky her textbook. Pottle calmly snatched it off Lucky's desk and slapped it back on the girl's desk.

"Miller, where is your textbook?" he snapped.

Several class members moaned. No one wanted trouble for Lucky. Not the Swim Champion, pride of Encino High. Not hunky, handsome, dumb-as-a-mushroom Lucky. He shouldn't be in this classroom. He should be on the set of a TV series featuring underwater treasure hunts.

"I just didn't realize we'd need our book today, Mr. Pottle," he said. The boy sounded once again like Eddy Haskell.

"You need your textbook every day, Miller. Had you taken your book home with you, would you have studied? And had you brought the book back to class, would you be capable of finding and reading me the answer?"

Lucky smiled. "I had swim practice until late last night, sir. I'm sorry. I'll go get my book from my locker."

"You will do no such thing."

Pottle leaned against the blackboard and pulled slightly on

both ends of his suspenders. "All right. Can anyone else tell Mr. Miller one rudimentary thing derived from the Constitutional Convention? One accomplishment. One fact. When you deliver the answer, tell our swim champion, not me."

I almost felt sorry for the doofus. Pottle should never embarrass a student by picking on him. Why would any teacher dump a load of humiliation, even on a dumbass like Lucky?

I thumbed through my new textbook, impressed by the color maps, the table of contents, the timelines, and the appendix. I assumed he would not call on me. I was new. It was my first day. Obviously, I did not know the assignment, nor had I even been given the textbook until a few minutes ago.

"Mr. Hodge?"

Shit!

"Do you know the answer? If so, illuminate us."

"Me?" I asked, incredulous. I prayed there was more than one Mr. Hodge.

"Your file says you're from a private academy. Bon-vah-deen?"

"Yes, sir. Bonvadine Academy."

"Can you tell us one accomplishment, one feat, something, please, from the 1787 Constitutional Convention? Do not keep us waiting."

Panic ran through my head. Why pin this on me? Shit, shit, shit. Why is it always me? I should transfer out of this class and take Advanced U.S. Government. I want the transfer now! I'm damned if I do, damned if I don't. If I give a good answer, Lucky's animosity toward me will only increase, but if I give a stupid answer, I'll—well, Pottle will think I'm as dumb as everybody else.

"Mr. Hodge? I'm waiting."

"I know a little. Not much," I replied.

"Give us whatever tidbits of information you have."

I had promised myself I would do my best to fit in, but how would I do that when nearly every student in this class failed the quiz? Should I purposely act stupid so I could be part of the crowd? I tried finding a middle ground.

"We're waiting."

"Mr. Pottle, it's my first day here, and I haven't read the textbook. From my limited background in this history, I remember one of the objectives of government included securing the right to life, liberty, property, and the pursuit of happiness."

I didn't think this was a very good answer, but Mr. Pottle clasped his hands together, stood away from the blackboard, and bounced up and down on his heels.

"Excellent answer. Why couldn't you come up with this answer, Mr. Miller?"

Pottle raised his arms up in the air and bowed at me, as if I were the Sultan of Encino. Then, he glanced at Lucky and pointed his pencil at the boy's forehead.

"Tomorrow, Mr. Miller, Mr. Phillips, and Mr. Levine will be in the hot seat. This kid didn't even read the textbook. By George, this is his first day in class, and he knew an answer! I expect all of you to thoroughly reread the chapters tonight and answer my questions correctly. Because if you don't study, you won't pass my class."

He winked at Lucky.

I wished Pottle had not embarrassed Lucky in front of everyone and made me seem smarter. This would have been outlawed at Bonvadine. Most of the time we worked in an atmosphere of encouragement, not disparagement. Clearly, Pottle believed you could make students work harder through humiliation and intimidation. In my mind, this was a fireable offense.

I knew better than give Pottle a piece of my mind. I had no intention of starting trouble. More importantly, I thought I should let Lucky know how I felt about this. As much as I believed I should create distance between me and the doofus, I could seize this opportunity as a moment to repair the damage done and offer my services as a tutor and book report writer.

After class, I darted out into the hall, searching for Lucky. I sorted through a whole bevy of possible scenarios. With my help, he'd have no trouble completing high school, and if he started community college, he'd earn a deferment and avoid the draft. Who knows? I might save his life!

By the time I organized the thoughts in my head, Lucky and his band of hooligans had marched past me. I felt big hands shove me across the hallway. My arm hit a bank of lockers, I lost my balance, and I crumpled to the ground.

Lucky stopped, assessed the damage, and laughed. "Judy, I didn't hurt your vocal cords, did I?"

My arm was bloodied. My brand-new history textbook, with its beautiful colored maps, had been tossed across the corridor, its pristine cover bent and torn. I could feel Lucky's bad breath on my face as he laughed. I pulled myself up off the cement, but Lucky fiercely put his hands on my shoulders and pushed me down again. "You're not going anywhere. Stay. Good dog!"

As they walked away, his buddies howled with laughter, as did many other kids rushing by, desperate to make class before the bell rang.

I stuck my hand in my pocket and felt for the dime. Should I call my aunt? Maybe I should call my uncle and spend the rest of the day at his office. I sat there, sprawled on the cool cement in the covered hallway, angry at myself on several levels. One, I was wearing the wrong shoes. If I'd had tennis shoes on, maybe I wouldn't have skidded across the cement floor as if I were on skates. I was also the skinniest kid in this school, as light as a feather. No wonder gangs of kids could take advantage of me. I could blame Miriam Hodge, or I could take the responsibility myself. Get fit. Gain some weight. Put on some muscle. Secondly, I had turned down a prime opportunity. I should have written the entire book report for him. Why did I stick to my high morals? What is wrong with me? I asked myself. My damned ethics have no place in this town. If I'm surviving this move, I must cheat, steal, rob, and who knows, beat up other kids and toss them in ditches! This is the Wild West, not New York City.

"You hurt?" a voice asked.

Some old lady stood over me. She helped me up from the ground and escorted me to the nurse's office. Her flowery scent made my head spin.

"What's your name?" she asked.

"Haskell Hodge."

"Son, you have a bad bruise. My oh my. I'll put Mercurochrome on it, but it will sting."

And sting it did. She also dipped a cotton ball into alcohol and rubbed the wound so hard I almost flew out of my chair.

I gathered she must be the sadistic school nurse who used hypodermic needles as hair pins.

"So, what happened here?"

"Some kids knocked me against the wall."

"I'm reporting this."

"It's all right. No need."

"What are their names?"

"It's my first day here. I don't know any names."

I may be many things, but I am not a snitch.

"Should I call your parents, have them pick you up?"

"No, I'm fine" I told her. I was fine. She put several Band-Aids over the wound. When the bell rang again, I thanked her and sprinted off toward my next class. Well, not sprinted—hobbled.

Could the day get any worse?

12

THE BASEBALL GAME

I was standing in the east section of campus, staring at the torn, crumpled piece of paper that listed my classes and their locations. Good thing I had stuffed it deep in my front pocket. My next stop? BIABC4. What the blazes does that mean? I had lost the paper map Vice Principal Freed gave me. I had already missed one of my classes. I nearly broke my arm. I had no friends. The day had gone so horribly, how could it possibly get any worse?

And then I heard a voice over my shoulder.

"Need help?"

Angelic, sweet, sonorous, her voice was the birdsong healing my world. I turned to see who had spoken. She had on a red T-shirt announcing in thick black lettering: "Macbeth Arrives January 1967 Encino High." She was very pretty with brownish hair under a cute cap and a few adorable freckles. I pointed to the odd combination of numbers and letters on my sheet.

"Oh, Industrial Arts," she says. "How silly of them. Back Campus Industrial Arts Building C4. Easy, huh?" She pointed in the opposite direction from where I had been walking. "It'sway away uildingbay atway ethay arfay endway ofway ampuscay."

What the hell was that?

"It's a building at the far end of campus."

"Hey, thanks. I appreciate it."

"You from New York?"

"Upper East Side," I told her. "Only been here a week."

"Eventysay-irstfay andway exingtonlay. Eliaday Acobsonjay. I'm working on my Pig Latin."

Jesus, am I in the Encino mental ward?

"I lived at 71st and Lexington. I'm Delia Jacobson."

"Haskell Hodge."

We shook hands. She had the softest skin.

"Both displaced New Yorkers. What brought you here?" she asked.

"My mom dumped me at my aunt's house while she went off to Europe with her boyfriend."

"That was pretty bold of her."

"I guess you could say that."

"I'm here because my dad got transferred. He's in aerospace. If I never see a cold winter again, I'll be fine. You like it here?"

Don't screw this up. She's nice and smart. In her own way, very pretty. Cute might be the better word.

"I think so."

"I'll show you around some time. Sound good?"

"Yeah. Yeah." That's Southern California for "yes." I gotta get the hang of it.

"I'm trying out for Lady Macbeth. You into acting at all?"

My God, she speaks my language.

"I am."

"You should try out. Tryouts are next month."

"Sure. Why not?" I said. *Macbeth*, huh?

"Maybe we'll bump into each other at lunch or nutrition?"

"Sounds groovy. And bitchin'!" I've heard these words a lot.

Delia! DEEL-YA. I didn't care how unusual she was, I wanted a friend and an ally. The fact that she was trying out for Lady Macbeth was a real plus. She was kind and personable. I couldn't say people had been too kind lately, and I didn't know if it was me—some aura about me—but I was so pleased she showed some interest.

My list of things to do must include becoming fluent in Pig Latin.

"I gotta run," Delia said. "Or I'll miss my test in English. You a senior?"

"Yes!"

"Emay ootay."

"Emay ootay too," I replied. I caught on fast. A friendly person who enjoyed drama—I would learn any language if it helped me get close to Delia.

I headed toward Building B at the very back of the campus, apparently near a swamp. I smelled algae, garbage, sewer water, wood chips. Inside the warehouse-like structure, everyone was working on some balsa wood animals. Today must be lacquer day. The fumes made my head spin faster than the perfume I had smelled on the school nurse. The teacher, wearing overalls and a Builder's Emporium hat, said his name was Mr. Woodrow.

I'm not making that up.

"New boy, everyone!"

Not one kid raised his head to see who walked into the room.

I barely spent more than ten minutes in the class before the bell rang. Then, Mrs. Olson's science class, where we assembled Styrofoam balls into our version of a solar system. Then lunch where I ate alone, wandering through the massive cafeteria while munching on a hard meatloaf sandwich. After lunch,

French. The French teacher? More breathtakingly beautiful than Mrs. Green. Only problem? Mrs. Dubonet only spoke French.

"Vous êtes nouveau. Non?"

"This is beginning French, right?" I asked. "French 101, Miss Dube-ah-net?"

I always thought I was good with languages, but the only one I had tackled at Bonvadine was a dead one.

"Monsieur Hodge? *En français, s'il vous plaît. Vous devez parler en français. Sinon, je ne répondrai pas à votre question.*"

"Um." I was baffled. Could a beginning French class be this advanced in a couple of weeks?

"Est Doh-meh-neigh. Nous parlerons après la classe. Allez au laboratoire de langues avant ou après l'école."

I was glad when I landed in PE, the Land of the Encino High Braves. My teacher was Mr. Vance. A few inches shorter than me, Vance wore the tightest T-shirt, maybe two sizes too small, showing off bulging pectoral muscles and massive biceps. On his right arm was a tattoo of a ship's anchor. "Suit up, Hodge!" He handed me a pair of shorts, a T-shirt, a jock strap, and a locker number. I had paid a gym fee of twenty-five dollars when I registered, so this must be what I'd purchased. His shaved head glowed in the sunlight, and when he smiled, his perfect white teeth gleamed brightly as if he were posing for a toothpaste ad.

I wrote the locker combination on one hand with a pen.

"Can I just watch today?" I asked.

He completely ignored the question as if he had not heard a word I said, so I stuck my clothes in the locker and suited up.

Afternoon temperatures roared into the high nineties. Despite the heat, Vance insisted we run, do pull-ups, jumping jacks and push-ups, all outside on the hot asphalt. Then, after calisthenics, Vance announced we were playing baseball. Our class versus Mr. Rattigan's.

Though I'd never played baseball before, I was at least familiar with the rules and the vocabulary. Innings. Strikeouts. Three outs. If the ball crossed a certain line, it would be considered a home run. I understood the basic terminology. Hey, I even knew what a pinch hitter was.

Lucky Miller pitched for Coach Rattigan's team. I mean, what better way to end the day than getting hit by a fastball thrown by my bitter enemy? Or not getting hit at all.

I had been playing center field on and off for the past half hour, and no balls came my way. I thought about Delia, the bright star of the day. I also noticed another kid on the opposite team, standing on second base. He looked familiar, though he kept pulling his hat over his forehead, shielding his eyes from the sun, and I couldn't be sure it was who I thought it was until a ball finally came toward me, and I planned to tag the runner on third base. I must have heard that phrase a million times. My uncle loved hearing Vin Scully on the radio. Who would think the vocabulary I picked up from listening to Dodger games would ever come in handy? The ball bounced a few times on the grass. I grabbed it and ran toward third base. I think I should have thrown the ball to the third baseman, but the runner had already reached third base. What was the point in throwing it now? I knew I should now throw it to the pitcher, but the kid on third base looked so damned familiar, I couldn't help staring at him.

"Hey! I think my aunt knows your mom. Sheila?"

I ended up a few feet away from third base.

"I'm Haskell."

He scratched his head and scrunched his eyes. "You're the actor from New York!"

"Well, you're more the actor than I am, but I am from New York."

"Miriam Hodge is your mother?"

"Yes!"

"And you're the Sugar Flakes kid? I used to love those commercials. You still do them?"

The third baseman interrupted. "Hey, are you fags having a tea party? Throw the frickin' ball back to the pitcher."

I threw the ball and moved backwards into center field, grateful Henry didn't roll his eyes or say anything mean. I couldn't hear his words, but I read his lips—"Talk later," he said, winking at me. Why did I have this crazy feeling of relief? A buoy thrown at me while adrift. I was so glad my aunt knew his mom. With our mutual interests, we might become good friends.

Next inning, I sat on the bench, never got called to bat, and when it was our team's turn to field, I stood there, once again in center field, watching Henry in the dugout. He waved at me a few times, but I couldn't wave back. I mean, how would that look?

No balls came my way. Two-ten p.m. Two-twelve p.m. Two-fifteen p.m. Soon the bell would ring and, thank God, this school day was nearly over.

Score was four to four. My team—now in the batter's box. Two outs so far. Next player up hit a single. Next player? Another single. Soon some heavy-set guy—dubbed a power hitter—batted the ball far into center field. Bases loaded. Two outs. Five minutes left. Three men on base. Two-thirty-nine p.m.

"Hodgeman, you're up!" I heard someone yell.

God, make the bell ring! Please. Make it ring right now!

Although I had the baseball lingo down—this would make my uncle proud—I had never actually hit a ball before or swung a bat. I watched baseball on TV many times, but I had never participated in the game.

BAT-TER, BAT-TER, BAT-TER, BAT-TER, BAT-TER, BAT-TER, BAT-TER.

The chanting of this word, over and over, reminded me of the Voodoo songs sung in *Hercules and the Snake People.*

BAT-TER, BAT-TER, BAT-TER, BAT-TER, BAT-TER, BAT-TER, BAT-TER.

If only the bell would ring so class would end and I wouldn't embarrass myself at the plate.

BAT-TER, BAT-TER, BAT-TER, BAT-TER, BAT-TER, BAT-TER, BAT-TER.

The sun created this shimmering effect, as if we were on the surface of Mars instead of in Encino. I tasted brown-red dust on my tongue. I smelled sweat and the stench of my own body. My eyes stung from the toxic air.

Lucky swung his arms in circles, his face one big grimace.

I am striking you out, you little FAIRY, he seemed to say.

"Hey, Judy! You hold the bat like you're a little girl!" someone yelled. No, not just someone. Someone from my own team! Words travel fast.

Lucky was all snarly and ferocious, kicking the sand with his left foot, a mad, smiling bull. Any minute now the bell would ring, the session would end, and if I could make contact with the ball before the bell rang, I'd be the hero. If I struck out, I'd be Judy forever.

Much depended on the outcome of this game.

Lucky spit in his glove, raised his leg, and threw the next ball.

It flew past me.

"Strike one!" someone shouted.

Sitting on the bench, Vance bowed his head, scratched his nose.

Say something, Mr. Midget Muscle Man!

Lucky smiled again, cocky, arrogant, his eyes firmly planted on me.

The ball flew past me, and I swung anyway. Dummy! What's the matter with you?

Strike two.

The grin on Lucky's face now turned into a full-spread happy, gleeful, malicious smile. I guess elbowing me in the hall was not enough. Calling me Judy in front of my classmates? Not fulfilling. Striking me out would make his day, and if he accomplished this fast enough, his team would be up next, and who knows? Seconds before the bell rang, he'd hit a home run and change the score. It would be five to four, and he'd be the hero of the day.

Please, dear God! Do not let me strike out.

Henry, playing at first base, gave me a thumbs-up. If I made a single and brought a runner home, his team would lose—and yet he encouraged me.

Aren't you man enough to hit that ball, a voice said inside my head? And if I hit the ball and ran, would Henry catch the ball before I even made it to first base and tag me out?

But where do my feet go? How should I stand? How do I hold the bat? What's my strategy here? I turned around and hunted for some encouraging faces, but my team players just sat on the bench, staring mindlessly into space. Finally, Mr. Vance looked up from his thick paperback book. He was reading *The Carpetbaggers*.

"Mr. Vance?" I asked. "Could you help me?"

Vance rose from his chair, a painful expression on his

face. Did he suffer from hemorrhoids, or was he dreading the opportunity of making a difference in a boy's life?

"What's the problem?" he asked.

"Obviously, I have no idea what I'm doing. Would you help me?"

Now my whole team laughed. I should write jokes for Johnny Carson.

"Oh!" he said. It was as if Vance had been asleep this whole time. Couldn't he tell I was struggling? "Your feet should be parallel. Now align them directly under your shoulders." He turned and spat onto the ground. "You left-handed?"

I nodded.

"Okay, your right side should face the pitcher. There you go. Keep your knees bent. Plant your back foot. Line up your knuckles."

What a heavy load of instructions!

"Come on, Haskell. Don't strike out, you dork head!" someone screamed.

"Get at least a single!"

And then in the outfield, I heard members of Lucky's team chant, "Judy, Judy, Judy. Strike out already! What's taking you so long?"

"Don't let the voices annoy you," Vance told me. "Keep your eye on the ball. Didn't your dad ever practice with you?"

I shook my head. My dad? I barely ever saw my dad. He doesn't know the first thing about parenting or playing baseball.

"It's all right. You can do this," Vance said in a surprisingly warm, comforting voice. "Let the bat hover over your shoulder. Keep a straight line. Now when he throws the ball, swing."

Glancing briefly at the runner on third base and then back at me, Lucky threw the ball with force.

I swung.

I felt the bat make contact with the ball. I did not see where it landed. I just ran, like bloody hell, overrunning first base. The runner on third came home, and our team scored the winning point. Henry smiled. I could read his lips. "Good job!"

When I turned around, saw the boys on my team screaming and hollering, jumping up and down with excitement, I joined in and screamed, "Hallelujah!" Several boys patted me on the back. "Good job, Hask." "You're not bad, goofball." I was thrilled. At least I proved I could hit a ball—I was not completely helpless. Lucky might now accept me not as some dorky uncoordinated idiot but as a kid who tried his hardest.

Henry tapped me on the shoulder. "Let's meet maybe after school. I have a bus to catch. See ya!"

He ran ahead of me. Lucky, who was only a few feet on my left, stuck his nose in the air, refusing to look my way. If I were to try for a truce, this was the perfect moment.

"Lucky?"

No answer.

"You pitched well."

"Fuck off."

His team lost. He wanted a win. I could see why he might be upset.

"Do you still need help on your paper?" I asked.

"Not from you, Judy. Get lost."

"I'm sorry we got off on the wrong foot. I'll help you with the book report if you want. I'll even tutor you in Government, so you can pass that class. Okay?"

I sounded so pathetic.

He rolled his eyes and began walking faster.

"And really, all I want in return is peace, man. Peace between us." I surprised myself I could even talk this way. I was no hippie. I never attended a love-in or peaceful march. Still, he ignored me. As soon as we entered the locker room, he disappeared, and I wandered up and down the aisles searching for my locker.

Fortunately, I could still read the locker number and the combo on my hand. I opened the locker, removed my clothes, and started dressing until Vance yelled at me. "Hodge? Did you shower, yet?"

"No sir. I don't want to miss my bus."

"You're not leaving here until you shower," he said.

"Sir, the bus comes in ten minutes."

"That's not my problem. Next time, move faster."

Lucky and half a dozen Neanderthals now stood naked in the shower, throwing soap at each other. Didn't they also catch the bus? I didn't think the day could get any worse, and yet the idea of showering naked with these guys petrified me. We didn't even have PE at Bonvadine, let alone open showers. I was self-conscious, not only over my skinny skeletal body—but my dick was a grower not a show-er, and when soft, it was so tiny, it disappeared, leaving only its head, as if it were a mushroom. Their dicks? Longer, bulkier, rope-like. Why did I get short-changed? I looked the other way, and yet, how could I not stare? If they saw my shrimpy penis, I'm sure I'd never hear the end of their taunting and teasing. I waited and waited. I better get this over with, I thought. I removed my clothes, stuck them in the locker, and reluctantly walked naked down the aisle holding my two hands in front of my privates.

I found a spot on the other side of the large, room-size shower. I soaped up, stood under the shower heads, cupped the water with the palms of my hands and slapped it on my face. A tattooed, bald, big bellied old man—kids called him Wolfe—sat on a chair with a pile of white towels on his lap. I noticed when kids exited the shower that he made sure they were soaking wet before he handed them a towel. One kid was only half wet, and Wolfe barked—"Soap up!" The poor kid would go back into the showers and get totally soaked.

Don't make a big deal of this. Say nothing. Just follow the rules.

Just as I made my way across the tiled room toward the shower exit, Lucky and his fellow Neanderthals started urinating on me, aiming their dicks directly at me, spraying me with a strong flow of dark yellow urine, laughing so hard one of them slipped and fell on his rear end.

For a hygiene-obsessed freak like me, I was irate that no one intervened. Not Vance. Not this old bald man with a pile of towels on his lap. How did those boys get away with urinating on others? This was totally nasty and unhealthy.

I went back and washed myself off and grabbed a towel.

I could handle this once. I couldn't imagine, however, going through this day after day, five days a week. I would say something. I would not shower in PE if students were allowed to do this to each other. The urine smell stuck in my throat, and I gagged until I dry heaved into the toilet.

I finally galloped over to my locker. This time I couldn't remember my combo, and the numbers were smeared on my hand. I kept moving the spindle left and right. Henry stood a half dozen lockers away, just in a pair of underwear. No wonder he got all those parts. He had a near-perfect physique, olive skin, much darker than mine. I wasn't sure how he handled violating school code by wearing his hair long, but I could see why he'd get cast as an Indian or, for that matter, a rugged pioneer boy. Granted, he was older than me, as most kids were in my classes, but still I wished I had his handsomeness. If I did, all my troubles would be solved. I'd not only be more respected, I'd be more desired—and not just by casting agents. The girls would swoon all over me.

"You okay?" he asked.

I couldn't get my locker open, and as I struggled with the numbers, glancing periodically at him, trying not to look, I felt my dick grow longer and harder.

What the hell is wrong with me?

I tightened the towel around me. I had the feeling Henry saw the uncomfortable position I was in, but he said nothing. There was something slightly cruel lurking in his gaze. Or maybe I just read into it.

I attempted softening my now very erect dick by tilting my head backwards and rummaging through titles of every gruesome horror movie I could think of: *The Tingler. Blood of Dracula. The House on Haunted Hill.*

Please, please, please make my erection go away. Can this day get any worse?

I was so relieved when I finally got my locker open, quickly removed my towel, and put on my underwear without Henry (or hopefully anyone else) noticing my erection.

Frankenstein. The Werewolf. The Fall of the House of Usher. The Pit and the Pendulum.

I came up with as many titles as I could until I finally threw on some clothes, grabbed my sweaty shorts and T-shirt, my books and notebook, and I ran onto the sports field, across the campus, onward toward the bus stop.

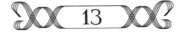

AN ENCOUNTER AT THE BUS STOP

I stood in one of the lines of students snaking across the parking lot where the buses would eventually line up.

"You taking the bus home?" It was Henry shouting across the lot, running toward me. "Are we on the same bus?"

"Yeah, yeah."

"Bitchin'! Let's sit together."

"Bitchin'!" I said back.

"Hey, can I butt in front of you?"

The girls behind us giggled. "Butt all you want," we heard one of them mumble, and Henry raised his eyebrows and smiled at them. We were about to have a conversation when, at that very moment, Lucky darted in front of us, nearly crash-landing into me.

"Oh, sorry. May I jump in line in front of you ladies?" He started sniffing me. "What's this I smell? Eau de Pee?"

His group of hooligans, creeping up behind him, thought this was the funniest joke Milton Berle ever stole.

Henry again put his hand on my shoulder. "That kid is such an asshole. Ignore him."

At least a couple dozen other kids stood in the various lines, and some of them must have heard what Lucky said because I heard one boy tell a girl—"They peed on him in the showers"— pointing to me, of course. The girl covered her mouth with her hand, muffling her hysterical laughter, as if she too thought this was great fun, worthy of a skit on *The Hollywood Palace.*

My first day at EH, and I was getting repeatedly humiliated. When will this day ever end?

"Hey, Judy! Did I hurt you this morning?" Lucky circled around me.

"What did you call him?" Henry asked.

"It's none of your business, Stoneman. Was I talking to you?" Lucky wiped his mouth and blew a strand of hair out of his eyes.

"No, but this is a friend of mine, and I don't appreciate you picking on him."

"You're friends with Judy? Did you make her Carnegie Hall concert?"

Again, his fellow hooligans broke down laughing. I expected this from spiky-haired Winston, but even Nice Nate was smiling, and I found that disappointing.

"No, but if you keep this up, you'll be hugging the sidewalk in a moment." Henry said. I hoped Henry's brashness would intimidate Lucky.

"Bug off, four eyes! You wearing a little pony tail! Isn't that the cutest thing?" Lucky attempted touching the small roll of hair Henry had rubber banded at the back of his head.

"You're a frickin' moron. Go get in the back of the line, Lucky."

"You have a problem with me butting in front of you, four eyes?"

Henry did wear glasses, but they weren't nearly as thick as mine, and with the wire frames and the tinted glass, he looked fashionably "in," as if he belonged not on a school campus but behind a drum set in a hippie rock band.

"I'll bug off after you shut the hell up!" Henry continued. "I don't want you calling him those names again. It was probably funny the first time you said it. It's not funny anymore."

Lucky shook his head and smirked. "What a bunch of little faggots you both are! Look at you fairies hanging out together." He said this in a sing-song voice, loud enough for his voice to carry across the parking lot area. I was hoping Henry would just ignore it. Instead, he stood up to Lucky, their faces inches apart from each other.

"Tell me, Mr. Miller, what do *you* know about faggots?" Henry asked him, poking his index finger against Lucky's chest. "Why don't you tell us all about faggots?" By now, there must have been at least a few dozen kids circling around them. It grew very quiet. A few more deep breaths. My heart raced. I felt this horrible clamminess seep through my skin. I didn't want Henry defending me. Still, what choice did I have?

"If you're so convinced we're faggots, Lucky Miller, you must know quite a bit about faggots. Because I haven't a clue. Why don't you share with us—with everyone here. What does Lucky Miller know about being a faggot?"

I held my breath. I couldn't believe he was taking on this hoodlum. What was he thinking?

Winston covered his mouth with his hand, probably to keep from loud laughs, and Nice Nate too looked as if his eyes might spill out of their sockets. Maybe they had never seen their Big Leader so humiliated.

Lucky was definitely startled. He kind of shuffled his feet, shifted his glance around the crowd now surrounding us, and his face turned a bright red.

"I'm sorry. I didn't hear you. What—do—you—know about being a faggot? I'm sure you're familiar with the saying: It takes one to know one?"

The crowd grew eerily silent. Lucky turned crimson, his hands curling into fists, his breath accelerating. Now nearly everyone was holding his breath wondering who would throw the first punch.

We stood a few yards from Dr. Freed's office. The California flag drooped in the still air. We saw no bus. No school administrator. No teachers. Just a crowd of nearly four dozen students, surrounding Henry and Lucky. Winston and Nate stood directly behind their leader, and I was behind Henry. Were we about to get into a brawl? A second felt like an hour, and then Lucky smiled, signaled for his pals to move before he raised his fists in the air, obviously preparing for a fight. Lucky took the first swing, but Henry grabbed his arm before it made contact, kicking Lucky in the stomach. Lucky immediately fell to the ground. Before he could get back on his feet, Henry put the heel of his foot onto Lucky's forehead. The other hooligans did nothing. Winston stood there, his jaw wide open, and Nate trembled, as if he feared he might be the next victim.

It happened so fast, I think all of us were shocked, maybe even dazzled by Henry's quick self-defense.

Bending down on one knee, Henry spoke into Lucky's ear, almost in a whisper. "Listen, Monsieur Miller. If you ever lay another hand on Haskell, you won't be just lying on the ground. You'll be in the hospital, with broken arms, broken legs, and broken ribs. Is that clear?"

"Yeah, who's going to do it to me?" Lucky asked, his voice barely audible.

"I am, you moron. Who else do you see volunteering for this job?"

Henry pressed his heel harder on Lucky's forehead until the poor dweeb screamed. "Stop it!" Lucky's arms swung at Henry's leg, but Henry jumped, his two legs landing hard on Lucky's arms. The doofus screamed again, an excruciatingly painful expression on his face.

"You want up? Apologize, right now."

Under his breath, Lucky mumbled, "I'm sorry." As the doofus rose to his feet, he took another swing. Henry caught Lucky's fist with his right hand and twisted the arm hard behind his back until the poor hooligan screamed louder than before. "All right! All right! Enough!"

"I learned self-defense because of idiots like you. Now leave my friend alone."

The bus finally arrived. Henry and I sat together in the front as we watched Lucky dust himself off and board. Before he made his way past us, he tried punching Henry in the shoulder again. Henry dodged it by merely moving his shoulder in the nick of time—and poor Lucky, his knuckles hit the metal bar above the seat with such force, I wondered if he had broken his hand. It must have hurt like the devil because he let out a loud, painful yowl.

"You better put some ice on that as soon as you get home!" someone shouted.

"It's going to swell up big time."

"Someone I know is going to need some X-rays!"

"And his mommy."

"She'll make it all feel better. No worries."

"Mommy will kiss his little boo boo!"

"And sing him some lullabies so he'll go fast asleep."

And these girls—the same ones who had stood behind Henry and me in line—began making all sorts of baby sounds and noises. Really annoying. I was glad they took my side now. I couldn't say I felt sorry for Lucky. I felt relieved he was getting a dose of humiliation. See what that feels like, you doofus! Still, I didn't think any of this teasing was necessary.

I waited until the bus headed out of the parking lot before I thanked my hero. "That was very brave of you. I appreciated your help."

"Your first day at school and you've made an enemy. How did you manage that?"

I shrugged.

"How did you become so lucky?" He laughed at his own pun and then lowered his voice. "Talk to me, buddy boy. Why did he call you Judy?"

I didn't want to answer him for fear he'd stop liking me. I shut my eyes for a moment. The strange feeling that ran through my blood was a weirdness I couldn't identify. Only one other person had ever been this nice to me. Once in school I was asked to accompany Annie Freedman on the piano, and since I played by ear and knew every popular show tune, we did a whole repertoire during an assembly. It was very rewarding. Lots of girls thought I was "incredible" and "amazing," but afterwards, during recess, Mark Tucker, a fellow thirteen-year-old, mimicked the girls and kept complimenting me in a girly voice. He also made fun of my big ears. "Fly away, Dumbo!" I put up with the teasing for a few days, and perhaps it would have gone on for weeks had Mr. Varnish not overheard Tucker and told him he must stop his taunting. "If I hear one more tease coming from that mouth of yours, you'll spend a half day in the hallway wearing the dunce cap. Is that clear?"

Apparently, not clear enough. Tucker harassed me in the hallways, after school, and at lunch until Varnish caught him flicking my ears as I bent down for a drink of water at the water fountain. "That's it, Tucker!" Varnish made him sit in the middle of the hallway actually wearing a dunce cap, a tall triangular hat, white with red stripes, made of metal. Though it resembled a birthday party hat, it was much larger, maybe the size of the cone you might see blocking an intersection. Varnish made him stay on the stool wearing the dunce cap two whole hours, and during the breaks, kids crept past him, often laughing and pointing fingers. When his punishment ended, Tucker ran out of the school and dashed into his father's limo. That evening, Mr. and Mrs. Tucker insisted on a face-to-face meeting with the Headmaster and Mr. Varnish, and I can't say exactly what went on there, but Varnish turned up the next morning, bright and early, and little Tucker never showed his face again.

We later heard he was enrolled in a military school in upstate New York.

Bullying at Bonvadine Academy was taken very seriously. Maybe that's why I loved Mr. Varnish so much. No one had ever rescued me in that way, until Henry, my one-time rival, kicked Lucky Miller in the stomach.

I needed to say something. He asked me two questions, and I would answer at least one of them.

I cleared my throat.

"So here's the scoop. You ready?"

Henry nodded. "Go for it."

"Lucky was nice to me when we first met. We both liked the Beatles. He went kind of berserk when he heard I had purchased a copy of the latest Beatles album for Hope with the rare butcher cover."

"I don't know what that is."

"The four mop heads are dressed in butcher smocks, surrounded by pieces of raw meat and plastic doll parts. Anyway, it's a rarity, and he was impressed, and he was all 'Let's hang out, bud.' Wanted to see my comic books, my posters. And all was just fine until he insisted I write his book report for him, from start to finish. I said I'd help. I wouldn't write the whole thing. That's cheating."

"I don't blame you."

"And then he threatened me. If I didn't write the book report, he basically said I'd be without a bodyguard, opening myself up to getting killed by gangs of ruffians who would leave me for dead in a ditch."

Henry shook his head. "The guy's a complete moron."

And now I wondered if I should address the other question— regarding why he called me Judy—and I figured, why not go for broke?

"Before all this happened, Lucky spied on me one day while I practiced making baskets. I was a bit clumsy and yet determined to figure out the best way of tossing a ball into the basket. While I did this—I don't know what got into me—I started humming."

"What's wrong with that?"

"Well, you got me. I was doing my own rendition of 'Somewhere Over the Rainbow.' Sang some of the lyrics as well. He heard me and made some crass comment to his sister and my cousin."

"Figures."

"Yeah. And then in my government class today he said out loud, so the whole class could hear, 'Hey Judy, when you singing at Carnegie Hall'?"

"He's a fucking idiot."

"In front of the whole class! Well, I'm glad you agree." I let out a deep breath. "I mean, who doesn't like Judy Garland? My uncle likes Judy Garland. Mr. Varnish, my history teacher, said she had the greatest singing voice in the twentieth century."

"I think she's great, too." Henry grinned.

Well, that was a relief.

"And you know, Haskell, I used to enjoy watching her TV show. I was so sorry when they cancelled it."

"Me too. Love the episode when she sang songs from *A Star is Born*."

"Can't beat 'The Man that Got Away.'"

"Right? What a moment, when she sings that in that smoky nightclub?"

"She really got ripped off. The Academy Award belonged to her."

"I know. What was the Academy thinking, giving the trophy to Grace Kelly for a good but not remarkable performance?"

We both sat back, our heads against the smooth plastic seats of the bus, smiling and laughing. I had a pal who loved movies, appreciated one of my favorite singers, and was willing to stand up and defend me.

He reached over and squeezed my hand.

"You're going to need some self-defense lessons, buddy boy. I don't know why Lucky takes this bus. He has a car, but for whatever reason, he's on my same bus a couple times a week. I'll tell you what," he said. "You help write my term papers, help me study for tests, tutor me in math, write *all* my book reports. In exchange, I'll teach you everything I know about self-defense. Fair enough?"

Now he was making fun of me.

I didn't care. I had what I assumed could be a good friend, something I'd wanted all my life. A friend who loved theater and movies and acting. A friend who could teach me self-defense. Someone who appreciated me and hopefully understood me better than I understood myself. I sat back in my seat, closed my eyes, and crossed my fingers, making certain my words remained in my head, quite silent, so I didn't embarrass myself: Please, let this become what I hope it becomes. A friend. A real friend. Someone I can trust and depend on. A life-long friend. A person I can be honest with and share everything with, even my heart-breaking humiliations and my embarrassments. Finally, I had an ally who would help me fit in.

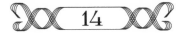

14

HENRY STONEMAN'S BEDROOM

As soon as we entered the kitchen, using a side door, Henry shouted, "Mom? Monsieur Hodge is here! Remember him?"

His mom shouted back from far across the house. "You have your piano lesson in three hours! I haven't heard you practice for more than a few minutes," his mom yelled back.

"I am fully aware and ready, Mom! I'll be fine. *Ho praticato e sono pronto.*"

Henry spoke Italian. What did this kid not do?

He led me up the stairs, and we entered an attic room with high ceilings, pitched with octagonal roof lines. On his walls were pictures of various movie stars—his idols, he said: John Wayne, Randolph Scott, Spencer Tracy, Cary Grant, and dozens of others.

"I'll change. I'll be right out." He disappeared into his walk-in closet and reappeared a short while later in a pair of jeans and a T-shirt with a massive portrait of Beethoven on it. His jet black hair was barely long enough for a mini-pony tail, loose strands falling partly across his eyes, and he had the deepest dimples. It wasn't that he was just good looking; his features made him extraordinarily exotic. He told me he was half Arab and half Sephardic Jew. His father's family was originally from Casablanca, dating back hundreds of years, and his mother's family was Muslim, originally from Tunis. He could have easily passed for several nationalities.

I didn't want him catching me staring, but I couldn't help myself. For one thing, he had a darker complexion than most boys at school, his skin near perfect without any blemishes or pimples. He had a slight cleft in his chin, not deep but certainly noticeable, and his small ears were for the most part unseen because his hair nearly covered them. When he shook his head and his hair swung to one side or the other, I saw ears that were flat against his head, not protruding out all Dumbo-ish— like mine. He also had bluish eyes and long eyelashes. It was as if God had anointed him as a near-perfect example of male handsomeness, and I wasn't sure if I merely envied him or I wished I could trade places and be him.

Maybe he had a girlfriend. I wouldn't ask. Why wouldn't he have a girlfriend? Who wouldn't want him as a boyfriend? Or maybe he wasn't into girls?

"I thought EH had a strict haircut policy. Nothing below the earlobes? How do you get away with wearing your hair long?" I asked.

That got me out of my head for a moment.

"Dr. Freed made an exception since my long hair often gets me my TV roles." He sat down at his upright piano and removed the rubber band holding his pony tail together, allowing his hair to fall naturally a few inches above his shoulders. "I'll play something for you. I'm working on this Chopin mazurka. I've been practicing it slow. For you, fast speed?"

"Why not?" I said.

I had played this piece myself, so I was quite familiar with it.

The difference between our two versions? I played the music with my shirt on.

He pulled his shirt over his head. I wasn't sure if he was showing off his lean physique or if he took his shirt off so he'd feel unhampered.

The shirt now lay on the floor, Beethoven staring up at me with his cruel, dark, penetrating eyes.

"I get sweaty when I play, and I don't want my shirt all wet."

Oh, that explains everything.

On one wall were pictures of him when he was a few years younger. He had changed. Transformed would be a better word. Weight lifting, gymnastics, karate? What did he do to make the muscles stand out, especially in his abdomen? Or make the blue veins thicken in his arms? I was breathing fast, and I closed my eyes, hoping I could distract myself.

His fingers flew across the keyboard. It was a black upright, a Steinway, and he played with fiery passion and feeling, with wondrous energy and spirit. At one point, he slowed down, and the melody grew softer and more poignant, exerting such exquisite control, it brought tears to my eyes. My face reddened. I almost stopped breathing. Technically, he was far better on the piano than me, and he was probably a much better actor, and certainly more of an athlete. I wondered—the hours he spent practicing piano, taking karate or self-defense lessons, as well as preparing for his auditions—when did he ever have time to study?

"So, what did you think?" Henry asked me, after he finished. "Originally, I studied piano for my role as young Chopin. I'm in the film for less than ten seconds. Most of my part was cut. In the meantime, I fell in love with the piano." No question, he was a talented musician, and of the many musicians I knew, none of them—at least not at Bonvadine—had a body like his. What would it take, I wondered, to have a physique matching Henry Stoneman's? I wanted my body to look like his. Simple as that. It was like when I'd peruse the Charles Atlas advertisements, poring over befores and afters of men who miraculously changed from skinny to muscular after following the instructions, which promised results in less than fifteen minutes a day.

"You play so well," I said.

"You think so? Interesting how I slowed it down, huh? *Un movimento lento e facile.*"

I blanked out for a moment. I had no idea what he was talking about.

"Play something for me."

"I don't think that's a good idea."

"Play something. Anything, Haskell. Please."

Reluctantly, I sat down and played the beginning of Rachmaninoff's *Prelude in C-sharp minor*. This piece is said to have sections in it that are the loudest and the softest in music literature. At one point it opens with a three-note motif at fortissimo, imitating the pounding clang of chiming bells, and then it goes pianissimo, as if bells have stopped and we hear only the soft silent air of Moscow. I tried to instill all this feeling into my playing, though Henry had little reaction. I didn't know if he enjoyed it and it left him speechless, or he simply had nothing to say, one way or another.

Still on the piano bench, I turned so I could face him.

Henry sat in a chair near the piano, still bare chested, and put his hands behind his neck. I wasn't sure if he was showing off, or simply waiting for me to say something as I stared at the tiny strands of black hair in his arm pits.

"You're really good."

I nodded.

"I'm thrilled to meet someone who shares my hobbies. I like acting, but I prefer piano-playing. It's solely dependent on me, and I don't have to worry about a director or someone else telling me what to do."

"Acting's not a mere hobby for you. I saw you in *Westward*. You were scary good."

"One line. That's all I had. I'm eager for a real role. A meaty role. Something that entails more than a few words of dialogue."

"I'm sure that will happen soon enough."

"I'd love to quit school. I begged my dad to just let me work with a tutor, focus on my acting and piano, and forego all this school nonsense. Now I'm glad I didn't do that."

"Why?"

"I met you."

I drew in a long breath. I felt as if my whole body had gone limp with wonder. What did this mean? Had a miracle just happened? This may have been the worst day of my life, but I met someone who liked me. Maybe more than liked me.

He laughed. "Does that surprise you, Monsieur Hodge? I've always wanted a friend who knew a lot about movies and plays. We will have so much to talk about."

I nodded my head. "I guess."

"You took that acting class in New York. The Hogan method? How did you get in?"

"I tried out."

"Well, I'm hoping you'll give me some tips if I ever go on another audition, and I'll teach you some self-defense moves so you don't get trounced."

"Sounds good."

"You'll be my first pupil."

"I'm all for that."

"So, the sooner we start, the better. Agreed?"

"Yeah. Thanks."

"Like you, man, I arrived at school a skinny, scrawny mess."

"I'm a mess?"

"Yeah, you're like a stick figure in one of those early Disney cartoons. But that's all going to change. Let me ask you something."

He sounded so serious my heart skipped four beats. What would he say next? He lowered his voice to a whisper.

"Haskell, how old are you?"

"Me?"

"No, I'm talking to the kid down the street."

"I'm eighteen."

"No way, Monsieur Hodge. How old are you really?"

"Sixteen."

"That's what I thought. And you're a senior?"

"I skipped kindergarten. My mom was used to having me in an all-day preschool, which allowed her to do her real estate work, and when she'd pick me up, she'd dump me at Mary's house, and I'd break things left and right. I always got in trouble, so she found this private academy that would allow me into first grade. They had after school care."

Henry sat back in his chair so that he balanced himself on only the back legs.

"I'm eighteen, almost nineteen."

"Lucky is almost nineteen too."

"Yeah, I think he flunked a grade. I didn't flunk a grade. I missed a whole year, or what would have been ninth grade, traveling with my dad. We went all over India and Pakistan and most of Europe. I speak four languages."

My eyes blinked wide open. "That's unbelievable."

"And I have friends all over the world. In São Paulo, Brazil. In Lucerne, Switzerland. Even as far as Reykjavík, Iceland, but no one here in Encino, where I live. So, let's be clear, Monsieur Hodge. We must be friends, as long as you do one thing."

"What is that?"

"Stay alive."

"I don't think I'll have a problem with that."

"Me either, but just in case, I will be your sensei. I'm not advocating fighting. But make no mistake about it, you will need to defend yourself. Everybody gets in fights, especially at this school, and it's just part of the game. Plus, you're a bit odd, Monsieur Hodge."

I laughed. No use disguising my true self. Madame Scheherazade would be very proud of me.

"You ever play baseball before today?"

I shook my head.

"You were clumsy out there, but good for you. You hit the ball."

"Finally."

"And your team beat our team."

"Yep."

"And you pissed off Lucky Miller. He can't stand you."

I shrugged. "Maybe I should have purposely struck out."

"No. You did the right thing."

"As you can tell, I'm not very good at sports."

"I was always good in sports, and I'd usually be one of the first to get picked for a team. But I came here to Encino—filled with almost all white people—and because of my darker skin color, everybody thought I was Mexican or from some South American country. And when kids found out I was half Arab, living here in Encino? That made me a real outcast. Can you imagine what I went through?"

"I have no idea."

Actually, that was not exactly true. Reynaldo, whose mother was Guatemalan, father half black, half Puerto Rican, and half Cherokee—so what if the numbers didn't add up—told us stories about unrelenting bullying he faced growing up in the Bronx, complicated even further by his penchant for wearing eye liner, makeup, and his mother's blouses to school.

"Did you get in fights at your school in New York, Monsieur Hodge?"

"Never. We weren't allowed to get in fights. If we did, we'd get thrown out of school."

"I got in a fight almost every day my first semester here. I was a bit overweight, and I got tired of kids calling me fat hippo, camel jockey, sand nigger, diaper head—they were so ignorant. And my dad would have none of it. 'This nonsense must stop,' he said, in Hebrew. That's his native language."

"You speak Hebrew?"

"And French. Some German, Dutch. I pick up languages easily. One afternoon, some creeps threw me in a garbage can. I didn't break my arm, but I sprained it badly. Couldn't play piano for a few weeks. My dad made a big deal out of this near-catastrophe and spoke to Dr. Freed, who ended up doing nothing. It was my word against this gang of idiots who said I started it."

"Then what?"

"That very afternoon after a meeting with these kids' awful parents and Dr. Freed, Dad dropped me off at a martial arts studio, and the rest is history."

Henry raked his fingers through his hair.

"Monsieur Hodge, we'll work on this, all right? Once or twice a week? And you should consider enrolling in Burt's Studio, where I go. And practice every day. Practice until you're worn out. Is that clear?"

We practiced for at least an hour. He made me focus on using my legs to kick the center of the wall. I did this probably a few dozen times before I got the hang of it. We wrestled too, and each time he pinned me down, I gradually got better releasing his hold on me until I became so tired, I simply didn't move.

"You had enough?" He was hovering over me, pinning my arms to the carpet. I could feel his warm breath on my face. His nose an inch from mine, maybe not even an inch. I looked up and saw his dark blue eyes staring into mine, and I thought for sure he'd make a move. He'd lower his face and kiss me. I let my body relax, take in his scent, the sweet aroma of sweat and his natural skin odor and whatever deodorant he had on—Old Spice?—but instead he rose, got on his knees, and put his hand on my forehead.

"You're burning up, Monsieur Hodge. Should I turn the air conditioning on high?"

It was not particularly hot in the room. My face was flushed because I was embarrassed and humiliated by my uncanny attraction for him.

"I'm going to teach you a few jab punches, you ready? Come on, stand up." I could move, or I could remain still. I decided I'd make no effort to stand up. I just lay there, closed my eyes for a moment. He reached down, held both my hands, and attempted to pull me up off the floor.

"You're such dead weight. You tired? You had enough?"

I finally stood on my feet, and now we faced each other, maybe a foot apart.

I imagined his cheek grazing mine. Maybe he'd position his face so that his lips and my lips would finally meet.

"Did I hurt you?" he asked.

"I am a bit woozy."

"Maybe we call it a day?"

I nodded my head. "Can I use your bathroom?"

He pointed to the door near the closet.

My shirt was drenched, but I was too embarrassed to take it off. Fortunately, his little attic room had its own bathroom with a sink, a toilet, and a small shower. I threw some cold water on my cheeks and forehead and stared at myself in the mirror.

I lusted after Henry Stoneman. I had this insatiable desire to kiss him, just as I kissed that other boy a few weeks ago in New York.

This was an unmistakable feeling I hoped I could keep hidden. We had just met. We had shared a moment on the baseball field, a wonderful conversation on the bus, and now this wrestling match.

I wanted him to peel my shirt off and feel his skin against my skin, his lips against mine, his whole naked body on top of my naked body. I visualized us rolling across the floor of his room, kissing and hugging and laughing.

I really must be crazy.

I took a long pee, and as I stood there, I wondered if this awkward moment would end our wonderful budding new friendship. I didn't want him realizing I enjoyed the physical contact.

What is the bloody matter with me?

I heard a few knocks on the door and then Henry's voice, outside the door.

"Monsieur Hodge? I'm worried about you. Your dizziness all right? Did you fall down the toilet?"

"No. I'm okay!"

I heard the doorbell ring, heralding the arrival of the piano teacher and offering an exit from the awkward situation.

"I'm putting on my shirt and going downstairs. My teacher will be up here in a moment. I'll be right back."

I could hear him, his mother, and a woman with a loud Italian accent chatting away downstairs.

I noticed on the sink a stack of three-by-five black and white polaroids of Henry. He was wearing jeans, a cowboy hat, and an unbuttoned shirt. You could see most of his beautiful muscular chest. His hat tilted over his forehead, and he had one hand on his hip. Standing next to him was the Duke himself, John Wayne. I didn't know what got into me—I felt freaking jealous of his success. It's one thing to have talent; it's another to have the look casting directors desire.

I stuffed one of the photos into my back pocket, opened the door, and walked into the bedroom. Moments later, Henry entered with an older woman following behind him. With her all-black dress, nearly down to her knees, and her silver hair, wound like yarn above her head, she appeared as if she had stepped out of some old melodrama, playing—not a piano teacher—but a rich empress recently widowed. I did not shake her hand. I merely nodded and excused myself. "I should go," I said. "I have a test in calculus tomorrow."

"Wait one moment!" Henry turned toward his piano teacher. "This kid is on the back of the Sugar Flakes cereal box!"

"Oh *mio Dio!*" she said.

"He was the kid in the Sugar Flakes ad who danced with the animated tiger! And he also was in *Medea* with Judith Anderson!" Henry boasted.

I was somewhat embarrassed by his boasting. "I had no

lines. She slit my throat, eight performances a week. I got the role when I was nine."

It apparently did not matter how modest I was, the piano teacher squeezed her cheeks with both her hands, blew an air-kiss at me, and said, "Oh *mio Dio, ho visto quella meravigliosa produzione!*" From the little Italian I learned from Mr. Arturo, my piano teacher, I think that meant, "Oh my God, what a prestigious production."

"You'll coach me in my acting, right, Monsieur Hodge?" Henry asked.

"Why not?" I asked.

"And I'll coach you in self-defense. We'll have the perfect partnership, you think?" He held his hand out to shake mine. "Do some push-ups! Okay? I want to see some muscles on those arms!"

I ran almost the entire way home, nearly two miles. I removed the wrinkled polaroid and stared at it.

What if he counts his photos every night and discovers one gone? What is wrong with me?

I had never felt such infatuation for anyone—boy or girl. I knew I had to do something. Either I speak with Henry and share my feelings, or I go out of my way to avoid him, if that's even possible.

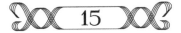

15

SOMEDAY MY PRINCE WON'T COME

I decided to do neither of these. I'd wake up in the morning, do my hundred push-ups, and practice the moves he taught me. I joined the martial arts studio and began taking classes, and since they all knew I was Henry's "protégé," my instructors often spent a good ten minutes before and after class making sure my form was impeccable.

During our after-school time together in his attic bedroom, Henry and I talked about tests, term papers, and acting. We were busy, poring over our copies of *Variety*. One afternoon we discovered an incredible opportunity. I mean, really something I couldn't have dreamed up. It was a great distraction. An open call for a new Hollywood film entitled *Lost at Sea*, about a boatload of school boys marooned on a desert island, surrounded by cannibals and dinosaurs. The ad said they were looking for fifteen boys between the ages of fourteen and twenty-one. Some acting experience required. And it would be directed by Reginald Warwick and produced by my father, Tony Pawlikowski.

"It's *bashert*," I told him.

"Yes, it's meant to be," Henry said. "How come your last name isn't Pawlikowski?"

"My mom wanted my last name to match her stage name."

"Isn't that unusual?"

"My mom is very modern. She had an affair with Barbara Stanwyck once."

I quickly changed the subject. *Lost at Sea* would be filmed on location in Buenos Aires, so I told him it would be exciting for the two of us if we learned some Spanish.

"I speak Spanish. I'll teach you."

What language did he not know?

"And there are fifteen parts. Fifteen! And we *have* acting experience! And it's Warwick Productions!"

"And my deadbeat never-pick-up-the-phone dad might have his hand in producing it!"

"Surely, we'll both get cast in this film! Monsieur Hodge, we have it made! If we get these parts, we can leave Encino High, make our great escape and travel to Argentina together! Didn't I say this might happen?"

What would come next? He'd take out a pair of castanets and a red rose. Maybe he'd invite me to dance, and at one point throw his arms around me, squeeze me close, and kiss me passionately.

"Oh, Haskell, it's not always easy being us, but this will be so much fun!" And this is when, after wrestling and being sweaty in his room for a full two hours, he gave me this intense, long hug.

I had no sense whether Henry desired me or not. He did not make any intimate moves toward me when he had the chance. Was this a romantic hug, or a hug like you'd hug your uncle or your brother?

I had to eliminate the idea of romance in my head. Henry was not being intimate. No way.

Why, however, would one boy take off his shirt in front of

another boy and flaunt his muscles, as he did that first day we met?

And what did he mean when he said it wasn't easy being us? Why wouldn't it be easy being us? Because we both favored singers like Judy Garland? Because we were into acting and music? Because neither of us spent Sunday afternoons glued to the Zenith watching football? Because our favorite movie—we came to this consensus—was *There's No Business Like Show Business* starring Ethel Merman with Marilyn Monroe?

I wished there were a stamp we could have on the back of our necks identifying our sexuality. Gay. Semi-gay. Fully gay. Partly gay. Fully Outright Heterosexual. How were we supposed to know who we were and who others were? Was it all guesswork? Must I ask this question: Henry Stoneman, are you attracted to me?

I was afraid if I asked him if he were queer and he said no, and then he asked me if I were queer and I said no, or I'm not sure, or "Would it matter?" it could easily endanger our friendship. Ruin it. Destroy it.

No. This was just one of those subjects better left unspoken, unless Henry brought it up. And, of course, that was never going to happen.

● ● ●

Over the next few weeks, we spent much of our free time during our morning break and lunch practicing the script of *Lost at Sea*. Henry's agent had loaned us a secret bootleg copy, though it was an early draft and many scenes seemed either incomplete or missing. Still, we could act it out. Henry loved the film's high concept: High school kids on an educational tour of the Galapagos Islands face catastrophe when a terrible storm pulls the boat into a remote area and shipwrecks them off the coast of a mysterious island. The adult leaders in charge die in the wreckage, but Demetrius, the part Henry had his eye on, is the eighteen-year-old son of a Greek shipping tycoon, and he survives along with twelve of the other boys. Handsome and fit, Demetrius bullies the other kids unmercifully. Eventually, he convinces the pack they should sacrifice Oggy (the part Henry thought I should consider) to the human-hungry cannibals in hopes this "meal" might save the rest of their lives.

I was not gaining thirty or forty pounds for the part of fat Oggy, nor did I think this film, in its current script form, could ever get made. I enjoyed rehearsing with Henry because I wanted his company. At one point, I suggested he change the spelling of his name from Henry to Henri, an idea he treasured. "Superb, Monsieur Hodge! Much more sophisticated with an 'i.' French, right? Henri Stoneman." He repeated his name several times, saying it with a thick French accent. He wrote it out, smiled, spread his hands out and reached over, giving me a big bear hug.

I could feel him sink his fingers into my skinny back.

I was thrilled he liked my idea, and with his arms around me, squeezing me tightly, I had another tantalizing image of him finally turning his face, our eyes meeting, our lips touching.

Why am I even going there? Again.

I came home in the afternoon and buried myself in my room, pretending I had a ton of homework and tests. At dinner, I used Hope's tactic and said I didn't feel social.

"Would you mind if I brought dinner into my room, please?"

My aunt did not seem to mind and did what she had done for Hope, bringing me a tray of macaroni and cheese and a salad.

I figured a good hour alone allowed me some contemplation time.

"I'm developing feelings for you," is what I would tell him, although I couldn't quite classify or pigeonhole exactly the feeling.

Was it love? Lust? Infatuation? I had never felt this way before. It felt strange and intangible, like I had been possessed by some supernatural homosexual entity, tightening its tentacles around my fast-beating heart.

I shut my eyes. I stretched my legs out on the bed, my hands behind my head. And as I pored over this dilemma of mine, struggling how best to handle the Henry situation, I heard the door to my room fling open so hard it hit the wall with a loud bang, almost sounding like a gunshot.

Standing in my doorway was Cinderella, dressed for the ball. Her blonde hair was stuffed above her head, large brown hair pins keeping it from disentanglement. Her eyes and face were in full makeup, with thick red lipstick and thick eyelashes. Of course, she wore the lovely white silk dress with its wide skirt shaped over a few petticoats, not a hoop. The hips had what I think were called pouty swags.

"What do you think, Has-skull Bas-skull?" Hope asked. "I'm going as Cinderella for Halloween."

This was Wednesday, October twenty-six. Time certainly travelled fast. This holiday was only five days from now.

"I am preparing because there's a contest at school for best costume. Think I have a chance of winning?"

"They don't have a real good Satan outfit at Woolworth's, do they?" I asked.

"How did you know? I've seen the outfit with horns and a red cape. I'm sure it comes in an adult size. Why don't you buy it?"

She threw herself on the bed.

"What's up, Has-skull Bas-skull? Why weren't you at dinner?"

"I'm not feeling well."

"What kind of snarky wacky werky jerky day did you have?" She stared at the plate, still half full of macaroni. "You didn't eat your dinner, bad boy."

"I told you I wasn't feeling well. I'm not hungry."

"You gotta eat. You got keep your strength up. You never know when you might get beat up by Lucky. Vanessa tells me he wants revenge."

"For what?"

"For whatever you did to him. You should have seen his hand. It was all swollen and black and blue."

That happened a month ago. This was old news.

"I didn't do anything to him. He did it to himself."

"Is that why you're practicing judo? I hear you jumping and bashing your head against the wall."

"It's not judo, and I'm bashing my foot against the wall. It's called kicks. I'm practicing so I can defend myself."

"Well, good luck with that. If I were you, I'd get out of town. I'd move to Tombstone, mister. I'd find myself a cave."

"That's probably not a bad idea."

"Lucky's such a pill. Even Vanessa can't stand him. You know what? She asked him to help her with her spelling test, and he told her some really nasty words. His father yelled at him, and his parents took away his car keys. They're always taking away his car keys."

"I saw him driving today, Hope."

"Well, I'm glad you noticed because in order to win back his keys, he had to test Vanessa on her spelling words."

There was a long, uncomfortable silence. "What does that have to do with me?" I asked.

"I need your help."

Oh, what is it this time?

"I want help on my spelling test. What do you think?"

"I thought your mom was helping you."

"She already tested me on the words so I know how to spell them, but she won't help me put them in sentences."

That's right. Every Friday she had a series of tests. Math, reading, and spelling. This was actually good. Up to now, I'd been sulking in my room. Helping Hope would take my mind off my troubles.

"What do we have to do? Where should we start?"

"Here are my words, including the bonus words. I get extra credit for those. I have to write a sentence for each word, and the sentences must form a story."

"What kind of story?"

"Just any story. She told us to be original and different."

"All right." I looked over the words:

1) Always	5) Chimney	9) Parties	BONUS WORDS
2) Touch	6) Hair	10) Royal	13) Caterpillar
3) Different	7) Beautiful	11) Branch	14) Delightful
4) Ordinary	8) Horse	12) Mysterious	15) Gorgeous

"I have to put each of them in a sentence, and it has to form a story."

"Show me the exact directions."

Hope pulled out a wadded-up mimeograph sheet with instructions she had stuffed in one of her glass slippers. It said: "Write a story using all the spelling words. If you can, make up a story about your Halloween costume."

"This sounds like fun. So how do we get started?" I asked.

"All right. You come up with the first sentence. *Beverly Hillbillies* comes on at eight, so we gotta work kinda fast. Mom said I can't watch TV until my story is written."

We had an hour.

"Does she know I'm helping you?"

"Yes."

"I'm helping. I'm not writing it for you."

"Well, I'm not able to do this all by myself, so let's start already."

"Fine. Why don't we say, 'This will not be an *ordinary* story.'"

She wrote it down and misspelled ordinary.

"Hope, it's A-R-Y, not E-R-Y."

"Oh, I got it." She turned her pencil around, erased the "E" and rewrote it. "Now what?"

"Once upon a time, there was a young *royal* prince who fell in love with Cinderella."

"He fell in love with *gorgeous* Cinderella. That's two of my spelling words, including a bonus word!"

"Excellent job, Hope. How do you like that? I'm very proud of you. You write the next sentence."

"'Cinderella had a wicked stepmother who wouldn't let her go to the ball.'"

"Very good, but we need to use one of your spelling words."

"Cinderella had a *delightful* and wicked stepmother."

"How about this? Cinderella had a wicked stepmother who was mean and *delightfully different*. Can we turn an adjective into an adverb?"

Hope scratched her nose. "Sure. Why not? And all of a sudden, her fairy godmother shows up and . . . and . . ." Hope slouched in her chair and grimly folded her arms across her chest. "Haskell? This story is boring. I mean everybody knows the Cinderella story. How do we make it, oh I don't know, strange?"

"Let's change it a little bit and make it original. She meets the prince in the forest while playing with *caterpillars*, and he invites her to several *parties*."

"All right. Then what?"

"And the prince falls madly in love with her, telling her she has such *beautiful* golden hair."

Hope feverishly wrote all this down. "Then what?"

"And every Saturday, Cinderella visits him at the castle with the towering *chimney*."

"Good, good, good!"

"The prince wants to marry her, but Cinderella is very *mysterious* and turns him down."

"Oh, this is really good. Thank you."

Hope scribbled all the sentences down and read the entire narrative from her sheet. I corrected a few misspellings until we were caught up to this last sentence.

"He could not understand why she was *always* turning him down, and he remained quite sad until he asked her, 'What's wrong?' And she said. 'Prince, I just want to be friends.'"

"I love it! We still have to get *horse* and *branch* and *touch* and we're done."

"Okay." I wondered if I should go for broke and write an unhappy ending or fix it so that the prince and Cinderella live happily ever after. I figured I'd go for the more realistic ending. "'The unhappy prince rides on his *horse*, but he wasn't paying attention. He got hit in the head by a tree *branch*, and died when his head *touched* the ground.'"

"Oh, perfect! We got everything in, even all the bonus words. Thank you!"

"You're welcome. What about your math and your reading?"

"Mom said I can do that later after I watch some TV. I'll be back, okay?"

My aunt came in a few minutes later holding Hope's story in both her hands. I was still lying on my bed, my arms folded across my chest. At first she said nothing. Aunt Sheila merely shook her head, staring at me as if I had done something brutally wrong. "You wrote this?" she asked.

I sat up. "Hope and I collaborated."

"Hope cannot turn this story into her teacher."

"She wanted to make it different. We gave the old fairy tale a creative spin. It was her idea."

"'I just want to be friends?' What is that about? At eight years old, how would Hope know a phrase like that?"

"You'd be surprised. Hope's very precocious."

"There are appropriate and inappropriate stories. Just like the record album, you need to think before you do things like this. Killing the prince with a tree branch? Mrs. Barlow reads these stories out loud in class, and I don't think she will appreciate that violent image. This is third grade, not high school."

"I'm very sorry."

"Think things out next time. You're a smart kid. I know you've never lived with an eight-year-old before, so it may take some getting used to."

"I'll be careful. I promise."

"I'll help her rewrite it, but neither of us are happy about it." My aunt reached over and pinched my cheek before she turned around and trotted out of the room.

Clearly something was wrong with me. I was channeling my own frustrations with Henry and inserting them into my poor cousin's spelling homework. I was sure he just wanted to be friends. Nothing more. Why fantasize that anything more would come of it?

I decided I'd zip it. It was over. I would simply erase any feelings I felt for Henry, and if necessary, avoid him as much as possible. I certainly could not, under any circumstances, take my feelings out on poor Hope.

But then several hours later, I changed my mind. What if you're missing an opportunity?, a voice said inside my head. Maybe Henry feels the same way as you do. How would you know unless you ask him? After all, in the story, the prince sees Cinderella acting mysteriously, and he calls her on it.

By midnight, though, I had talked myself out of having any conversation at all with Henry, knowing full well it would turn out disastrously. Even if he said he loved me, even if he decided to pull my clothes off and seduce me during one of our martial arts sessions, even if we both agreed we loved each other and wanted to spend the rest of our lives together, it spelled disaster in every single way, and here's why.

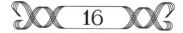

THE THREE REASONS

Reason One: It was very dangerous to be homosexual. My mom's hairdresser may have been the closest I had to a gay friend. Reynaldo Jesus Rodriguez held court at our apartment on many snowy Sunday afternoons, often inviting some of his friends over, as he, Mom, and his buddies drank martinis, skewering the world as a homophobic cesspool and declaring war on all people, government agencies, and religious zealots who put down mankind's natural desires to love others of the same sex, of different races, or different religions.

"They're all phonies. They all preach love and Jesus while hating anyone who is different," he'd say. "Some of the worst homophobes, you know, are gay. All the way up high in government. I've had some trysts with a few senators and district attorneys. That's the God's honest truth!"

I looked forward to his visits and, in fact, adored his outlandish behavior, sashaying around the house wearing one of my mom's boas and flowering hats. But outside on the streets of New York, this kind of behavior got him arrested several times, and he learned to "tone it down." One Saturday night, however, Reynaldo did what he often did; he visited a bar in the Village, leaving around two in the morning, and hadn't even walked a block before he met some man in an alleyway who turned out to be an undercover cop. The story we heard? The cop arrested him for "lewd and indecent behavior," locked him up in jail, where a group of hard-ass criminals beat Reynaldo to death that very night.

My mom identified his body at the morgue, although she said he was barely recognizable. His face had been punched so hard, all the muscles had been flattened.

My mother cried for days. I thought she would never recover.

His memorial was attended by hundreds from all over the city, maybe because his death symbolized the horrors of being queer in New York in 1965. The arrests. The suicides. The bludgeonings. The loss of employment if the boss discovers his employee visited one of those male-only bars. Homos couldn't teach school. Homos couldn't work in businesses. Homos couldn't work in Hollywood. And not that I was interested in ever working for the federal government, but Reynaldo said back in the 1950s, there were mass firings of all homosexuals working for the United States government. I would pretend not to listen to Reynaldo's diatribes in my mom's kitchen, but how could I not hear them? Even in my bedroom—with the door open, of course—I heard every word, and I swore I'd never ever ever ever be queer.

Reason Two: With Reynaldo dead, I did not have any gay friends or know any happy gay people. I didn't know any male couples who lived a happy life together. For that matter, I had never even seen two men together, holding hands, kissing, or showing any form of intimacy. Didn't see it in the movies. Never watched it on TV. Certainly never saw it among Reynaldo and his buddies. I was also unaware of any famous gay celebrities.

The few who were "outspoken" were people like Truman Capote with his wispy feminine, child-like Southern drawl, rolling his hands and touching his cheeks as he shared stories on *The Tonight Show*. Or Dracula-like Andy Warhol, his face a kind of bleached white, speaking with a weird lisp, and showing off art that most people thought was not art at all. A painting of a Campbell's soup can? Please. Though Reynaldo said there were many wonderful, incredible heroic men and women all through history who happened to be homosexual, I was unaware of any live ones who could function as mentors or role models. And without role models, I swore I'd never be queer.

Reason Three: Homosexuality was illegal. I had no idea how the government could justify arresting someone for having sex in his own home, but these laws were on the books. Even the psychiatrists at their annual meetings still declared homosexuality a mental illness. One of Reynaldo's friends said he had become so tired of relentless bullying at school, he tried cutting his wrists with a piece of glass. When his parents got wind of the injuries, they insisted he endure shaming rituals at their church and then finally institutionalized him, where he endured several bouts of shock therapy. After hearing that story, I swore I'd never be queer.

My one glimmer of hope came from a man named Alfred Kinsey. Reynaldo had talked a lot about this Kinsey Scale. Since I was too cowardly to ask questions about what this meant, I snuck off to the New York Public Library one afternoon and perused the Reader's Guide, looking up every article I could find on Kinsey's research.

I was fourteen.

One article spelled the whole thing out: the Kinsey Scale measures a person's sexual orientation based on their experiences or responses. The scale ranges from zero, meaning the individual is totally heterosexual with the desire for sexual activity only with the opposite sex, to six, where the person is exclusively homosexual, with a desire for sexual activity only with the same sex. The writer of the article assured the reader that all human beings fall somewhere on this scale: some at the start, some at the end, and many in the middle.

This report became very controversial. Few people believed the average man or woman might have even a tiny, minute attraction to the same sex. Whoever heard of such a thing? However, if my sexual impulses landed somewhere on the lower end of the scale—let's say a two, even a three—I might have a good chance of living a heterosexual lifestyle. It was not unusual, one report said, if straight men felt a small attraction to the same sex. This might be perfectly normal. In order to survive, the male simply conceals or subverts these impulses so that he can fit into normal society.

I had my own theory of how I might harness my desires.

I would go out with Delia Jacobson, this girl whom I had become friendly with, and if the date went well, it would convince me I was no worse than a "two" on the Kinsey Scale. In time, she would drive the homo out of me. As a result, I'd live more comfortably in this hetero world. I'd get married, have children someday, and get so busy as a hetero, I'd have no time for homo thoughts. It all made sense, a very logical, mature way of thinking.

I had no intention of sharing this with Henry. In fact, I gave up the idea of being honest with him. Instead, I might cleverly drop hints I was dating Delia and see whether or not this made him jealous. If it did, then I'd switch strategies.

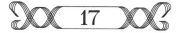

17

THE DATE WITH DELIA JACOBSON

The healthiest option was to avoid Henry for at least a week. I'd see him in the hallway and duck into a classroom until he ambled by. I'd take a different bus. I'd make sure we weren't in line at the cafeteria at the same time. For the whole week I took a brown bag lunch—cold lasagna or cold Salisbury steak or cold macaroni and cheese—and ate it on the lawn.

This grew tiring. One afternoon I gave up avoiding him and met him at the cafeteria. He wore his long, exotic hair down instead of bunched into a tiny pony tail, black jeans and a black and white T-shirt advertising Burt's Studio.

I had a hard time breathing.

"Where have you been, Monsieur Hodge?"

"I've been here and there." We sat down at one of the benches, and I shared some Kentucky Fried Chicken with him. I told him my uncle had called the principal and got me out of PE. That's why he didn't see me there. "Whatever Uncle Ted told Freed, it worked like abracadabra, and now I'm in Study Hall."

It was great having an uncle functioning as a father, and today I decided I'd treat Henry like a brother.

"I've missed you, Monsieur Hodge."

"Well, here's the latest. I'm going on a date tonight."

"With who?"

"A girl in my English class. Her name is Delia."

"Delia Jacobson?"

"I didn't know you knew her."

"Last year she ran for student council and made some crazy speech all in Pig Latin. Yeah, I know of her. Where are you taking her?"

"I have designed the perfect date. A double feature at the Encino Theatre. *How the West Was Won*, fresh off its exclusive engagement at the Cinerama Dome, paired with the movie version of the Broadway musical *A Funny Thing Happened on the Way to the Forum*, a comedy set in decadent Roman times and featuring Zero Mostel as the wily slave scheming for his freedom by uniting his young, smitten master with a virgin courtesan."

I was quoting directly from a synopsis I read in the paper.

"What's a courtesan again?" he asked.

"A prostitute, and yet, in this musical, she's a virgin."

"But she lives in a brothel."

"Exactly."

"And you're taking Delia on a first date to these two movies, one of which is set in a whorehouse."

"I'm a bold kind of guy." I figured six hours of movies, sitting together, eating popcorn, talking during the intermission—what could be better? Plus, the second film was a musical. And the first film had Debbie Reynolds singing and playing the accordion.

Henry rolled his eyes. "You're crazy! First of all, Haskell, how well do you know Delia Jacobson?"

"We're in a class together. I help her study for tests." I had transferred from lovely Mrs. Green's class into the Honors English class just so that I could be with Delia.

"I will not spoil it for you. I'll let you discover Delia Jacobson for yourself. She's odd."

"I'm odd. We'll be a pair!"

"She's more than odd. Shall I be honest with you?"

"Be honest."

"You've heard of Peter Mathieson? Only kid ever at this school to get a perfect score on his Math SAT?"

"I never heard of him."

"He got early admission and full scholarship to MIT. Delia sort of dated him. Basically, she used him. She got him to tutor her, for free of course, in first-year algebra. She promised she'd go to the prom with him, but she backed out at the last minute, giving him some phony excuse like she got food poisoning. He was not just disappointed, he was heartbroken."

"I'm not going to be heartbroken or disappointed. It's just a movie, and she said she'd meet me there."

"You're not picking her up?"

"I don't drive—at least not yet—so the plan is she'll meet me at the theater at seven."

"Chances are, if she shows up, she'll be hours late, and then you expect her to sit through that Western movie? It's like four hours with an intermission. Plus, there's another movie? What time does it get out? Two in the morning? You're nuts," he said.

I figured Henry was jealous. Maybe he wished I had invited him, not Delia. If he were jealous, I was glad. Even if he tried dissuading me from going, I'd go anyway. Delia would love these two movies. I knew she would. She was a New Yorker. I was a New Yorker. She liked *Macbeth*. I liked *Macbeth*. We had a lot in common.

This night of our rendezvous, the eleventh of November, I would meet her at the Encino Theater. She said she'd be there around seven with bells on her toes.

"Iway ightmay ebay away ittlelay atelay. Ontday aitway. Abgray owtay eastsay," which translates into "I might be a little late. Don't wait. Grab two seats." I was even getting good at Pig Latin.

I did just as she asked. I got us two seats in the middle section. I bought us a large popcorn and an extra-large Coke with two straws, and I waited. Seven o'clock. Debbie Reynolds sings with her accordion. Eight o'clock. Jimmy Stewart courts Diane Baker. Nine o'clock. Edge-of-your-seat suspense, as George Peppard chases the train robbers across the top of a moving train. No Delia. Soon *A Funny Thing* began. Half the audience walked out once they realized it was, frankly, a dull musical. I stayed, growing steadily depressed and weary. Where was Delia? If she were late, let's say by half an hour, no big deal. But it was now eleven, four hours late, and I decided it was hopeless. She wasn't showing up. I walked home alone, depressed and disappointed.

As soon as I opened the front door, I spotted my aunt sitting in her usual chair in the sunroom, sipping a brandy and smoking a Chesterfield. "How'd it go?" I didn't answer her. I merely trudged into my room, removed my clothes, and buried myself under the covers. The smell of her cigarette soon wafted across the air above my sheets. Was she standing in my doorway? Maybe she hovered over the bed? I did not move. I pretended I was asleep. So humiliated and embarrassed, I didn't know what to say. I would never admit the truth to anyone.

All right. I couldn't keep my anger contained.

"Delia didn't even show up!" I blurted out as I sat up in bed.

My aunt snuffed out her cigarette in the glass ashtray she was carrying. Then she pulled up a chair, sat by my bed, emptied the ashtray into my trash can, and remained silent for a good long minute. I couldn't stand the silence.

"Why are you just sitting there?" I asked.

"I'm waiting for you to say something."

"All right. What is wrong with me? Why did I think this might be a perfect date when it was, as Henry predicted, a perfect recipe for disaster? When will I ever learn? Am I destined to live a life where I'm constantly humiliated?"

Aunt Sheila stroked her neck and then let out a long, deep sigh.

"You had a no-show. It happens."

"What could have been so important that she'd not call me a few minutes before the date and say something?"

"Why don't you ask her?"

"I don't ever want to speak to her again."

"Then, I guess an explanation is not important to you. Don't say a word. Keep it a mystery."

"There is no way I can live with this mystery hanging over my head!"

"Well, then say something." My aunt softened her voice as she smiled gently. "You so remind me of your mother sometimes. She would get equally agitated."

"Is that supposed to make me feel better?"

"No. I'm merely offering some advice. My suggestion? Don't take your anger out on the poor girl. Ask her what happened. Pause. Wait for an answer." She pinched my cheek. "I hope that makes sense."

I nodded my head.

"Good. Now get some sleep."

This was the first time I could remember my Aunt taking a real, solid interest in me, and it did calm me down. I was glad she was here in my room, even though she left this terrible cigarette odor floating over my bed.

I stuffed my face into my pillow. Although I did appreciate Aunt Sheila's advice, and I found her words very comforting, I feared I would be unable to contain my wrath when I faced Delia on Monday morning.

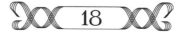

18

YVES' LAST ADVENTURE

I saw Delia in the hallway at school on Monday, and I readied myself for a confrontation. What excuse could she possibly come up with, justifying no phone call, not even a follow-up apology for her absence? I was so angry and perplexed. Why would anyone not show up for a date and not call first?

Delia ran toward me and threw her arms around my neck. "Oh Haskell, I am so sorry. You have no idea how terrible I feel." I didn't put my arms around her. I was truly pissed off.

"Where were you?" I asked, disgusted.

"My dog got sick, and I had no way of contacting you."

"Your dog?" Honestly, this was the lamest of excuses. "I didn't know you had a dog."

She started crying. I mean, actually wailing in the hallway. Kids passed us by and glared at me, as if I had done something to her.

"Is the dog all right?" I asked.

"I was up all night with him, and early Saturday morning, he died in my arms."

Her voice cracked, more sobbing. If she were inventing this excuse and making the whole thing up, I'd congratulate her. I'd give her a ten for realism, maybe a six out of ten for imagination. It fell into the "The Dog Ate My Homework" category, but her performance? Convincing. Maybe her acting chops *could* pull off a cunning, ambitious, conniving Lady Macbeth.

"He'd been in my life since I was a few years old. We grew up together. We had so many adventures."

"I'm sorry," I told her, coldly. I still didn't believe her.

I watched her swallow and catch her breath. "While Yves was vomiting all over the carpet in my room, I lost track of time. And when he started spitting blood, I mean, I assumed you were already in the theater. What could I do?"

She was right. Even I would miss a double feature if my dog was spitting blood. Though I've seen movies at the Encino Theatre a few other times, I didn't expect managers to track me down in order to deliver a phone message.

Delia was still sobbing hard. "You want to talk about this later?" I asked.

"No, no, it's okay. You forgive me?"

What could I say? I nodded.

"I'm so glad."

"You know, there's a dog graveyard just up the street from my house. Are you interested in burying him there?" I wasn't sure if I should mention it, but I just blurted the words out. I figured this would determine if she were telling the truth. I expected a laugh, maybe a "You're kidding, right?" Instead, she surprised me.

"I think that sounds like a really good idea."

I had no idea if I could even bury a dog from a different neighborhood in the burial site. It was owned by our neighborhood. I figured there were some restrictions on which dogs could enter and which dogs could not. What if the requirement was that any dog buried in the cemetery must be owned by a person who lived there? Then what would I do?

"Will I have to pay for the plot?" she asked.

"I'll find out. Let me check with my aunt, okay? What kind of dog was it?"

"A Bichon Frise."

"Is that a big or a little dog?" I had no idea. I was not up on my dog sizes since my mom never allowed me to have one.

"No, very small. In fact, I'll purchase a tiny casket and be over, maybe tomorrow, after school? I'd like to spend a bit more time with Yves before I say goodbye."

She was buying Yves his own casket?

"We could just dig a hole and put the dog in the hole. That's what everybody does around here. I never even heard of a dog casket."

"I could not possibly consider that, Haskell. He would need a pine casket, and I think I know where I can buy one."

"All right," I told her, still not sure if she was pulling my leg. This sounded eerily reminiscent of the scene in *Sunset Boulevard* where Norma Desmond actually hires a funeral service to bury her monkey. "I'll call you."

My aunt didn't see a problem with burying a tiny Bichon Frise in the graveyard. Most of the dogs had been huge. German Shepherds. Great Danes. Labradors. "I'm sure there's plenty of room for a small dog," she said. "What's her name?"

"You mean what was *his* name? Yves."

My aunt blinked. "What kind of name is that for a dog?"

"It's a French name, like Yves Montand. Yves Saint-Laurent."

"Make sure you spell it correctly."

"We'll work it out. I'll take care of it."

So my next date with Delia was Tuesday afternoon. We met

in front of my house. She was only an hour late. Delia carried her pooch in a picnic basket, covered in a Scottish print blanket, and we walked up and around the Tara mansion on our cul-de-sac until we came to the animal graveyard. Delia was dressed all in black, including her socks, and in her backpack she had a small pine box, barely large enough for her dog.

"You know, Haskell? I just got him out of the freezer and, by the way, this is the nicest thing anyone has ever done for me," she said.

"I'm sure that's not true," I replied. I pointed toward a small spot that would be shaded by a crape myrtle on sunny days. "We can bury him there."

I'd say the entire graveyard was about the size of a typical kidney-shaped, Valley swimming pool, and there was quite a bit of room for more dogs. We spotted gravestones for Jeanette, Al, Cary, Roman, Mae, and Joan—dogs once owned by the famed director and apparently named after popular movie stars of the day. On the other side of the graveyard—the non-Hollywood side—we spotted Pooky, Rags, and Shadow, names of local dogs. I had brought with me a stake and some cardboard in case Delia wanted a temporary gravestone.

She shook her head when she saw me carrying the materials.

"That won't be necessary," she said. "As long as we mark the grave and people know it's a grave, we can put up a headstone a year from now." Delia spread out the blanket, set her dog on one end, and rolled up the cloth until the dog was fully covered. "It's fleece. Yves was allergic to wool," she said, winking at me. Delia then laid her dog gently in the casket, and I dug a hole with the shovel I'd brought. The soil was wet, so the hole opened up quickly. We placed the casket inside.

The whole time, I was bandying back and forth in my head

the question: Why would we wait a whole year before she puts up a headstone? I'll be away at college, hopefully at NYU! Or Harvard? Yale? Again, I begged myself not to ask, and yet the words tumbled out of my mouth carelessly.

"I'm just curious. Why wait a whole year before you can put up the headstone?"

She answered without a pause. "In the Jewish religion, we don't actually put the headstone on until a year after the death."

I swallowed a few times. "Your dog was Jewish?"

"Well, I'm Jewish. I think that makes my dog Jewish. Aren't you Jewish?"

"I'm half-Jewish. I don't think my father was Jewish. Funny, the subject has never come up."

"Well, following Jewish tradition, Yves' nameplate will not be set for another year. That's just the way things are done."

She squinted her eyes and smiled.

"He was very special. We spent our whole life together. When I talked to the rabbi this morning, he said each soul is judged immediately after death and undergoes the appropriate purification process, which takes about twelve months. So, we'll wait on the nameplate. I'll compose something special."

"You called the rabbi for burial instructions?"

"He also said that by waiting a year, we can make certain the dog will not be forgotten. Also, it will give me time to think about what I want written on his headstone. Don't look at me that way. Lots of people do this in Los Angeles."

I knew if I argued with her and began debating whether the dog was actually Jewish or not, I'd lose the battle and maybe start a war. Delia could tell, though, from the flabbergasted expression on my face, that I had a hard time comprehending her enthusiasm for religious ritual. Next thing you know she'd insist on sitting *shiva*, maybe requiring ten dogs to show up for a *minyan*.

I mean, the girl was a nut job. How long should I let her spend time with me? It might be better if I let her finish the ceremony, wish her well, and call it a day. Forget Delia.

Soon, a sullen, uncomfortable silence reigned, broken only by a plane overhead.

Delia had brought a tape recorder with her, and she put on her dog's favorite musician—Fats Waller—and his rendition of "Ain't Misbehavin'." It didn't work at the right speed, though. The batteries were probably old, and poor Fats sounded as if he were drowning. Delia turned it off.

"You know, Haskell, I'm actually glad we have no music since it would only make me cry harder. If you wouldn't mind, I'll say the *Kaddish* after we shovel soil on the grave."

Why not? The tinny sound of raindrops started plopping against the coffin lid. And as the rain grew stronger, the smell of leaves, dirt, pine needles, and grass pervaded the air. It smelled fresh and good, not like at home on the Upper East Side.

"You know, when my mom and I left New York a few months ago," I said, attempting some small talk, "we were in the midst of a massive garbage strike. It gave New York a rotting-fruit smell, and before you knew it, we had rats in the kitchen and ants and cockroaches crawling up the walls. This is so much more beautiful, and the smell is much nicer."

I was desperate to come up with something to say.

Another airplane roared overhead, giving off a loud crack as the underbelly opened, releasing its landing gear.

"Are we near an airport?" I asked.

"Encino is in the flight path. You hadn't noticed that before?"

"I rarely spend time outside."

"Well, I have a feeling neither the rain nor the airplanes are coincidental. It's all in the scheme of things. God works in mysterious ways. Wouldn't it be lovely if the rain stopped?"

And stop it did, almost as soon as she asked this question.

At this point, she picked up the shovel, dug it deep into the mound of dirt, and threw a pile of wet soil onto the pine box. We did this alternately until the box was fully buried. Delia recited the *Kaddish*, a Jewish prayer of mourning. I was surprised she knew it by heart, but she said she often went on Friday nights to temple with her father and memorized most of the prayers.

She brought out a blanket, laid it across a mound of dirt, sat cross-legged, and patted a space beside her.

"Please sit. Let me tell you how much I appreciate your help and acceptance today. Some people would think I'm a lunatic."

"Really?"

"I can be a bit *meshuga*, I suppose, but I really loved Yves. Have you ever loved anyone so much you would do anything for them?"

I shook my head. "Not really. I once felt pretty close to my mom. Not anymore."

"I'm not talking about mothers or fathers, or relatives. I can't explain it. It just feels like I've lost my best friend." Again, tears streamed down her cheeks.

It was the oddest feeling, for in some ways I could empathize, feeling a certain loss myself. True, Henry didn't die, but the love I hoped we might share remained unfulfilled. I was still reeling from the torment of being a homo hopelessly in love with a boy who would never love me back, stuck with a girl who spoke Pig Latin and sat *shiva* for her dog.

"I brought some lemonade. Would you like some?" she asked.

She removed a thermos and two glasses from her backpack. We sipped, sat back on the blanket, resting on our elbows, and stared at the sickly yellow haze obscuring the mountains and darkening the sky. My eyes burned from the smog.

"You're the best, Haskell. Thank you again." She lay back and reached over and held my hand. "You're so nice and thoughtful . . ."

I suppose my silence could be interpreted this way.

"Haskell? Would you mind helping me with something? Remember that original sonnet we had to write for class?"

"That was due last week."

"I'm just a bit behind. Would you mind writing one for me? I have a draft, but I can't seem to finish it."

"Did you get permission to turn it in late?"

"No, but it will be all right."

She handed me a sheet with just a few lines, and I began scribbling away.

"Oh, and you should probably make sure it's addressed to a boy, not a girl. Mrs. Dunlap gets all bent out of shape if we don't make certain it's written to a person of the opposite sex. She says this is America, not France."

I did not mind redrafting her sonnet, nor did it bother me that it was addressed to a boy. In fact, the fourteen lines poured out of me.

"Oh my God, Haskell. You're so creative. You wrote this so fast! I love the line about his long raven hair falling below his earlobes."

"I thought that was a nice touch."

"And 'four languages' and 'bandages' does not exactly rhyme."

"I'll fix that."

"And you seem so at ease writing to a young man."

"Well, you know Shakespeare wrote 126 sonnets to a young man. Men can write poems to men."

"Thank you. I am very appreciative."

The lemonade was delicious. I loved the smell of pine needles. The sound of the airplanes overhead made each of us giggle. At one point, she swung an arm around me and said, "You are so talented and so smart. I really like you."

"I really like you too," I told her.

"I think forgiveness is such an important trait in a human being, and I so appreciate your ability to show understanding."

"That's all right."

"At school tomorrow, please join my friends and me for lunch. There are other guys in our group, you know. Nate? You know Nate Netherland right?"

I did actually like Nate, even though he was part of Lucky's clan.

"And Alice Michaels? And Sarah Nuel? And Kathy Heath? And Margaret? There is a group of us drama kids that sit together, and since you did some acting—they'd all love to meet you and talk to you."

"Sounds good to me."

"And you know what I did? I took out a book from the library that showed vintage pictures of cereal boxes, and I found one with your picture on it. I'll bring it to school."

"You're the best, you know that?"

Ordinarily, I might have agreed with Henry's consensus. This girl was simply using me not only as her official pet funeral director but as a cheat, helping her fulfill an assignment she had failed to turn in on time. So what? I had learned my lesson.

There are some things one has to do at this high school if you expect to survive. And think of the perks. Delia invited me to join her table during lunch and meet all her popular friends. I was thrilled. One of the girls—Kathy Heath—was the President of our senior class. Another one was a track star. Several of them were vying for roles in *Macbeth*. How exciting was that? I felt content and fortunate. I would finally be included and not excluded from the popular crowd. I found someone who cared about me and wanted time with me.

She now wrapped both her arms around me and gave me a kiss on the lips. "Haskell, you have no idea how special you are." Her eyes filled with tears and her lips formed a splendid smile. "Iway inkthay ou'reyay away eryvay extraordinaryway ersonpay," she said, and not knowing precisely what it meant, I merely replied the one phrase I knew by heart— "Emay ootay."

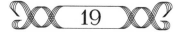

19

MY DARLING DELIA JACOBSON

I squeezed onto the bench among nine girls, including Delia, at lunch the next day. All of Delia's friends seemed excited to see me.

"Oh my God! You got murdered on stage on Broadway?"

"You were in the Sugar Flakes ad?"

"You had a part in *Medea*!"

"Your mother was Miriam Hodge?"

She still was Miriam Hodge.

"My mom and I watch her movies on the Late Late Show on weekends a lot. My favorite is *Love in the Parthenon*."

"No, no no. It's called *Love in Athens*."

"Trudy, I know what it's called. I've watched it half a dozen times."

"That's not the title. It's *Love in Athens*, and it's *Love in a Paris Post Office*, and it's *Love in Brooklyn Heights*. I keep a journal, and I write down every TV show and every movie I've ever seen. I know this."

So, I was a popular kid at lunch, at least with these girls. I was grateful when Nate joined us. Yes, he was one of Lucky's hooligans, but he once encouraged me when we played football in the cul-de-sac several months ago. He was kind of a good guy. He also was a very talented set designer. I was impressed by the drawings he created for the sets in *Macbeth*, and since many of these girls wanted parts in the school play, they were curious as well.

His plan was to design an actual forest with mist and trees and rocks. The trees would be on tiny wheels so they could be taken off stage easily. His design would even include trap doors for the witches to come in and out and large castle walls on rails that could slide off the stage.

I appreciated him showing up because otherwise, day after day, I'd sit with a group of girls jabbering away, sharing sandwiches, laughing and acting silly, and I'd be the only boy. True, on some level, I was the go-to boy for a group of girls who were struggling to figure out the male mind. "Why doesn't he call me back?" "Why is he ignoring me?" "Frank told me he just wants to be friends." I had some insight into these perplexing situations.

With Nate there, however, I felt the pressure fall off of me, and he could help answer their questions, too. Though I don't think his answers were any better than mine.

As expected, Lucky would pass by and scowl. He had lunch the same period as us, and you'd think he'd do everything in his power to impress some of these popular girls. They were pretty. They were smart. Their faces brightened when he approached. Some of the girls even offered him sips from their thermoses and bites from their sandwiches. Surprisingly, the only thing Lucky wanted to do was make fun of Nate or me. "You enjoy being one of the girls, Natey Patey?"

"Shut up, Lucky. I'm showing them my sets."

"You're showing them your what?"

This would get a huge laugh from nearly everyone. I couldn't understand why the girls didn't find Lucky annoying.

Another time, Lucky returned to his old routine of taunting me.

"Did you girls know you have a Judy Garland impersonator sitting at your table? Judy, why don't you sing one of your signature tunes. Anyone have a harmonica?"

The key to stopping this behavior was to pretend I didn't hear it. If he knew it bothered me, which it did, he'd continue teasing me. I pretended I was fine with the teasing even though I wasn't. Though I worried if this teasing happened again and again, my silence would be construed as weakness. I'd be deemed a coward, and I'd lose my popularity with the girls.

I finally sought Henry's advice. I knew he was in Study Hall in the library, and I tapped him on the shoulder and asked if I could chat with him on a bench outside. He was no longer taking the bus home every day since he often walked directly from school to his martial arts studio. If I didn't talk to him today, I figured I might not see him until after the four-day Thanksgiving weekend.

"Ah, Monsieur Hodge. I never see you anymore. What's up?"

"You've been really busy."

"No, you've been very Mr. Popular. Good for you!"

I explained to him that Lucky had started taunting me again, this time in front of Delia's friends, and I didn't know what to do.

"What's there not to do? You're ready, Haskell. All you have to do is stand up, tell him enough with the Judy Garland jokes, and if he doesn't stop, you'll make him stop."

"How will I do that?"

"I taught you some moves, and I know you've been learning

self-defense at the studio twice a week. Burt said you're good."

"I'm working at it."

"If Lucky knows you have the moves, he'll leave you alone. Trust me. You see how he doesn't say anything when I'm around? He's afraid of me."

"I don't want to start a fight. I try to pretend he doesn't get my goat."

"And how is that working out?"

"He gets my goat. I'm steaming mad."

"So, my approach? I've drawn a line in the sand with Mr. Moron. Now it's your turn. He has to become afraid of you. That's the only way you'll stop his taunting. You know some moves. If he gets overly annoying, say something first. And if that doesn't work, be firm. Tell him it's over. You're through taking his shit. If he throws the first punch, punch him back. We practiced this defensive move, and Phil said he worked with you a few times. He told me you're doing great."

"You've said that."

"Just keep it low key. Be only on the defensive. Don't start a fight and don't throw the first punch."

"And if none of this works?"

"If talk doesn't do the trick, if he insists on a fight, let's say, outside of campus?"

"Then what do I do?"

"I'm not a believer in staging a fight unless it's on the mat at the studio, and if worse comes to worst, you might have to resort to a meeting with the Millers and the Teitlebaums."

"I do not want to do that."

"A face to face might stop this nonsense in its tracks."

"I am not going to do that."

"It's not a pansyass way of handling it. He's your neighbor, right? You just say enough's enough. Tell his parents and your aunt and uncle that you're tired of it. The joke has gone on long enough, and he should grow up. Ask them what they think you guys should do, short of muzzling their son. I don't see a problem with that."

"I don't know Mr. or Mrs. Miller."

"Your aunt and uncle do."

"I don't want my aunt and uncle involved in this."

"As I said, it's a last resort. You decide if it is necessary to go that route."

● ● ●

Although I dreaded another encounter with Lucky, I would not let that ruin the holiday weekend. Aunt Sheila brought in a turkey dinner from Gelson's, complete with a unique garlic stuffing and a delicious pumpkin pie with a graham cracker crust. I feasted on leftovers Saturday and Sunday, and watched a marathon of movies featuring several movie musicals Uncle and I had selected over a month ago and various holiday-themed cartoons including Pilgrim Popeye and Pilgrim Porky Pig.

All of this kept my brain busy, and I almost forgot about the doofus who lived across the street. When he did in fact show up at the cafeteria, on Monday, and nonchalantly mumbled under his breath a few words like "homo" and "fairy," I stood up, hands on my hips, and reminded him of the agreement we had made on my first day at school. He had violated that agreement. "If you don't have anything nice to say, you should keep your big fat mouth shut."

"What the fuck did you say to me?" he asked.

Before I could open my mouth, Trudy immediately chimed in. "Don't you understand English?" Trudy asked him. "We're busy.

Haskell is helping us with our lines. Auditions are next week. Get lost!"

He put on a goofy smile and was about to say something—something really stupid, I feared—when Trudy stood up again and pushed him.

"DO YOU UNDERSTAND ENGLISH? GET LOST!"

I didn't think this helped the situation. Lucky pointed a fist at me, bit his lower lip and, as he strolled past us, raised both his middle fingers.

"You know, I can defend myself," I told her.

"I'm sure you can, but we don't want you in the hospital. We need your help." She rested her elbows on the table. "So, where were we?" Trudy beamed, proud of her bravery. "A group of us are trying out for the witches in the play. Will you help us with our line readings?"

Six of these girls wanted to play one of the three witches in *Macbeth*.

"The auditions are next week. Please, Hask? Will you help?"

Trudy had put together a list of times she believed would work for Coaching with Haskell Hodge. These included early hours before school started, the lunch hour, the fifteen-minute nutrition period, and after school.

"You'll be available for this, right? Help us with our line readings? I can't speak for them, but I'll pay you a dollar a lesson."

The money sounded good. There were record albums and books I could purchase, but I didn't like the idea of helping all six when obviously only *three* of them would win roles. Shakespeare wrote this play for *three* witches. If six competed for these three parts, my coaching would result in three wins, three losses.

I smelled disaster.

The next day in our English class, I came down with hives all over my arms and legs. Delia could see the huge bumps on me since we sat across from each other in class.

I told her I didn't want to go to lunch looking like this, and I didn't feel comfortable coaching her friends.

"No worries. I'll say you can't coach them because I'm trying out for Lady Macbeth. I have much steeper competition. I'm going against a girl who always gets big parts in shows. You'll help me nail this role, right?"

"The girls will hate me even more."

"They'll be fine. I'll tell them you made a commitment to me weeks ago. Eythay etterbay otnay ivegay ouyay away ardhay imetay!"

The Pig Latin was getting really annoying.

"I'm an actor, not an acting coach."

"You said you took acting lessons from the same teacher who taught Marlon Brando and Paul Newman, right?"

In the heat of excitement one afternoon, I had exaggerated Miss Hogan's credentials.

"And I'll make it worth your while."

"You'll pay me? Trudy offered me a dollar a session."

"No, I can do better than that. Why don't you come over Friday afternoon, and we'll rehearse at my house, uninterrupted in the confines of my bedroom. Maybe afterwards, we'll go swimming. Bring your trunks. What do you say?"

"Is your pool heated?" I asked.

It was now late November. It was sixty degrees or colder at night. Still, if the pool was heated, how much fun would that be to jump in her pool, maybe play Marco Polo, and kiss underwater? Afterwards, we could run upstairs, chase each other into her bedroom. I could coach her in her bedroom with the door closed. The suggestion came from her, not from me, and if that didn't sound like an invitation for sex, then I didn't know what was.

I now added Acting Coach to my previous duties as Sonneteer and Funeral Director. I figured all this would further extend the opportunity with Delia Jacobson to progress into the greatest love affair of all time.

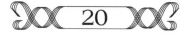

20

THE SWIM INSTRUCTOR

Of course, there was one slight problem. I didn't know how to swim.

At dinner one night with the Teitlebaums, I raised the dilemma. "I have a date this Friday night, December 2, with Delia Jacobson, and she invited me over to swim."

My aunt clasped her hands together and smiled. "*Mazel tov!*"

"But I need swim lessons fast. I have four days before the big date."

"Even if we found you a qualified, certified instructor and a heated swimming pool for practice, you can't learn how to swim in a week!"

"I don't have a week. I have ninety-six hours."

My aunt shook her head. "You can't learn how to swim in just a few days."

"Then what am I going to do? I don't want Delia to think I can't swim."

"You see? He wants to make a good impression," my uncle said. He rose from the table, scraping his chair on the marble floor. "Why don't I look up some names in the Yellow Pages. There's no reason why he can't learn to swim in a short period of time."

My aunt scoffed. "Ted, you're not going to find a qualified swim instructor in the phone book. They only list swim schools, and they're all closed until spring."

Uncle Ted pulled Hope off her seat and grabbed the thick, bulky San Fernando Valley edition of Yellow Pages that Hope sat on so she'd sit higher at the dinner table. "Look, Sheila," Uncle said as he flipped through the pages. "There are dozens of instructors."

"Fine. Fine. Trust a stranger to teach our nephew how to swim. If that's what you want to do, fine."

"I don't know what the big deal is. It's not like we're hunting for a psychiatrist or a brain surgeon. It's a swim teacher. He needs to learn how to hold his breath and learn the butterfly stroke."

"Theodore, I have no problem with him taking some lessons, but a few days is not going to do it. Miriam asked me to look after her son, and that's what I'm doing. If he's going to learn how to swim, I want him well prepared, with lots of practice, before he dives into a deep, most likely very cold, swimming pool—with a girl. If he catches his death, I'll blame you."

"He's not going to catch his death, for God's sake," my uncle shouted.

Aunt Sheila shoved her chair back and stormed out of the dining room, heading toward her bedroom. A door slammed.

I had heard my aunt and uncle bark at each other occasionally, but nothing as loud or edgy as this argument. I didn't want to create any more animosity, and if worse came to worst, I'd forget the swim lessons and jump in the pool with Delia, doing my best to tread water without drowning.

Uncle signaled for me and Hope to help clean up the dinner mess. I washed the dishes, Hope dried, and my uncle put things away. "Don't worry about all this. Mom's been a little tense lately. She misses her phone calls with her sister. She used to talk to her every Monday, and now it's been—what?—nine or ten weeks since Miriam left, and they seldom talk. It's so expensive."

Hope piled all the plates onto the table so her dad could put them back into the cabinet. "I have an idea. A really, really good idea," Hope said. "Don't look any further. I can teach Has-skull Rascal. I'm a real good swimmer."

"You're not a good swimmer, and you're only eight years old," my uncle corrected her.

"I'm eight and three quarters."

"I will call some of our friends and see if they have the name of a qualified instructor. I'm sure someone will recommend a good teacher."

"No, I can do it. Really, I can. Please give me a chance."

At this point, Aunt Sheila wandered back into the kitchen, her hair wrapped in a towel, wearing a terrycloth robe over pajamas. Without speaking, she threw her arms around my uncle. As she looked around the kitchen and noticed how spotless we had made it, tears came to her eyes.

"Heat our pool, Mommy!" Hope screamed. "Heat it now! I will give Haskell swim lessons! Please, please, please, please!"

"We're not turning on the heater in winter, sweetheart. You think money grows on trees?"

"It's for a couple of days, Mommy. I'll put the tarp on after we swim. I know I can teach him. I'm really good."

"That's very sweet of you. I think I know someone, but I only have her work number. I'll call her first thing in the morning."

"I can teach him! I really can. Please give me a chance. Please?"

I did not want this discussion turning into another argument, so I finally waved my hands and told them I didn't need swim lessons. "It's just for one night. If I wade in the pool or insist we just go in the Jacuzzi, it will be fine."

My uncle kissed his wife. "Sheila, let's give Hope the chance. It will be fine."

"Hope can't teach Haskell to swim."

"I will personally supervise."

"She barely swims herself."

"I will watch them. Look at me." As he squeezed Aunt Sheila affectionally, something happened. The squeeze produced a burst of tears, and soon my poor Aunt Sheila was sobbing hysterically. "Honey, it hasn't been easy for you, has it?"

"I miss my sister."

"I know."

"I miss her so much. I can't tell you. I feel an ache in my heart."

"Was I right?" Uncle winked at us as he squeezed her tightly and patted her head. "Well, she's safe. She's enjoying her time in Antwerp, right?"

My aunt nodded. "I don't know what's wrong with me. I miss talking with her because she is my best friend, maybe my only friend."

"Well, you're my best friend, honey. You really are, and so anytime you just want to talk, say the word."

"It's not the same thing, Ted. You're a guy. She's my older sister. There's something about sister talk that you and I can never duplicate, and I don't want anything to happen to Haskell."

"I'll tell you what," my uncle said. "I'll heat the pool. The heating bill will not put us in the poor house. I'll sit in a chair and watch the whole swim lesson. It will work out swell. Trust me. Hope's enthusiasm alone will turn Haskell into a swimmer."

"I trust you. But if he drowns, I'll kill you."

My uncle kissed his wife once again and pinched her cheek.

That night Hope cranked up the heater and put on a tarp.

The next night, I stuck my feet onto the first step of the pool. The water was still cold, and I saw no way I was going to get myself in. Hope began splashing me, though, until finally I forced myself down the steps and lowered myself into the water.

"Let's go at it," I told her.

"Oh, goodie. I will turn Has-skull into a fine swimmer. I will! I will! I will!"

She spent a good five minutes teaching me the breast stroke. We had a splash contest and then practiced the breast stroke again. She showed me how to float, hold my breath under water, and keep my body steady while floating. More splash contests. This was a far cry from the girl who once dubbed me a big dork. As long as I would allow some time for play, she patiently taught me swim skills.

What shocked me was how Hope remained rigorous, dedicated, and focused, making certain I not only swam but swam with correct form, including proper breathing techniques and the precise bend in my arms. She was not distracted by the moon, the stars, the aliens in the sky, or the *Beverly Hillbillies*. What had gotten into her? Why was Hope concentrating on me and not once demanding we stop so she could watch her beloved Jethro and Granny, leaving me stranded in the pool?

I was amazed at her power of concentration. Soon I found myself in the deep end swimming, quite confident I wouldn't drown. She even gave Uncle Ted pointers when during one of our sessions, he jumped into the pool and joined me for a few laps.

"Daddy? You need to reach as far forward as possible. Stretch those arms! Here, let me show you."

Of course, it was none of my business, but I decided I'd come right out and ask her anyway. "Are you taking something? You seem unusually focused and not the slightest bit distracted."

"I'm in therapy!"

This I knew.

"And Dr. Lax put me on Ritalin!" she screamed out loud. "It's a lifesaver!"

I had never heard of Ritalin.

"It's a pill that Dr. Lax said will help me stay focused and organized. My teacher also said I've become a much better listener."

God bless Ritalin! And God bless Dr. Lax! We practiced for hours in the pool, and in return, I promised I'd help her study for her spelling tests, assist her in constructing a map of Early California, and patch together a model of a California mission that rivaled all other California missions. It seemed no one ever did anything in the Valley without expecting something in return, and the sooner I settled into that idea, the easier it would be for me to fit in completely.

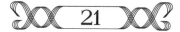

21

THE BIG NIGHT, PART 1

M y date with Delia was set for Friday night. I could hardly sleep Thursday night, anticipating the possibility of my first sexual experience.

And yet, I knew I was getting ahead of myself. She said we'd rehearse in her bedroom with the door closed, but I might be expecting too much. At the very least, I figured we'd sprawl across her bed and talk. What I liked about her was what we had in common. She told me she was originally from Great Neck, New York and had her tenth birthday party at Sardi's, the celebrity-watcher restaurant. Like me, she was a theater addict and avid museum-goer. She loved the Natural History Museum's rove beetle exhibition. Finding someone who appreciated the nine different species that evolved into mimicking army ants? Incredible!

At this moment, however, she was focused on final tryouts for the school's spring show, playing Lady Macbeth in Shakespeare's *Macbeth*. "You'll help me slay that performance, right?" My gut told me I would. She liked that I was a trained actor, and I gave my readings a professionalism other kids in her production didn't possess. I would not try out for any roles in the play. Instead, I'd play drama coach, preparing her to win the role of a lifetime.

We'd rehearse alone in her bedroom. I'd put my arm around her. We'd chat away until maybe, eventually, we'd kiss. I was projecting far into the future, but I found a roll of Trojan rubbers in an open locker at the gym and stole them, thinking they might come in handy. At least they would save me an embarrassing trip to the drug store.

Someday, if not this Friday, we would not only conquer our scene, we would conquer love.

I shaved my chocolate milk mustache, did a hundred pushups and jumping jacks and, in the little time left, swam laps. With a copy of *Macbeth* and a pair of swim trunks tucked into my backpack, I was ready for my date with Delia Jacobson. I left Aunt Sheila a note telling her I'd be home around nine and walked down the street toward Ventura Boulevard where I caught the bus, got off at Louise Avenue, and jogged the ten blocks uphill to the address on Heidi Avenue.

I was an hour early, so I wasn't sure if I should stroll around the block a few times, go back down to Ventura Boulevard and order a Coke at a coffee shop, or take a chance she'd be home and climb all the way up the four flights of stairs to her front door. The house itself seemed a cookie-cutter version of all the other two-story, A-framed, Swiss-themed homes on the street. I assumed each of them had spectacular views of the scenic San Fernando Valley. I could spot The Queen's Arms, a few multi-story office buildings, even a few private airports situated among fields of avocado and orange trees. Of course, the entire expanse was dotted with swimming pools. Quite breathtaking. I also could see why people might buy one of these chalets in a section called Rancho Encino, though I saw no ranch. It wasn't even in Encino. It was in the next town, Tarzana. Delia's house, like most of the others, was built on a high cliff, and every day, if you didn't park in the garage at the end of a high driveway, you had to climb the stairs, eighty-five of them, to the front door. Since I arrived early, I checked out her backyard. I found the pool and the Jacuzzi built right up against the edge of a cliff. The back of the house was held up by stilts embedded into the mountain. Water from the pool and Jacuzzi could, if filled high enough, pour over the cliff down the mountain.

Who would buy such a monstrosity in a state known for earthquakes? What if a terrible shift in the topography loosened the soil and the entire hill slipped cascading this home down the mountain?

These thoughts evaporated as I pressed my thumb on the doorbell and held it there for a few seconds.

Finally, a woman about my aunt's age, wearing an apron and carrying a large wooden spoon, poked her head out the door.

"Can I help you?" she asked. I could smell onions and gravy.

"I'm here to see Delia."

"Who are you?" she asked.

"I'm Haskell Hodge. Delia's friend. She invited me for dinner. Oh, and rehearsal. We're doing—I mean, she's doing a scene from *Macbeth* on Monday. I'm coaching her."

Still, a blank stare.

"We're in Honors English together." She still stared at me as if I were some Russian spy or, more likely, an encyclopedia salesman. "Am I at the wrong address?" I asked. "Delia said she lived at 4309 Heidi Avenue."

I waited on the porch until the woman unlatched the bolt.

"You got the right address, but Delia's not home. I'm her mother, Sharon Jacobson." Mrs. Jacobson opened the door and signaled that I could enter. "It must have slipped her mind. She's at Andrea's house. I'll call her."

The moment I stepped inside the house and smelled the delicious brisket and onions, my heart skipped a beat and a half. I took in a long, deep breath. Real food. Delia's mom was a cook. Though probably around my mom's age—mid-forties—Delia's mom had a much more voluptuous and curvaceous figure than my mother or my aunt, and it made me realize that someday Delia would probably gain weight and look exactly like this: irresistibly sexy, following in the footsteps of Ethel Merman, Simone Signoret, Marlene Dietrich, Mae West, maybe even, to a much smaller degree, Marilyn Monroe. I preferred this full-bodied look over women with tiny waists and slender hips and more or less boyish figures.

I think I lost my mind for a moment. I must have stared at plump Mrs. Jacobson for a good long minute.

"Is something wrong? You need some water? You look faint."

I suspected that if my relationship with Delia blossomed, as I hoped it would, might Mrs. Jacobson someday be my mother-in-law?

Wouldn't Aunt Sheila go nuts planning a wedding at the Queen's Arms and have everyone, including the bride and groom, dress up in medieval costumes?

Mrs. Jacobson handed me a glass of ice water.

"Sit. It's a bit hot out there today. Did you walk here?"

"Sort of. Yes."

I knew I was drawing wild conclusions, and I warned myself: Stop making things up! You barely know Delia. You're rushing into crazy fantasies. Still, awkward moments like these become lifelong memories.

"Why don't you make yourself comfortable in the den."

Ah, the den. Wooden cabinets, a Zenith color television set, shelves of hardbacks including some of the same books Uncle Ted displayed on his bookshelves: the Will Durant series, Churchill's books on World War II. *Exodus. Hawaii. The Collected Stories of Sholem Aleichem.* I felt at home here. Even a menorah sat on a shelf above the fireplace and shelves were strewn with black and white photographs of men with long, messy gray beards and women dressed all in black, their silk blouses suffocatingly buttoned all the way to the tops of their necks.

A few minutes later, Delia's mother stood in the doorway of the den, hands on her hips. "You sure it's tonight? I'm very surprised Delia's not here."

"Delia definitely said Friday. I'm a bit early." I examined my watch. It was only four-thirty. "Delia told me to come around five."

"Well, I made a lovely dinner, so I hope you'll join us."

"Sounds great."

"Let's give her a little time, shall we?"

Mrs. Jacobson clicked the remote, the TV came on, and the picture landed on channel two. Hundreds of thousands were marching in front of the Lincoln Memorial. Soldiers blocked the marchers. Canisters of tear gas were being thrown. One guy interviewed said, "We're aiming for the Pentagon. Kill the pigs! End the war!" One young man was dragged onto the curb, another beaten with a club. The journalist appeared aghast. "I've never seen anything like this!" he said.

This was truly distressing. If so many people were protesting this war, why couldn't we just end it?

"Ever see anything like this?" Mrs. Jacobson asked me. "Ronnie is in boot camp right now in Texas."

That must be her son.

"And Herb and I tried all we could to get him out of the Army. Hired a special doctor. Considered labeling him a Conscientious Objector. If he gets deployed to Vietnam, I might personally yank him off the base and drive him into Canada. You think that's wrong of me? Am I being unpatriotic? Marsha next door thinks I'm a commie. I'm not a commie. I love my son. I would do anything to protect him."

I knew little about Vietnam, and I felt quite guilty about it. I wasn't sure how to engage in this conversation.

"If this continues, as some wars do for years and years, guess who will be on the front lines?" She ambled forward, and her glasses fell to the tip of her nose. "You will. Better prepare yourself. Do your research."

"Hopefully, I'll earn a college deferment."

"Fine. Get deferred. Afterwards? What then? Have you seen the film of all the boys in body bags being transported onto the plane?"

I sat there watching more police officers beating the poor protestors, and my heart sank. What was going on? Why were they doing this? The sight of protesters being beaten—the chaos I was witnessing—was deeply troubling. Here I was in the comfort of this cozy den while all those kids were risking their lives protesting this awful war.

"Would you like a piece of *kugel* while you're waiting?"

I shook my head. My eyes were glued to the TV screen.

"You know we could probably find something a bit more cheery. I'm sorry, I'm on my soap box here." Mrs. Jacobson aimed the remote toward the TV and changed the channel.

It was worse. News footage of Vietnam, Americans torching villages, women and children screaming as they watched their husbands and fathers line up against a wall, facing Vietnamese soldiers with guns.

"Let me put something more appropriate on," Mrs. Jacobson said, as she kept changing the channel until she found *Love Is a Many-Splendored Thing* with Jennifer Jones and William Holden, one of my favorite movies.

"Isn't that better?" she asked. "Want me to see if there's a football game on?"

"I like sports, but while I'm waiting, leave it on the movie. Thank you."

We had landed on one of my favorite scenes where the two lovers change into their swim suits on a small beach. Jennifer Jones lets her hair down as William Holden reclines on a towel gazing at her. Suddenly, they swim across an inlet to an inviting home, owned by some friends.

I knew I shouldn't be watching this scene. It always got me too excited. William Holden was about the best-looking movie star in the whole world. I imagined Delia and me acting out the same scene in the hot tub. I'd be the handsome news correspondent; she'd be an exotic doctor. And who knew, in a few hours, we could be in water together. I could hold her in my arms and kiss her, a better kiss than any of the ones from my past. But the more I fantasized about it, the less I could visualize Delia. Instead— and I was so embarrassed by this—I preferred holding William Holden in my arms. In my imagination, I tried pretending I was spreading my arms around Jennifer Jones. No magic. No intense feelings. Yet, when I substituted her for him, I felt this warm electricity run through my body, as if my thermostat ignited and my blood stream grew hotter. My dick got hard, too. Why is my brain so miswired? I must make this dream sequence work in proper order, with the right wiring and the correct direction.

I inverted the fantasy.

Delia peels off her bathing suit.

"Take yours off, too!" she says. "What do we need bathing suits for? The lights are off. The night is young."

It's dark, not a full moon, and what chance will I ever have of being naked with Delia or any girl? I do not worry about interruptions . . .

I hear her say: "Am I a lovely lunatic? Or am I one of those insane lunatics? I'm glorious as Lady Macbeth, aren't I?" She wets her hair and pulls it back behind her head. Despite there being only a crescent moon, I can see the cool blue of her irises. She takes my hands and places them on her well-proportioned, luscious breasts.

"Let's swim through the inlet and meet my friends. But before we dive in, I want a long, warm kiss!" Delia mews.

Under my swim shorts I have on my Li'l Abner jockey underwear, and she twists her legs around mine and pulls them off, as if by magic. Her hands reach down and touch my penis. My hands tremble. My body aches with desire as I cup her breasts with both my hands.

"I think sometimes there's no one as weird as me. What do you think?" she asks. "Do you ever feel odd and weird?"

"Most of the time," I say.

"Being with you is about the best thing that's ever happened to me," she says.

"I feel the same way, Deeel-ya."

"Let yourself go. Put your worries aside. Let me take care of you. You have no worries when you're with me, for when we are alone, nothing can get in our way except our own minds. We must not let that happen."

This is not Delia speaking. Whose voice is this?

"Monsieur Hodge, lean back. Relax. You're in my arms now."

Monsieur Hodge?

Delia is no longer Delia. I'm not in her arms. I'm not even in William Holden's arms. I'm in the strong, muscular arms of Henry Stoneman, and the breasts are not hers, they're his pectorals, rounded and tight. He squeezes against me, kisses me, and reaches down to stroke me. I explode. White cream streams out of me and floats across the water.

I wake up out of this strange, erotic, exotic vision, soaking wet.

I looked down and lifted the pillow from my groin. Cum stains on Mrs. Jacobson's cushion!

"Haskell? Sorry! I forgot you were coming. What's wrong with me?" I heard Delia's voice. "I'm so sorry, I'm late. I lost track of time."

Oh, shit! What am I doing? What a time to have a wet dream! I was perspiring and trembling. This was the worst thing that had ever happened.

"Haskell?" Mrs. Jacobson stomped into the room. "What were you squealing about? Did you fall asleep and have a nightmare?"

Maybe they didn't notice. I clutched the pillow, cum-side down.

"I guess I fell asleep. Yes, I had a dream I was in the war."

I looked up, turned around, and saw mother and daughter hovering behind me.

"You fell asleep, did you?" Delia's mom had a deep-throated laugh, as if she used to smoke several packs a day.

I think they believed my story—at least I hoped they did.

"Well, look at you!" Mrs. Jacobson said. "You're all hot and sweaty. Why don't you clean up in the bathroom and then join us for some dinner. The little boy's room is down the hall."

I waited until the two of them left the den before I trudged off to the bathroom, holding the cushion over my shame. I hoped I hadn't stained the fabric.

22

THE BIG NIGHT, PART 2

Thankfully the bathroom was at the far end of the hall, so I assumed no one could hear the sound of the hairdryer. After I scrubbed my jeans and the pillow, I dried off the wet spots. When I strolled back into the kitchen, Delia gave me this oddest look.

"What took you so long?" she asked.

"I'm sorry, I drooled. The saliva dripped down my shirt onto my pants, and your mother's pillow got slightly wet, so I dried them with a hair dryer."

What else could I say? A ridiculous lie was better than the truth.

Mrs. Jacobson motioned us to have a seat around the dining room table. "Please, please, just sit down. You've had a little nap. I'm sure you feel a whole lot better."

Not really, I was losing my mind waiting for your daughter to arrive. Having an erotic fantasy about Henry Stoneman on your couch!

What the hell was wrong with me? But what the hell was wrong with Delia? Why would she forget our *Macbeth* rehearsal? Nearly two hours late! Perhaps we were, in fact, a match made in heaven. Such a pair of doofuses!

"Tell me about this play you two are doing." Mrs. Jacobson said. The table was set for six, although there were only three of us. "Sit, Haskell. I won't take no for an answer. You look like you could use a few pounds of brisket."

"Mom, it's *Macbeth*. You know the play. You saw the Orson Welles version years ago."

"Well, what is your involvement in it?" she asked me.

"I'm coaching her for her audition."

"You're not trying out?"

"No."

"I'm going up against Maggie Hamilton. I told you that."

"Didn't she play Juliet last year?"

"Yep. And Laurey in *Oklahoma*."

"I heard The Juilliard School offered her early acceptance."

"Mom, stop it. Yes. I have some stiff competition trying out for the part. Haskell is merely helping me create more depth and intensity so I can ace it. He was the kid who danced with the animated tiger in the Sugar Flakes commercial!"

Mrs. Jacobson bit her upper lip. "Really? That's very interesting. What else have you done?"

Before I could speak, Delia rattled off a whole list of credits I had never done like *Wagon Train*, *The Rifleman*, and even the recent John Wayne movie *The Comancheros*, all shows Henry Stoneman claimed were on his filmography.

"Well, what do I know? I'm just a lowly court reporter who makes meatloaf and brisket. I always set the table for six, in case Delia's dad comes home from work early and brings friends. I mean, you never know, right? My worst nightmare is that Herb shows up with his boss and a few salespeople, and I don't have enough potatoes. Believe me, in this household, no one ever starves. Although you look like you could gain some weight. Doesn't your mother feed you?"

Before I could answer, Delia chipped in her two cents. "He lives with his aunt, Mom. His mother is Miriam Hodge. She was in all those 'Love' movies in the 1940s and 1950s."

Mrs. Jacobson clasped her hands against her cheeks.

"*Love in the*—what do you call it—*Pantheon*? Oh my God. Herb and I love watching those movies on the Late Late Show."

"She sells real estate now," I added. "She's living in Belgium for a year with her married boyfriend."

I was giving too much information, but Mrs. Jacobson didn't blink an eye.

"Well, good for her. I'm afraid my husband and I were never much into travel. Herb gets terribly airsick and seasick."

When we finished dinner, I volunteered to do the dishes, but Delia pulled on my arm and told me I should follow her into her room. It was nothing like my cousin's room, which was very pink and Barbie-like. Hope loved dolls. Rows and rows of them filled her shelves. This room, on the other hand, was dark brown and had trophies from football and baseball and posters of Joe Namath and some other football players I did not recognize.

"I can see why you'd make a perfect Lady Macbeth," I told her, breathing in the testosterone.

"Don't be silly, Haskell. This is my brother's room. He's in the army. My room is so cluttered with junk—mostly my mom's junk—so I moved in here. Eventually, if my dad ever cleans out the garage, we can store all her sewing machines and work books, and I'll move back into my pristine room."

"I'm into organization too. I keep all my comic books in tightly wrapped boxes."

"I bet you do. Look, before we get started, let me ask you if you'd proof one paper for me, the one that's due Monday. I haven't typed mine up yet."

"Sure, why not?"

"And also, before we go over my lines, I have a couple of math problems I can't figure out. You're in Calculus, right? I'm only in Algebra II, so I'm sure you can help me."

She showed me a page from her math homework and handed me a blank piece of paper. She had not done any of the problems, and I guess she expected me to do all of them.

"While you're finishing that, I'll try and memorize my last speech, and then we can go over it. I really appreciate your help."

It took a good hour or more for me to proof her badly written, error-ridden essay on "Do not go gentle into that good night." I made some major rewrites, and then I basically did her math homework for her before she sat down and read me her lines from Act I of *Macbeth*. When she got to the particularly important part—the lines where Lady Macbeth says, "Come, you spirits that tend on mortal thoughts, unsex me here!"—she may as well have been asking Montgomery Ward department store to open early. It just didn't have the fiery emotion needed to put her natural femininity aside so that she could do the bloody deeds necessary to seize the crown.

In this room, filled with footballs, cleats, and tennis shoes that were once muddied and dirty, it seemed like she should be able to just breathe in the manly spirits and go for it. I offered her a tip: "Be fierce, but persuasive. In Lady Macbeth's mind, this murder makes perfect, rational sense." She read the speech again, now sounding far too spirited, almost dizzy with excitement, like she were about to ride the Ferris wheel at a county fair.

I didn't know what I should say, and I'm sure she saw from my expression that I was unimpressed.

"I'm not very good, am I?" she asked as she reached out and grabbed both my hands. It was the first time she had touched me all night, and though yesterday I anticipated and longed for some sort of intimacy, now I wondered—What was the point? I mean, did I even care, anymore? If I chose Henry over Delia even in my dreams, maybe this relationship was hopeless. I suspected Delia would never drive the homo out of me.

I felt desperately lost.

I should go home.

"How bad am I, Haskell? You can be honest."

"You need practice. That's all." I was attempting the politest voice I could muster. Rubbers in my wallet? What was I thinking? Dreams of sexual intercourse in a pool? I was kicking myself for being so stupid.

"Am I terrible? Do I sound, you know, amateurish? Am I not getting any of the lines right?"

Truly, why hurt her feelings? After some hesitation, I simply said, "Practice makes perfect."

"Be specific. How can I improve my line reading?"

"You need to put some fierceness behind your words."

"Explain. Give me some notes."

"I've been giving you suggestions and notes for the past hour! You haven't been listening." Here I go. For sure, I will blow it now. "I read you the lines the way Judith Anderson read them. Act I, scene five. I see her soliloquy as a 'pep talk' designed to help her bolster the most reprehensible parts of her character. You don't read it with enough brittle enthusiasm."

"But what does that mean? Explain it."

I couldn't hold it back any longer.

"Delia, I've not only explained it. I read it out loud to you the way I think it should be read. Maybe consider playing a different role in the play, one that fits your personality."

"No. I want to be Lady Macbeth."

"Well, what about Lady MacDuff? It's a small but significant part."

"I'm not switching roles. Tell me what else I'm doing wrong, and I'll fix it!"

"I've been very patient. I sat waiting for you for almost two hours. I did your homework for you. I proofed your essay. I practically completed your whole math sheet. And for the past hour and a half, I've given you notes on what I think are the psychological aspects of Lady Macbeth, and you've read the soliloquy each time without really changing a thing. I've run out of ideas. If your heart's set on winning this role, study it. Rent some records from the library. Use *The Reader's Guide* and hunt down some reviews that pinpoint what you have to do to become Lady Macbeth."

I felt such a relief getting that off my chest. Not only was I honest, but I thought I was being helpful, saving her from a humiliating audition, especially considering her competition had been accepted to the most prestigious drama school in the country. This was one of the great roles in theater history, and Delia was unprepared to tackle it.

"So, basically, what you're telling me is, I have to go to the library and rent records? And I have to research the role for hours? I don't have time for any of that."

She burst into tears. The Delia who, moments ago, declared the gods unsex her, now stormed out of the room and slammed the bathroom door. I waited for a few minutes, but she didn't come out.

I finally knocked. "Delia? I'm sorry if I hurt your feelings. This is the way I research parts. The library is open on Saturdays. I think it's open until six."

"Oh, go away!"

"I wasn't planning on hurting your feelings. Would you have preferred I not be honest with you?"

"I'm a dramatic actress. I can pull this off. I know what I'm doing."

"Well, then that's great. I hope you get the part. Why don't you come out now so I can give you a hug and say goodbye."

"You can say goodbye from out there. Goodbye."

I stood for a few minutes and knocked again.

"Leave already!" she yelled, still refusing to open the bathroom door.

I caught the eight-thirty bus and walked the rest of the way home that evening feeling stuck in a new reality. Not only had we not—as I anticipated—spent time in her Jacuzzi and pool, maybe turning hot tub time into intimate moments of romance, but I had destroyed any chance of even having a friendship thanks to my outspoken honesty. Why couldn't I have lied? Had I sabotaged my relationship with Delia on purpose? I had been looking forward to letting Henry know how wonderful this date went. I even thought about stopping by his house on my way home, but what would I say now? I blew it. I was a total idiot. I did what New York critics do all the time—I destroyed a fragile ego.

As I dragged myself home, all I wanted was someone I could open up to—a dad, maybe a real dad who could coach me for a change and help me with my issues. Being me comes with such frightening secrets, and I have no one to share them with. Certain things Uncle Ted and I could talk about—record albums, baseball, movies—and I had bravely brought up the urinating in the school showers. He called the principal and days later Vance gave a speech about shower etiquette. But there was no way I would feel comfortable talking about my orgasm on Mrs. Jacobson's couch. And, of course, I had no relationship with my dad who rarely called and never showed much interest in my daily goings on.

However, wouldn't it be something if my mother surprised me and said my real dad was not Tony, but Earnest Warner, the son of Jack Warner, who had hit the midsection of his life and wanted the truth to come out.

There are certain times in life when a boy needs his dad. A real dad. And what if Dad turns out to be the greatest, kindest, most charming Dad in the whole wide world? What if he asks me out on a dinner date. "Be honest, son. Tell me anything you want!" "Well, I had this slight accident in the den while I waited for Delia to show up—I came on her mother's sofa." "Oh, no worries, son. Those things happen. Don't give it another thought. Tell me, Haskell, are you interested in starring in our new movie with Jack Lemmon and Natalie Wood? I can tell you this—it's not some cheap cannibal, prehistoric monster movie like they produce at Universal. No siree!"

Now I'm really letting my imagination go bonkers. Enough, already! I was getting tired of feeling sorry for myself. I sat outside on one of the cement steps, took some deep breaths, and figured my best bet was to climb into bed, fall asleep and wake up in the morning, feeling fresh and alive, free of all these mental distractions. I waited until the light in my Aunt and Uncle's bedroom turned off before I made my way into the house.

23

LATE NIGHT WITH SHEILA AND TED

Once the light was turned off, I tiptoed into the house, past their door, toward my bedroom, hoping I could avoid drawing their attention.

"Haskell?" It was my aunt's voice. "I saw you sneaking by. How did the date go?"

I backtracked and stood in the doorway, noticing that my aunt and uncle, sitting up in bed, were wearing matching pajamas: white fabric with bright red candy canes, the kind of flannel pajamas most people wouldn't be caught dead wearing except maybe on Christmas Day.

"I had dinner there."

"And?" My aunt plucked a cigarette from her pack and lit it. How did my uncle deal with her smoking all the time? And in bed? "When will we meet this lovely Delia? I can't wait."

"You can wait."

"Did you swim?"

"We swam laps together. It was a good break from practicing her lines."

"Excellent. Glad to hear it."

"My eyes hurt from the chlorine. I better get some sleep," I told them.

Since moving to the Valley, I had never lied so much in my life.

"Wait one second." My aunt now waved her cigarette in the air. "Ted and I were just wondering if you'd like to invite her over some night."

"No. Things aren't good, I'm sorry to say."

"What happened?"

"I don't want to talk about it. I'm a little down."

"You're depressed?"

"I guess you could say that."

"Do you want to take something?" my aunt asked.

"No no, no."

"I have some Valium in the bathroom."

"No thanks."

"I thought you were enjoying school. Sometimes we all need a little pick-me-up. Let me get you something."

"I don't think that's a good idea. I'll be all right."

"Hold on a second. I have something on the table here." She removed a yellow capsule from a bottle.

"Can't I just give him one of these, honey?"

She turned toward my uncle who shook his head. "That's Nembutal, not a good choice," he said. "I have some imipramine. Maybe that would be safer."

"I'm not interested in taking any drugs," I told them. "Thank you. I'll be all right."

"You should be excited," my aunt said. "You found a girlfriend so quickly."

"We're probably not even friends anymore."

"Oh, Haskell, she'll come around."

"I doubt it."

"Did you ever make contact with your dad?"

"No, that's another bag of awful. He never called me. I left a message for him. Nothing."

"Not a phone call? Funny, your mom told me he was going to call you."

"I just told you, Aunt Sheila, he never called me!"

"Well, don't get all agitated. By the way, I spoke with your mom tonight."

I had not been avoiding speaking with her, but whenever we had short conversations, she just sounded so fucking happy, and that only made me feel worse.

I was on the verge of tears. My mouth felt swollen and numb, almost too thick to form words. I had handled the night so badly. I was hopeless, absolutely hopeless.

"Your mother said your father was in India. He'll call you when he's back in town."

"No, he won't."

"Well, her exact words were, he was in Punjab finishing a crummy remake of *Gunga Din*, and he's looking forward to seeing you the moment he lands at the L.A. airport."

"I've heard that before."

"Oh, Haskell. Don't be so hard on him. *Gunga Din* is the only thing on his mind these days. Your mom said it may even be a bigger disaster than *Cleopatra*, and that film bankrupted Twentieth Century Fox. The movie he's making next, though, sounds very promising. What's it called?" She turned to Ted, but I answered her question.

"*Lost at Sea*."

"That's right. Kids stranded on an island with prehistoric monsters."

I finally figured I better say something. I was angry and tired. Melancholy might be a good adjective. "My friend Henry and I read about it in *Variety*. The least my dad could have done was have his secretary call and invite me down for a screen test. But as I said, he's been in his own little world. Thanks for asking, Aunt Sheila and Uncle Ted. I'll hang my wet trunks outside. Now may I go?"

My aunt now repositioned her pillows so she could sit up a bit higher. "If it makes you feel any better, I read a whole article about it in the Calendar section this morning. They're struggling with weather conditions. Hard to build sets during a hurricane, but the weather will improve and so will your relationship with Delia."

"In the morning, things will look brighter," my uncle said.

"There you go. That's the spirit!" my aunt chimed in, yawning. "Your uncle always says the right thing. You'll be fine!" She gave me a thumbs up. "Invite Delia over. We can take you guys out for dinner."

"It's all right. I'll pass," I told her.

"No, forget The Queen's Arms. We'll go to The Sportsman Lodge. They have trout fishing."

"It's really all right."

"Trout fishing on a date! That is the most romantic thing ever. You catch a few trout. They skin them for you and put them in plastic bags or they cook them for you, right there, with garlic and butter. Just delicious."

"Aunt Sheila, we had a spat. Actually, it was worse than a spat. It was more of a rupture. Trout fishing is never going to save this relationship."

"Oh, never is a long time. Don't say that. First love?" She edged herself off the bed, feet on the floor. "I'm sure if you two had a little talk, Delia will forgive you. What did you think upset her so?"

"The truth is, Aunt Sheila, I offered her some suggestions for improving her performance as Lady Macbeth. She wouldn't follow any of them. I was critical, not cruel, and yet she took it so hard."

"Why would she be so upset?"

"She has her heart set on a role that goes beyond her capabilities."

"You were just being forthright and realistic. She'll forgive you. It's not like you cheated on her and broke her heart. Look at the bright side. You at least connected with a girl. It's early in the semester. Eventually, she might make a very good prom date."

"I guess."

"There, there. I'm proud of you for putting yourself out there. Get some sleep, why don't you? Believe me, she'll get over it." Aunt signaled for me to walk closer, and this time I did, allowing her to clasp her arms around my neck. "I love you, Haskell."

Up to this point, over a month into my life in Encino with the Teitlebaums, I had not experienced much affection from Aunt Sheila. I wouldn't call her ice-cube cold. She just wasn't touchy-feely as some moms are. She never wrapped her arms around me. This evening she did. Even kissed my forehead. "I'm very proud of you for making the attempt at making new friends," she said, quite lovingly. "I have the feeling everything will work out fine. The girl's probably mad for you."

"That is an interesting way of putting it."

As I walked out, I swear I heard her whisper to my uncle, "Guess what, Ted, Haskell has a girlfriend." Funny how she assumed a fight equaled the possibility of romance.

And Uncle Ted, who so far had not said much, replied, "Thank God!"

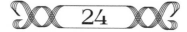

24

THE SHOWDOWN

Over the weekend, I stayed in my bed, pretending I was sick with a sore throat and a cold. I was so frustrated and confused. I begged everyone to leave me alone.

My aunt would knock on the door and ask if I wanted tea or a cup of coffee, and I would tell her all I wanted was quiet time.

At one point, she brought her usual tray of macaroni and cheese and set it on my bed. "You hungry? You haven't eaten all day."

"I'm not hungry."

"This macaroni is different. I made it from scratch. I took a class this morning, and I was determined to put my new knowledge to work. Boiled the noodles. Added the cheese. I crumbled bread crumbs on it and set it under the broiler. Absolutely out of this world. Please, eat."

I took a spoonful.

"Delicious?"

I nodded my head.

"Didn't I tell you? I know you prefer not talking."

"Thank you."

"And I haven't wanted to disturb you."

"Much appreciated."

"But I'm taking two classes. Yes, one in cooking but the other is called Alienation and Existentialism in World Literature. This morning I heard a wonderful lecture, and this sentence stuck in my mind."

I took another spoonful of the macaroni and braced myself.

"It's by Aldous Huxley, and he said, 'Do not brood over your wrongdoing. Rolling in the muck is not the best way of getting clean.' I think that says it all."

She leaned over my bed and kissed me on the forehead.

"Know that we love you, Haskell. We'll do anything. Say the word."

I suppose I needed some advice. What would I say, for example, when I bumped into Delia on Monday? I figured I could answer this question without her help. I should apologize. More importantly, I must never falter. Keep my chin up, my head high. I must stay out of my muck. Don't get all depressed. I realized the old Haskell was simply not functioning well in this new world. I must find another strategy.

The easiest way to solve this problem would be to tell Delia how sorry I was and make up some excuse for my ill-advised notes on her acting. I thought about your approach to Lady Macbeth, and you know, it works on a whole other level I had never considered.

This seemed the right thing to do.

On Monday morning, I made my way down the hallway toward our English class. Lucky Miller was strutting down the hall with his two hooligans. My new attitude will start right now, I thought. Be positive. Huxley's right. Stay out of the muck. I waved my hand and put on a big smile. "Hi, guys!" We hadn't spoken in weeks, and being friendly couldn't hurt.

I was the new me. Champion Haskell. Keep your chin up high.

Lucky once again lightly shoved me out of his way and muttered something under his breath that made Winston and Nate laugh so hard several other kids walking down the hallway asked, "What's so hilarious?"

"Hey, it's Judy," Lucky said pointing at me. "He just said 'hi' to me, sounding more like Judy every day."

Only a few weeks earlier Henry suggested I had some options. Which one should I choose? Control my rage or defend myself? I could feel the adrenaline build up inside. If I wanted to be respected by Delia and her friends, I had to stop acting like a wimp. Those days were over. I must be brave, aggressive, and lion-hearted.

I also had learned some tactical moves from Henry and my instructors at the studio. Use them.

"Miller?" I shouted. "Does making fun of other people make you feel better?"

This sounded so lame.

"I thought we had reached a truce, and if you remember right, we had an agreement: no name calling. You broke that rule, didn't you?"

Lucky shook his head wildly as if he could not believe what he was hearing. "You're such a fucking idiot."

"Are you talking to yourself? Because that's what most kids at this school think of you."

"Hey, faggot, I'm talking to you." He grabbed me by the shirt collar, and I twisted myself free, punching him right in the eye so that he fell against the wall in the darkly lit hallway, his head knocking against the hard cement.

"What did I just tell you? I am not taking this shit from you anymore!" I yelled, loud enough for teachers in their classrooms to hear. "Don't ever put your hands on me again, and do not call me names!"

I don't know where this courageous hostility came from. Was I bent on suicide? Swearing at school was probably punishable by suspension. If I started a fight with Lucky, I might even be expelled. Did I give him a black eye? I hoped so. Let him carry that with him all day.

Lucky pushed himself off the ground, now steadied himself on both his feet. He was a few inches shorter than me, and I would not be intimidated by his muscular arms. I was a warrior. I remembered moves Henry had taught me, and I had no choice. I would fight him off the mat.

The heel of my foot kicked him in the chin, another kick landed firmly in his chest, and thankfully, I knocked him down.

A group of kids began forming around us. I did not see Henry, though I did notice Delia running forward, squeezing her way through the crowd, ending up an arm's length from me.

"Haskell? What are you doing?" she screamed "Leave him alone! You will get in big trouble."

It was about seven-forty-five. Classes started precisely at seven-fifty. The warning bell would ring in four more minutes. Normally kids rushed up and down the hallway, eager to make class on time. But this morning, amidst all this commotion, Delia, Lucky's hooligans, and maybe ten other kids all surrounded Lucky and me. There was a show going on, and nobody wanted to miss it.

Lucky bounced back on his feet and wiped some blood off his nose.

"You're so dead, faggot."

"I'm very much alive, and this is the last time you'll ever call me names."

The two of us stood, a few feet apart from each other, fists raised.

"Unless you have some secret weapon on you, Judy, why don't you go onto your class and be a good little boy. I don't want to hurt you."

"I don't want to hurt you either, Lucky, but I'll hurt you if I have to."

Lucky laughed. "You will be sorry. I hate to say it."

There's a moment in the classic Western *The Big Country* when the city slicker (played by Gregory Peck) must face his worst enemy, a trouble-making, low-down, grizzly bully (played by Chuck Connors). Peck does not back down because he knows if he does, he'll be deemed a coward. The ranch hands will look down on him. His fiancée will think he's less than a man. And most importantly, he will not believe in himself.

This was my Gregory Peck moment. Henry stood in the back of the crowd, waving his arms, trying to get my attention. Delia screamed, "Haskell, stop it. Don't do this!" If I backed down, I'd continue being Haskell the Dork and the Laughing Stock of Encino. The faggot. The Judy. Any chances of resurrecting my friendship with Delia or anyone else in the crowd would be impossible. Word would get around. Haskell was a gutless weakling.

I was still nursing my shoulder when Lucky shrugged and once again muttered some nasty comment under his breath. "You're such a loser," is what I think he said.

I turned on my left foot, lifted my right one, and kicked him as hard as I could in his chest. He fell backwards. You could hear his thick head hit the plaster wall. I hoped blood would dribble down his forehead, cheeks, and chin. The doofus picked himself up again, wiped the blood off his mouth with the back of his hand and ran toward me. I stepped aside using a simple defense tactic Henry had taught me. Lucky's fist hit the opposite wall, and his scream echoed down the hall. As he cradled his fist with his other hand, he began yelling as loud as he could, "I'm going to kill you!"

Really? Where were the teachers? Why was no one in the hallway preventing this kid from murdering me? Again, if this were Bonvadine, Mr. Varnish would have rushed out of his classroom, grabbed Lucky by his arms, and pulled him into the Headmaster's office. He'd probably forego the dunce cap and simply kick the doofus out of school.

Here at Encino High? I didn't see anyone stopping us.

Why risk chances of retaliation? I jab-punched him smack in the chest, and the force caused Lucky to lose his balance and again fall backwards. I was surprised Winston or some other onlookers didn't cushion his fall. Instead, Lucky fell, and this time he sprawled across the cement floor. Fearful he might pick himself up once again, I sat on him, slugging him as hard as I could. I slugged and slugged. He jabbed back at me until I wrapped my hands around his neck and squeezed as tightly as I could, choking him as his head bobbed up and down. I heard Delia screaming. "Haskell! Stop it! Stop it now!" I heard Henry screaming, "That's enough, Hodge. You've made your point!"

But I didn't listen. I was too engulfed in rage. When I loosened my hands around his neck, I began punching him again, and I kept at it until his nose and mouth bled like a river. His skin turned bright red from bruising. His teeth were red with blood. I would have kept on punching, but I felt a hand pull me off of him.

"Okay, you two. Stop it this instant! Both of you, principal's office!"

You'd think with all that jabbing and punching, he'd be dead, but Lucky sprang to his feet, and Mrs. Green prevented him from pouncing on me.

"Stop it! Right now!" Beautiful Mrs. Green had a strong grip as she held each of us by an arm and pulled us down the hallway toward the administrative office.

The blood felt warm and sticky above my lips. My right arm ached, and I'm sure I had black and blue marks all over my legs where he kicked me. Nevertheless, I held my own. I defended myself. I hoped Henry saw enough of the fight so that he was proud of me. "Hey, Monsieur Hodge," he might say. "You beat up the swim champion of Encino High. Now everyone will leave you alone."

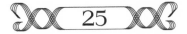

25

A PUNCH IN THE NOSE

Perhaps, I was getting a little ahead of myself. The day was not over yet.

We stood outside Freed's office—Lucky, me, and Freed's secretary, Miss Ito, who nervously handed both of us paper towels. The blood ran down our chins onto the linoleum. The janitor would mop up after us. I was glad blood dripped from Lucky's swollen face. I was proud of the hurt I had caused, and I truly believed this was the shining moment of my year so far at Encino High.

I won the fight.

"I am a rebel with a cause," I said out loud.

Miss Ito shook her head and frowned. "You're a student who will get expelled. I'll be back with some icepacks. Dr. Freed will be right out."

Miss Ito must have locked the outside hallway doors because Lucky and I saw a crowd of kids staring through the windows. The bell rang, but I assumed our fight had interrupted the normal start time for first period.

I knew I'd won, and if I were given a chance, I'd do it all over again. The worst thing he could have done was continue the fight, for there was no way would I ever let him beat me. Truly, my fear was this: My inner rage would overtake my reason, and I'd kill him, only to end up in jail and then in court and ultimately in the electric chair.

We stood for a good five minutes without saying a word. Finally, I said: "I almost killed you. I could have killed you. I was so angry."

Lucky rolled his eyes. "No way, Judy, would you have killed me. I was being easy on you. I could have punched you in the head and it would be all over, so shut the fuck up."

"You'll end up in Sing Sing someday!"

"Sing Sing? Is that where they lock up boys humming Judy Garland songs?" Lucky asked, grinning at his own cleverness.

I wish I had said Rikers Island.

I let out a deep sigh. This was not getting us anywhere.

"Let's just stop picking on each other. More specifically, stop calling me names. We don't have to be friends. Let's ignore each other. Deal?"

Again, he rolled his eyes. Why do I even bother? I should keep my big mouth shut.

"You like this back and forth we have? You want this animosity between us continuing? I am tired of it. We're both a bloody mess. Let's call it even."

He was breathing laboriously. I wondered if Doofus Head even knew what the word "animosity" meant. Or "laboriously," for that matter.

At this point, Mrs. Green ran toward us with icepacks and more paper towels.

"Will I be thrown out of school?" I asked her.

"You might be," she said, frowning. "If you started the fight, you could very well be expelled. You should know better."

"Why? I know nothing." If you had any idea what I've been through with this idiot!

She disappeared for a moment inside one of the offices.

"I'll tell you what," I said to Lucky. "I will take the responsibility for this catastrophe if you will admit your involvement. Just tell Dr. Freed you called me names, and I think ultimately, we may only get, oh I don't know, after school cleanup duty? I think if Freed knew the cause of my anger, he'd make an exception."

Lucky still did not utter a word. I figured maybe he was pissed he might get suspended, and if he got suspended he couldn't swim, and if he couldn't swim, the team would lose the state championship, and if the school lost the state championship, Encino High would lose an important trophy for its near-empty trophy case.

"Let's not do this again, all right? I think if we go into Freed's office and apologize, and we put our differences aside, leave one another alone, I'm sure you won't get suspended and hopefully I won't get expelled. Fair?"

He wouldn't even turn his head toward me, let alone utter a single syllable. He held the icepack against his eyes and continued his stony silence.

Mrs. Green opened an office door and stuck her head out. "Dr. Freed's almost done with his meeting. He'll be out in a minute."

The worst thing I could do, I suppose, might be insist I won this fight. I thought it best, in these circumstances, to admit fault. Accept punishment. Apologize profusely and come up with some compromise.

"So? We even? We both fought hard. Maybe, if we agree, we can save each other from expulsion."

Lucky merely rolled his eyes.

"This will not look good on my transcripts. Imagine, NYU, Princeton, Columbia? Trounced swim champion? They'll think I'm a loose cannon and dub me 'undesirable.' So, let's agree we will never fight again. If we agree we will never fight again, then maybe Freed will give us community service, and if we did community service together, it might, you know, heal the wounds, and we can hang out, like we were supposed—"

"Oh, shut the fuck up already!" Lucky screamed as he swung his arm backwards. He elbow-smacked me in the nose so hard, I crumpled onto the cement floor. I did not see this coming. I swear when he hit me, I heard the sound of nose cartilage breaking. I saw stars and moons and craters streaming across the sky. The moon crumbled into pieces, as I fainted.

What woke me was Mrs. Green screaming. "Oh my God! The blood splattered all over my cashmere sweater!" There was quite a lot of blood, a surprising amount, and not just on her sweater. All over the walls. All over me and Lucky. He must have broken one or more of my nasal corpuscles. Blood gushed out and wouldn't stop, and poor Mrs. Green waved her arms in the air, screaming and crying, seemingly helpless. "You ruined my sweater, and it was a gift from my fiancé!"

Obviously, bloody clothes was not a topic covered at Cal State Dominguez Hills Graduate Education Program.

Dr. Freed finally ran out of his office, and Miss Ito came to our rescue with another stack of paper towels.

Freed offered me his handkerchief.

"This might stop the bleeding," he said.

Like, who was he kidding? Nothing would stop the bleeding. It was as if the dam had broken. My nose opened up rivers of blood. The world turned black. Maybe I fainted again. When I opened my eyes, Freed and some other teacher had their hands under my armpits, guiding me into a car. I didn't realize when you bleed this much, you lose consciousness. I slumped in the front seat of this station wagon, holding my head back.

"Wake up, Haskell," Freed said. "No sleeping. Hold the cloth against your nose. Breathe through your mouth. I'll get you to the hospital in a jiffy. It's a few blocks from here."

I could not believe that doofus broke my nose. I might never breathe normally again. This could prevent me from auditioning for TV shows, movies, and especially commercials. I'd be unemployable, all because of his elbow.

Dr. Freed drove fast.

Rosemary Clooney sang on the radio something about coming over to her house where she'll give me candy and an apple and a plum and a fig, and who knows what other fruit before she'll do what? Love me? We all just want to love who we want to love without being bribed. At that moment, I desperately wanted silence, but if I released my hands from my nose and turned off the radio, buckets of blood would pour forth.

What lyricist on opium wrote this stupid song?

I loved it when she sang "White Christmas," but I hated these novelty tunes. If I released my hands from my nose and turned off the radio, though, buckets of blood would pour forth.

"Hold your head back, son," Dr. Freed told me. I suppose if I don't, I'll bleed all over his plastic seat covers. "We'll take side streets. It'll be faster."

"The music is killing me!" I told him, and thankfully, he turned the radio off.

As soon as Freed landed his station wagon at the emergency entrance, I saw my aunt standing at the glass doors.

"Did you break it?" my aunt asked.

"Did *I* break it?" I responded.

"Haskell, this is not the time for a squabble. I'm asking you a simple question. Do you think your nose is broken?"

"If it's broken, *I* didn't break it. Your across-the-street buddy broke it!" I was about to explode. She was blaming me? "Why don't you invite Mr. Miller over for dinner tonight, and he can tell you the whole story! Make him some of your famous Stouffer's lasagna!"

"Who are we talking about?"

"The coward swung at me when I wasn't looking. Lucky Miller did this!"

"That's not the story I heard. His mother said it was an accident."

"It was no accident. He was humiliated because I trounced him in front of all his Neanderthal buddies, and he couldn't handle the shame."

"Mrs. Miller said your nose got in the way of his elbow. She was very upset about it."

"She doesn't know squat what she's talking about. She's about as stupid as that Afghan of hers who keeps pooping on our lawn."

"Poppy is not her dog. He belongs to the Shapiro's. And Haskell, this is no way to talk."

Maybe upon hearing this weird exchange, Dr. Freed feared interfering with family drama. He waved goodbye and said he'd call later to see how I was doing. His duty was complete.

"Am I expelled?" I called after him. "You better expel Lucky! Do you hear me?"

He headed toward his car, ignoring my question.

That was smart because I wasn't certain how long until there would be another embarrassing eruption. My aunt's jaw tightened in mighty annoyance. She was probably worrying that her nephew would cause a rift with her neighbors. I surprised myself. I had never felt such rage toward another human being. I hated Lucky Miller. I prayed he'd get decapitated by a jackknifed truck, his head rolling down the 101, crushed by half a dozen eighteen-wheelers carrying tractor parts. How dare he justify this violent act by claiming it an accident! What a liar! And my aunt dared to believe him?

26

BROKEN NOSE—WOUNDED SPIRIT

"*Hola, hombre. ¿Cómo estás? ¿Qué estás haciendo aquí?*"
An orderly forced me into a wheelchair and wheeled me down
the hallway. "You talked back to your mom, man. If I did that,
my mom would have slapped me across my face."

She's not my mom, idiot. She's my aunt. I felt blood dripping
inside my mouth, down my throat.

"You in pain, *hombre?*" While I thought I answered his
question with my wincing and swearing, it was my fist
pounding against my thigh that got his attention. "Let me see if
I can get a doctor to get you something."

He draped a blanket over my knees and wheeled me into a
room, empty but for a chair and a small desk.

My aunt soon entered and pushed my wheelchair near the
desk. She eased into a chair, removing a cigarette from her pack,
though the sign on the wall plainly said, "No Smoking."

If you exhale, I will kill you.

"Please tell me what happened. I want every detail." This
was as close to a conciliatory tone as she could invent. "Haskell?
I'm waiting." She tapped her toe on the linoleum.

"Put the cigarette out, and I'll tell you."

She dropped it on the floor and stamped on it with the heel of her shoe.

I explained the whole story, from the start of the encounter in the hallway until he swung his arm against my face. I left out nothing. I told her he called me a faggot, and I was sick of it. "I'm not a faggot," I told my aunt, "and even if I am, it's none of his business, your business, anyone's business. I'll tell you what I want. I want Lucky run over by a humongous fleet of trucks, and I want to watch his guts eaten by vultures, and I want to watch the mommy vulture take his guts, bring them back to her nest, and feed them to the little vultures!"

My aunt swallowed hard. I don't think she realized how upset I was. Her face showed no expression as she removed another cigarette, toying with it as if it were her plaything. "When your mom gets back in town, we're going to have a little talk about the kind of movies you watch. She's been letting you see the most inappropriate films."

"Where is my mom? I want her here!"

"She's in Sicily, I think. Bobby was so busy she decided she'd travel a bit. They're having a wonderful time together."

"What is she doing in Sicily? I thought she's living in Antwerp."

"I don't know. Our conversations are so brief."

"Is she all right?" I asked.

"I haven't heard anything to the contrary. She's cruising in the middle of whatever body of water she's on. Someone invited her on their yacht. What ocean is near Sicily?"

"It's in the Mediterranean Sea."

"How do you know all these facts?"

"If you'd read more, you would know more."

At that moment, I saw our well-dressed neighbor, Dr. Hornstein, whip down the hall and enter another room. I had met him a couple of times as he often came over for cocktails. I had thought he was a psychiatrist. For example, if Hope put on a fit in the morning, refusing to get dressed for school, he suggested my aunt take her anyway, even if she was in her pajamas. She should not give in to Hope's tantrums. He would say stuff like that. Very psychiatrist-like.

"I don't need a psychiatrist. I need a surgeon to fix my nose."

"Dr. Hornstein is a plastic surgeon, silly."

"I don't believe you. Is he giving us a discount, is that why we're using him?"

"Haskell? Dr. Hornstein is a renowned plastic surgeon. Don't argue with me so much. I swear I have no clue how your mother put up with you."

"I don't want someone working on me who tells you to take Hope to school in her pajamas!"

"Haskell, stop it. You're so out of sync. You're acting very strange."

The pain was making me say the strangest things. She was right. I think I was mixing Hornstein up with the psychiatrist on *General Hospital*. They had very similar faces.

The orderly came back in, moved me onto a gurney, and wheeled me into a brightly lit room, a conflagration of fluorescent lights. Hornstein examined me, pulled the gauze out, probed and touched and asked if it hurt. I screamed out in pain and shouted at the top of my lungs, "I'm disfigured for life! I will never be the same! This is one big bag of awful!" With the full gravity of the situation finally sinking in, I realized I had lost my oddball adorableness for good, and the roles I once obtained so easily now were beyond my reach. No better time for a complete mental breakdown than now.

● ● ●

A nurse gave me what my aunt called a very strong pick-me-up. That was Encino language for painkillers. I slept for a few hours. When I woke up from a drug-induced slumber, Dr. Hornstein hovered over me once again, his beard neatly trimmed, smelling of Brut cologne and smoked salmon. He also had a dollop of cream cheese on his lip and onion breath.

"How you doing, Haskell?"

You just had a bagel, didn't you? I couldn't speak, I was in so much pain. I merely nodded my head.

"The musical last night was simply amazing, wasn't it?" he asked.

Was he addressing me?

"Weren't the flying carpets and harem girls something else? I thought the man playing the Wazir was excellent."

I was having a nightmare. I must have been asleep, dreaming all this.

"You know, Borodin knows his stuff, right?"

Borodin?

"Right you are, Eddy." It was a woman's voice, unmistakably the high-pitched, sing-song sound of my traitorous Aunt Sheila. Why is she here? And what the hell is he doing? I wondered why I felt nothing. When would the pain return? Was I dying? Where was the light? Doesn't a family member come for you before Death takes over? The man with a scythe? The Death card. I was going to die. And who was Borodin? Ah, maybe Borodin is my star-catcher, leading me through the gates of heaven! If I only have twenty-four hours left on earth, why am I on a gurney under such bright lights?

"So," Hornstein pressed a button, and the bed rose so he could face me. "Your septum is quite deviated. You awake? Can you hear me?"

I hear you, Blue Eyes.

He was as handsome as ever, this unbelievably gorgeous doctor from *General Hospital*, with his set of baby blue eyes—two, count them—behind thick black-framed glasses.

"I propose we repair it while we straighten your nose. What do you say? Two surgeries. A sort of double feature."

What is this "we" business? Was my aunt now assisting him in this surgery? She never went to medical school. And I've seen her cut carrots. I want her nowhere near my nose.

"You know, Eddy, I didn't realize this music was written seventy years ago. Now it's on the radio. Tony Bennett sings one of the tunes. What's it called? I forget."

"I can't remember it either," the doctor replied. "Hold still, Haskell. I'm almost done here. We can't operate on you today—too much swelling. I suspect by late next week, it will be fine."

I couldn't speak. It felt as if my lips were frozen shut. Was my aunt having an affair with Dr. Hornstein? Did he take time off from his TV show to do my surgery? Was he the most unqualified doctor in the world?

"When the swelling goes down, we'll have you back here," the doctor said, winking with one eye. "A month after surgery, you'll be as good as new."

"I bet Haskell would know," my aunt said. "He knows every musical. Haskell, honey, what is the name of this song?"

She hummed a tune so off-key I was surprised I could even figure it out. It was "Stranger in Paradise," based on a melody from—ah—I got it now—Alexander Borodin's opera, *Prince Igor*. It was all coming together. *Kismet's* music is based on the melodies of Borodin. I wasn't dead. I was being examined, and last night my aunt and uncle took advantage of their four-seat subscription to the Philharmonic and saw *Kismet* at the new

Los Angeles Music Center with their neighbors, Elena and Eddy Hornstein.

"What's the name of that tune, Hask? You know it, don't you?" my aunt asked, eagerly.

I do, and I'm going to make you stew over it.

"I think we better wait," the doctor told her. "He's on a heavy sedative."

"It's driving me crazy, Eddy! What is the darn name of that song? Hold off on the sedative until he tells us the title! Don't keep us waiting, Haskell. Please, oh, please."

My Aunt Sheila. You gotta love her, right? I was prodded and jabbed, blood in my throat, nose cartilage shattered, and beside me, my poor aunt feeling tortured, desperately searching for the title of a song she could not remember. I knew where Hope got her tantrums from. And you know what? My lips were sealed. You could stick needles in my eyes, torture me with novelty tunes—I wasn't budging. You couldn't remember something? It gnawed at you until your insides hurt. Old people in their forties and fifties were particularly vulnerable. Gosh, what's the name of that composer? Nuts, why can't I remember his name? Crap, what's the name of this person I'm talking to? Shit, on what table did I leave my keys? Fuck, where did I park my car?

I hoped my aunt's forgetfulness plagued her so radically that her insides ruptured and her spleen exploded.

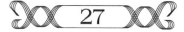

27

MY AUNT MAKES A PROPOSAL

A few nights later, I was tucked nicely in my bed in my own bedroom watching a documentary based on the *The Rise and Fall of the Third Reich* when Aunt Sheila strolled into the room, an unlit cigarette in her right hand.

"Again, I don't see how this kind of show is healthy for you, considering your state of mind."

"It's about Nazis. I'm always interested in studying that period in history."

"Well, not in this house." She turned off the TV and sat on the edge of the bed, cigarette still in hand. "How are you feeling? Did you have a nap?"

"Yes, and I'd feel better if you didn't light that damned thing."

Too late. She had lit it, but quickly snuffed out the cigarette in my trash can.

"I hope that won't start a fire," I said.

"Let's discuss a few things, if you wouldn't mind."

"I do mind. The elves are pounding hammers on my cerebellum. Maybe tomorrow."

"Sometimes you exude drama. Did you take your pills?"

"I can't take the narcotics. They make me hallucinate, and I get nauseous, and I get constipated."

"Do you want some aspirin for the pain?"

"No. Watching this documentary makes me realize things could be a lot worse. If I had been born in Poland in the 1930s, I'd have died in Auschwitz. And it keeps me distracted from thinking about my pain."

"We're not watching Nazis right now! I have something to discuss with you."

"You heard news about Mom?"

"Yes. Your mom is fine. I'm sure we'll hear more from her sometime next week. She's having the time of her life. Loves Sicily. Loves the yacht trip. She's very happy."

"How do you know?"

"We talked for a good ten minutes. Must have cost a fortune. She's eating lots of pasta and dancing in clubs at night. Stop worrying about her. She's now at sea, heading toward North Africa. Bob's busy at work. I doubt she'll find pay phones in the middle of the African ocean."

"That's a very dangerous ocean. And by the way, it's the Mediterranean Sea."

"It's no more dangerous than any other ocean. She'll be fine."

"That inlet between Sicily and Morocco? Lots of capsized boats."

"Haskell, stop it."

I knew I was being ridiculous, but not having heard a peep out of Mom in eleven days was scary. Instead of cruising the seas, why didn't she fly home and visit me, especially after this catastrophe? I worried that the new yacht they were on would tip over and she'd drown. You read about that happening all the time. Who visits Sicily anyway? Or Morocco? Or Fez? Why couldn't she be happy coming here and visiting Catalina? I sounded more like her father than her son. What was the matter with me?

"Pay attention. You know you're having surgery on Friday. The doctor said he'll fix the septum and straighten your nose, maybe even shorten it a bit. The surgery will give you a subtle improvement, and while he's at it, he'll pin back your ears."

"Why?" I asked. "Lucky punched my nose, not my ears!"

"Haskell, you can be so disagreeable. I'll be blunt. Kids have called you names for years, haven't they? Dumbo? Fly Away Haskell? Elephant Ears? These surgeries will help eliminate the teasing and taunting. You'll already be under anesthesia, and he'd include otoplasty for very little extra money. What's a few more stitches, right?"

"Stitches where?"

"I already told you. Eddy is recommending you have your ears pinned back," she repeated. "It will be very subtle. Most people won't even notice the changes. However, with the ears pinned back, the nose straightened and the septum fixed, you will breathe and look a hundred percent better. You will have girls crawling all over you. This Delia will be a thing of the past."

"I think I already accomplished that."

"Oh, I don't know. She came by the other day. You were sleeping." My aunt paused and rubbed her forehead. "Frankly, you can do better."

"Why didn't you tell me she had visited?"

"You were fast asleep. That actor friend Henry was with her too."

"They came together? Why didn't you say anything?"

"They stayed for maybe ten minutes. I told them about the

surgery, and they both agreed. Otoplasty? Very popular. Delia said her brother had it done when he was nine."

"Her brother never acted. He was a football player. These ears are my calling card. I got jobs based on flappy ears and my slightly bent nose."

"What was adorable at six may not be so adorable at sixteen. If you're serious about Hollywood, just remember, first impressions make all the difference in the world."

Plastic surgery struck me as something criminals do who want to hide from the law, and I feared I'd be completely altered and unrecognizable like Humphrey Bogart in *Dark Passage*.

"Roles once out of your reach now will be within your reach. When casting directors see your new photos, they'll no longer see the oddball. Instead, they'll see an attractive, smart, normal-looking, all-American boy."

"What if he goofs and cuts my nose off by accident?"

"That's not going to happen, Haskell."

I was incoherent, my thoughts numbed by pain. What if I woke up and was ugly? What if, when Hope saw me, she squeezed her hands against her cheeks like that poor man in the painting "The Scream"—except not with a silent scream, with real screaming?

"He crushed my nose, and I will seek revenge."

"You will do no such thing. Stop talking such nonsense."

Aunt Sheila handed me a couple of pills and a full glass of water. "Okay. Let's summarize. Three surgeries. One after another. Bump removed from nose. Septum fixed so that the whistle sound you make when you're snoring will disappear. Also, your ears will be stitched back so that they're closer to your head. I promise you, when your mom returns from her adventures, she'll be absolutely surprised and delighted.

■ ■ ■

Here was my fear: After all this plastic surgery, I'd lose my uniqueness. I'd spent my life running away from who I was. What I should really have done was face my critics and say: This is me! Like me or not! Why give in to becoming somebody else—ears delicately bunched against one's skull, a nose carved slightly and upturned, nostrils that breathe oxygen in and out without even the slightest noise? Reynaldo once said it was his snorting and snoring that finally landed him a single dorm room at Ohio State. There are advantages to a deviated septum.

On the other hand, I also saw the numerous advantages of having my nose fixed and my ears pinned back. I could cut my hair short and not worry about my ears sticking out. I could do sleepovers and not fear I'd wake up the whole household with my snoring. It might even open me up for boy-next-door roles I thought were out of reach. I even had this weird notion that if girls found me attractive and I had a lot of dates and opportunities for hot, heterosexual sex, this would further drive the homo out of me. I'd get married and live a "normal" life like everyone else, without the fear of being arrested and beaten to death in a jail cell. I figured if Henry approved, the doctor approved, Delia approved, Uncle Ted and Aunt Sheila approved, maybe this surgery couldn't be such a bad thing. As much as I hated to admit it, I wished my mom were around so she could also give me her two cents.

28

THE RETURN OF MIRIAM HODGE

It was a few weeks before Christmas, and all through the night, I tossed and turned, never waking once, until around midnight, when I smelled an acrid, pungent, choking stench enter the room. I sat up and a strange mist moved across the carpet. I peered through the haze at a faint, indistinct vision. This was a true apparition, maybe a ghost. She wore lipstick, a pearl necklace, lacquered black high heels, a dark maroon kaftan over a navy blue blouse, and a white pleated skirt. But her skin was a translucent, stark, grayish blue, and she smelled fishy, like bad sea water on a hot day. Not a wrinkle on her forehead or a bag under her eyes, but when she opened her mouth, her tongue was the size of a small trout and the color of dead salmon.

"Mom? What are you doing here?"

"I'm offering advice. I only have a few minutes. That's all they're giving me, so let's make the best of it."

As she approached my bed, the smell got worse. I squeezed into the corner of the bed, and my knees shook, knocking against my chin.

"What happened? I thought you were at sea with friends?"

"No, honey. We had an accident."

"What kind of an accident?" My heart raced. This was not good news. Something had happened. Sea water was definitely not her perfume.

"Well, if you must know, we were swallowed by a whale."

Now I realized I was asleep. Once I figured that out—a nightmare, precipitated by watching *A Christmas Carol* earlier in the evening and reading the Classics Illustrated comic version of *Moby Dick*—I searched for hidden meaning. What did the whale symbolize? Why was mom's tongue shaped like a fish tail? Did I wish my mother were dead? I figured the answers were forthcoming as soon as I woke up. I blinked several times, even squeezed my cheeks, pinched my forehead. The ghost still would not disappear.

"You asked for my two cents. Here they are."

She sat herself on the edge of my bed, and I moved over against the wall.

"I wish you'd sit on the chair. You're getting my bed all wet."

"Stop being so fussy. I came here with a mission. I'm showing you what you'll look like after you have these surgeries."

"You're the Ghost of Future Surgeries?" I asked, trembling.

"Exactly. We'll start with the bandage."

She snapped her fingers and instantly a mirror appeared. She showed me my face wrapped in thick tape and bandages. I resembled a mummy found in the ancient caves of Encino. "Unwrap yourself," she said.

In this weird nightmare, the doctor had bandaged me up tightly from the neck up, leaving me only two small dots for my nostrils and slightly larger holes for my eyes. I recklessly followed her instructions. I unwrapped my head, ears, and forehead until I had a wad of gauze, tape, and bandages in my hands.

Then I raised my chin and stared into my mother's red, watery eyes. A whale, huh? I mean, whoever heard of people getting swallowed by whales these days? A whale's tail might turn over a boat. Maybe a whale might bite off someone's leg. But eat the person whole? Who ever heard of such a thing? It's the 1960s, not ancient Roman times.

"Am I hideous?" I asked.

She pulled a cigarette out of her purse and lit it.

"I don't think you should smoke here, Mom."

She shook her head. "Believe me, no one will notice." Her eyes widened as she shook her head. I detected a wry smile, a grin. I was preparing myself for the worst. Whatever she saw, she didn't like. I'm not sure I cared since she was a phantasm, but nevertheless, I waited for an answer.

"Oh, Haskell. What did my sister do here? How come you didn't consult me first? My, my, my. For goodness' sake!"

"It can't be as bad as all that, can it?"

"Oh my, oh my, oh my!"

"What?" I asked. "Hand me the mirror. What are we talking about?" I shouted. "Let me see what I look like."

"Oh my God!" She squirmed awkwardly, biting her upper lip, or what was left of it.

"How bad is it?" I asked.

"Oh, Haskell. This puts chills down my spine, and I don't even have one."

When I looked at myself in the mirror, I saw a botched job. Ears uneven. Nose slanted downwards and upwards. My skin discolored. My eyes crossed. Whatever Dr. Hornstein did, he must have been drunk while he performed surgery.

I had become a monster.

"Frankly, I think this will open up lots of doors for you," my mom said, holding back laughter. She shook her head, puffing smoke into the air and choking on it. She extended her gray index finger toward me. "If Tony ever does a remake of *The Hunchback of Notre Dame*, they need not look any further. You're their Quasimodo!"

She chuckled until she almost choked.

"I have a good lawyer. You will have a huge lawsuit on your hands, and whatever money you collect, you'll live on for the rest of your life. Let me give you some motherly affection before I depart."

She climbed further onto my bed, but the smell was so putrid I pushed her off. I could feel the slimy fish skin on my hands.

"Mom, go back where you came from. You have no idea how upsetting this visit is for me."

"I'm just giving you some motherly advice."

"I don't want it. That deformed monstrosity you're showing me is an illusion. It does not exist. I have received good medical advice, and I will follow it."

"From whom?"

"I have family here I rely on. My new family, and I'm going ahead with the surgery."

"All of a sudden my opinion doesn't count?"

"It's been a few months since you moved me here, and I have made some adjustments and discoveries. I have an aunt and an uncle who are often here for me at any hour, not only after midnight."

"What is that supposed to mean? I find this sudden lack of allegiance somewhat discomforting."

"I've also learned to start making my own decisions, apart from you."

"Well, listen to you!"

"And so this visit is over. As long as you're dead, please never show your face in any of my nightmares again."

I forced my eyes open, catching myself before I fell headfirst off the bed, causing further face damage. I was drenched with sweat. I wasn't in a hospital. I was in my own bedroom on the Thursday night before surgery.

The dream was merely a creation of my imagination. My mother, who was very much alive, didn't hear any of this. I had subconsciously created what one might call a devil's advocate, and I wasn't going to listen to her. Dr. Hornstein assured me the changes would be subtle, so minimal, and yet make a positive difference. I climbed out of bed, strolled into the kitchen, made myself a strong cup of Yuban coffee, and imagined a life where I'd never be teased or taunted or bullied. Not only would my appearance no longer provoke cruel laughter, but with my new self-defense abilities and my new-found muscles and strength, I'd be more attractive and invincible.

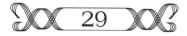

29

THE UNVEILING

A week following the surgery, after much anticipation and fear, I prepared myself for the unveiling. I merely repeated in my head good thoughts. I will look just fine, and I'll be grateful for Dr. Hornstein's expertise and skill.

My aunt drove me to the doctor's office on Van Nuys Boulevard. We took an elevator to the fourth floor and sat in the visitor's lounge.

"You ready for the unveiling?" she asked.

A nurse signaled for me to step forward. "You'll be in room seven."

Aunt Sheila followed me into the exam room. Several nurses prepared the tray with the scissors, a tiny mirror, and a bunch of other metal instruments.

Then the doctor walked in, wearing a white cloak and plastic gloves.

I crossed my fingers.

My aunt grew surprisingly quiet as she watched Dr. Hornstein gradually unravel the tape, then the bandages, and then some gauze, until he had removed all of it from my head, ears, and nose.

"How bad is it?" I asked. Fake nose. Fake ears. Fake sinuses. Flyaway Haskell. Elephant Ears. Dumbo Boy. What would they come up with now? Plastic Kid? Fake Face? Faggot Face? Queer Head?

How far could I run this time?

My aunt clasped her hands together as if in prayer and gasped a few times. This couldn't be a good sign.

Really bad.

Once the nurse had cleaned the dried blood from my face, my aunt stepped back and slapped her hands against her cheeks.

Oh, this was not good.

"My *God!*" she screamed.

"Oh my God!" eked out of my mouth.

"Oh Eddy. He looks wonderful. Oh, he will be so handsome!" Then, removing her hands from her cheeks and clasping them together, she announced, "Oh Eddy, you outdid yourself."

"He's very swollen, but once the swelling goes down, it will look so natural," the doctor said.

"Terrific job. Oh, Haskell. You should see yourself."

"So, why doesn't someone hand me a mirror?"

She took a few steps back, her arms behind her back, admiring the handiwork with such excitement. Any stranger looking on might suspect she had performed the surgery herself, and the doctor was her mere assistant.

Dr. Hornstein said, "It's swollen, so use your imagination. Think of what your face will look like when the swelling goes down."

He handed me a mirror. I was horrified by how wide my nose appeared. The nostrils were two large tunnels in a long narrow mound of nose flesh. I was one big, puffy face.

"As I said, it takes time." The doctor dabbed my face with alcohol-smelling cotton balls. "You're very swollen."

I asked a few questions about the congestion, the mucus, and the pain in my sinuses, and he said all that would go away with time. He handed me more pills. "Take it easy for the next two weeks, and get lots of sleep. I'll see you back here in ten days."

Two weeks after my unveiling, I invited Henry over. I was nervous, of course, by what his reaction might be. I made sure to put on my new contact lenses and even straightened my hair with a chemical straightener. Unfortunately, he arrived a few minutes earlier than expected, and I couldn't remove all the chemicals no matter how many times I rinsed. I got dressed for the first time in days, deciding not to wear my usual corduroy jeans and orange-striped shirt. I put on a button-down madras shirt my aunt had bought me and a brand-new pair of blue jeans before meeting him in the kitchen.

His jaw dropped as he stared at the swollen creature with the wet, greasy hair.

"Monsieur Hodge, is that even you? You look like a drowned rat."

I told him of my efforts at straightening the curls.

My aunt greeted Henry with a big hug. "No worries. I'll have Paulo at my salon take all that goop out of your hair. You should have let him straighten it."

The last thing I wanted was to be seen in my aunt's beauty parlor getting my hair straightened by Paulo. But she was right. I had no idea what I was doing. I had used a lot of the creamy serum and made a complete mess of it.

"What's new with you, Henry?" my aunt asked.

"As a matter of fact, I'm very excited, Mrs. Teitlebaum. My agent got me an audition for *Lost at Sea*, and it went well. Now they want me back for a second call. Haskell should try out for a part."

"Why not?" my aunt said. "I will leave you boys alone," she added, lightly squeezing Henry's shoulder. "There are some escalloped apples in the oven. Enjoy!"

They smelled delicious.

"And I also made a lemon torte. Absolutely divine." My aunt wore a pink chiffon dress with pink high heels, an indication she had attended some fancy luncheon earlier in the day.

We wasted no time and cut ourselves some torte, scooped vanilla ice cream on it, and poured the hot cinnamon escalloped apples over the ice cream.

"Your aunt is a great cook." Henry said lapping up the last of the apple gravy and gobbling a chunk of torte.

I would not reveal my aunt's secret recipe—everything we were eating came from cartons of frozen food. One of the rules I'd follow now that I had become a new me: Watch the words falling out of my mouth. Be careful what truths I revealed. Omission was not the same thing as lying. I figured I'd practice this method more often and avoid trouble. In New York, it seemed people were too honest, often flinging insults, hardly ever caring if they hurt someone's feelings. Get over it! Don't be so overly sensitive, you big jerk! Here in Los Angeles, respect must be paid. People were thin-skinned. Saying nothing was preferred over saying something honest and forthright.

After dessert, Henry proposed we head toward my room.

"I found another part for you in the film. Not Oggy. They already cast that part with Marley McNeice, a British actor. As

Liam, you won't be devoured by dinosaurs. You can basically play yourself."

I carried a desk chair from my uncle's study into my bedroom. This way we could sit beside each other as we read from the script. I didn't expect him to lie beside me on the bed.

Henry began by summarizing the story once again, this time focusing on a new character named Liam.

"Liam is in the entire picture. He doesn't get eaten by a Tyrannosaurus early on like some of the other characters. Now the actual scene I did for the audition was with Oggy. If I'm called back, they said they want me read the scene I have with Liam, so let's do that. This will help both of us 'cause I expect it's down to me and one or two other guys."

I was not excited about the film. Almost every week, Charles Champlin in the *L.A. Times* reported dreary news about the numerous delays. A disastrous hurricane destroyed some of the set. The script was still being revised, this time by a whole staff of new writers. The producers weren't happy with the director and were threatening to replace him. Champlin's take on it? The film was cursed, and every day it suffered one or more defeat. This convinced me, more than anything, that I should stay clear of *Lost at Sea*. But if Henry won a part, wouldn't it be great if I could join him for four months in Buenos Aires? And yet, I was tired of pretending Henry might some day fall for me when it was plain as the new nose on my face he saw me purely as a platonic friend.

Wake up, Haskell. Smell the ether.

Maybe I'd hoped he'd see my new surgically improved face, feel attracted toward me, and say something. No, he's not going to do that, and why am I pretending he will?

"I have something for you, Monsieur Hodge."

I wished he wouldn't call me that. He handed me a "Get Well" greeting card with signatures from students in my class.

"That was so nice of everyone!" I said. Delia had even written a little note apologizing for her behavior at her house and wishing me a fast recovery. She wrote: "Bravo, Haskell! You're my brave hero!"

This was a relief. I didn't want her hating me forever. Curious, though, I asked how she recovered after losing the part of Lady Macbeth.

"Oh, she didn't lose it. After your coaching session, or what there was of it, her parents hired a real acting coach. What can I say? She aced it."

"She won the part over her Juilliard-bound competitor?"

"Yep, and she said if it wasn't for you, she never would have hired someone to help her, and of course never would have landed the role. She's very grateful."

"And what about Lucky Miller? Did he get suspended? Fill me in on what I missed."

When I had asked Hope about Lucky's fate, she played dumb. "He was expelled, Hodge Podge, but that's all I can tell you."

What a strange thing to say. If he was expelled, I'd be happy. And yet, there was something my family and friends weren't telling me. When I asked my aunt, she told me I had more important concerns. "He doesn't deserve your attention," she said. Even when I asked my uncle—my reliable, wonderful, upbeat uncle—he told me, "You don't want to know."

"What don't I want to know?" I asked Henry. "Something happened, but no one will divulge the truth." I wondered if he were dead. Did my punches do permanent damage, and weeks later, he died? And yet if this were true, why wouldn't they tell me? What was the point of keeping silent? Did the bruises I inflicted on him cause lasting damage? And if they had, why hadn't police officers or detectives come to the hospital or my home to investigate?

"Is he brain dead?" I finally asked, hoping I didn't sound too optimistic.

Henry shook his head and laughed. "No."

"Well, then be a friend and tell me what's going on. Why is everyone keeping it a secret?"

"I don't think anyone knows exactly what will become of Lucky. Leave it at that."

I was still lying on the bed while Henry sat on the chair. At this point, for some odd reason, he crawled onto my bed, and sat on the edge, his hands nearly touching mine.

"You will find out anyway, so I may as way tell you." He kicked the shoes off his feet. "On the day of my audition for Demetrius, I met Lucky at the studios."

"Why was he there?"

"As you know, it's an open call. Fifteen parts. Maybe even some nonspeaking parts. Plus, they haven't even started casting the cannibals."

"Lucky's no actor. He's a swimmer."

"Well, nevertheless, he answered the ad for an open call."

"But he has no acting background, no acting talent. I am not even certain he knows how to read. Why would they consider casting him?"

"Because he looks good, Haskell. He's very handsome! His swim coach mentioned the audition in front of the entire team. What can I say, it's Hollywood! They need some beefcake in the movie."

"So, what's going on. Stop teasing me," I finally demanded.

"He auditioned for a part in *Lost at Sea*, and they turned

him down. Right then and there. They said he was not right for the role."

I let out a big sigh of relief.

"He probably flubbed his lines. He's such an oak."

"I heard he wasn't that bad."

I could read the worried expression on Henry's face. He was keeping something else from me. The hesitation in his voice made my throat tighten. I also felt queasy and a bit dizzy.

"I talked with Lucky after the audition. I asked him why he slugged you, and he felt bad about it. He was ashamed because you trounced him hard."

"I took everything you taught me, and I used it on him. Aren't you proud of me?"

"Come on, Haskell. You're supposed to keep all those moves on the mat. They're for self-defense only."

"What choice did I have? I *was* defending myself?"

He wiggled off the bed and returned to his chair.

"Lucky said he punched you on purpose. He wanted to get expelled. If he got expelled, he would no longer attend high school. No more Pottle. No more tests. Simple as that. By punching you in the nose, he figured he'd move on with his life. Study for his GED."

"That's ridiculous. He was humiliated by his defeat."

"That may be true. You're right."

"And so is he off somewhere? Pumping gas? Washing dishes at Mike's Pizza?"

"No. After he got expelled and tried out and lost a part in *Lost at Sea*, someone arranged for an audition at ABC TV network. They're currently casting a new Tarzan series, and with Lucky's swim background and his hearty physique, they think he might make a good young Tarzan."

"You mean like Johnny Weissmuller?"

A former Olympic swim star, Weissmuller had made at least a dozen Tarzan movies. I couldn't imagine mush-head Lucky acting as Tarzan in a major TV series. Then again, Tarzan, raised by apes, is kind of a mush-head.

"How is this possible?" I asked. "He's an idiot."

"Long story short, he won the part."

"The lead part?"

"Yes, he's ABC's new Tarzan."

We live in a corrupt society where the bad get rewarded and the good go punished. Lucky should have been expelled and forced into a prison for juvenile delinquents, not an ABC Tarzan series. He should not be wearing a loincloth. He should be wearing striped pajamas. And instead of swinging across hanging vines among the anthropoids, he should be on a chain gang, chopping rocks into tiny pebbles. The villain should always get his just punishment.

"I can't believe he landed the starring role in an ABC series."

"Haskell, the world's a strange place. There's no rhyme or reason to what happens in Hollywood."

I sat up with an icky taste in my mouth. Kill me now. Strike me down. I cannot live in a world that gives this dolt, this imbecile, a role on a major TV show. I rocked back and forth until I could feel the bile in my stomach move up to my throat. I hoped I'd drown in my own vomit.

"Where is my bottle of pills? I'll take a dozen."

"This is why no one shared the news. You're heavily medicated, and we knew it would upset you." Henry now sat on the floor. "You will be fine. Nothing makes sense in this town. Who would think anyone would go see *Billy the Kid Versus Dracula?*" Henry laughed. "The Vietnam War makes no sense. Lyndon

Johnson makes no sense. The infringements on civil rights in this country make no sense. People shouldn't behave the way they behave. It's not right. The world is a crazy hellhole! It's all one big absurdity. I'll tell you what, why sit on the sidelines and let Lucky Miller get all the fame? You should at least try out for *Lost at Sea*. Liam is a great part."

I'd pored over the character description on the first page of the script, and I didn't like what I'd seen.

"He's an Irish kid from Dublin," I told him. "I'm not much with accents."

"Well, you'll get coached."

I thumbed through the script.

"It says he has only one leg?"

"Yes, he gets one of his legs chewed off."

"By a shark?"

"Well, it's actually a sea turtle. It's a prehistoric sea turtle the size of a whale."

"That's a little far-fetched. A plain white shark might make more sense."

"The film's a fantasy. Some of the animals—lizards, sharks, even sea turtles—grow into enormous beasts, because it turns out years ago the U.S. did nuclear testing near the island. That's why dinosaurs roam the land."

"Who wrote this?"

"It will be great. It's derivative of a lot of other films out now, but that will only make it more popular. This is a great role for you, honestly."

My mind was still stuck on Lucky. I couldn't imagine my nemesis winning the main part in *Tarzan* while I was stuck playing an Irish one-legged kid, attacked by a radioactive turtle on an island of cannibals. Yes, Mr. Miller had the Tarzan body.

And yes, he had been a swimmer, like Johnny Weissmuller. Yes, he was just dull-witted enough to play the ape-raised Tarzan. Still, it wasn't right. It wasn't fair.

Henry was back on his chair, sitting beside me, both his hands on the screenplay.

"Well, in the meantime, wanna read lines together?"

We read several scenes from the screenplay. I made no negative comments about Henry's performance as Demetrius, even though I thought he was wooden and strangely paced with staccato pauses and random jumps in pitch. What did I know? I had underestimated Delia's abilities. Maybe Henry's reading was everything they were looking for. I told him he did a great job. I wished him the best of luck. "I hope you land the part. I really do, Henry with an 'i'! Call me the second you receive the phone call announcing you got the role!"

I sounded too enthusiastic. I felt disgusted with myself.

Mr. Varnish once hammered into us, "Hard truths can be dealt with, triumphed over, but lies will destroy your soul." He gave us examples of politicians in the Royal Court of King Louis XIV who would falsely compliment their king and fawn over him excessively in order to curry favors and win his loyalty and support. Most often the king saw their true motives, realizing they were flattering excessively. The words describing these liars? Varnish wrote them on the chalk board:

liars—sycophants—toadies—parasites

In bed that night, I wondered if I were becoming one of these horrible creatures. It stunned me that I would ever sink this low.

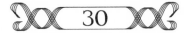

30

THERE'S NO PLACE LIKE HOME

Instead of focusing on *Lost at Sea*, I spent a good portion of my time home recuperating and watching old movies. I also got the royal treatment from the Teitlebaums. Aunt Sheila brought me food on a tray, never squawking about my insolence or bad attitude. My uncle even "borrowed" an actual projector from the studio and a half-dozen films from his company's vault and let me watch movies in my bedroom at my leisure: *The Jolson Story, The Sea of Grass, Adam's Rib, The Man Who Came to Dinner*. Hope could hardly sit through any of them. "So boring!" she screamed. "Can't we watch *The Wizard of Oz*? It's my favorite. Please?"

"Improve your grades," Uncle Ted said, "and I'll see if I can get that film!"

So while I was out of school for the last two weeks of December and the first two weeks of January, I completed all my assignments—even dashed off a few term papers—and in my free time, I tutored Hope.

We were on a mission.

A month or two ago, Hope's third grade teacher, Mrs. Barlow, sent home a progress report that was truthful but heartless.

She wrote, "Hope is still not listening in class and rarely turns her homework in on time. Her reading scores are low, and in math she scored the lowest in the class—forty-two percent. She's falling increasingly behind, and if I don't see an improvement soon, we may have her repeat the first semester of third grade in the spring."

I watched my aunt read the note while she sat at the kitchen table, sipping a cocktail and smoking a Chesterfield. After tearing the sheet of paper into tiny pieces, she sat back, closed her eyes, and without any warning, slammed her fists so hard on the wood surface of the table, I expected it to crack in half.

I was no mind-reader, but I was pretty sure my aunt was worrying that if things continued on this same course, Hope would be twenty-five before she graduated high school. Matriculation, like the word for God in Hebrew, was rarely spoken out loud in the house. But that night, Aunt Sheila said the word.

"What will we do? Hope can't be held back. She must matriculate!"

So that's how I became Hope's tutor and coach. During Christmas vacation and even after she started back in school in January, we studied every day for at least an hour at a time. When she did well, I put happy stars and stickers on her homework. I offered her incentives, so she'd work harder, such as, "If you get eighty percent on this next test, I'll sit and watch *Bewitched* and *Get Smart* with you. I'll make sure your mom gives you an extra hour of TV." Or: "You complete this exam? Four stars, and I'll take you to see Disney's *The Ugly Dachshund*. However, if you score below an eighty, you have to clean my room, make my bed, and do all the dishes after dinner. Deal?"

Hope fell for it. Turned out, she aced the tests I wrote for her, all based on her homework assignments. I had her make up all the missing work and complete an extra-credit book report on *Charlotte's Web*. We created flash cards for math, and she memorized all the answers. Mid-January 1967, a few weeks before final report cards, Hope skipped into the house, happy as a bouncy Winnie-the-Pooh. Not only had she passed her reading proficiency test with a seventy-five percent, but she scored in the seventieth percentile on her math. Mrs. Barlow even awarded her a certificate for improvement and wrote a note saying she could complete the second semester of third grade.

You'd think Hope had won the lottery.

That evening, as we sat around the dinner table gobbling my aunt's homemade meatloaf, made from a delicious recipe on the back of a Lipton onion soup box, Hope declared for all to hear, "I could never have done this without Haskell's help!"

"The Duke of Dorkdom has his uses," I said dryly.

"I will be his loyal subject forever," Hope replied.

What Mrs. Barlow—and my aunt for that matter—did not understand was this: Not all children are motivated by the same things. Some work hard purely because they are self-motivated and see no alternative. Others score high marks because they're born smart or have an innate drive. Some just care about learning. Hope followed none of these patterns. She did best when she was bribed. Uncle Ted had promised her a treat if she scored well on her exams.

That weekend he brought home all four reels of *The Wizard of Oz*.

My cousin was ecstatic.

"What was your favorite part of the movie?" I asked Hope, after we watched the film.

We were sitting outside on the patio while Uncle Ted rewound each reel in the living room.

"When they're dancing and singing 'Ding-dong the witch is dead.' And suddenly smoke appears, and the Wicked Witch shows up. It's so scary! I root for Glinda. She's so beautiful. She always helps Dorothy get out of trouble."

"I kind of agree with you."

Hope's face lit up.

"You do?"

"I do. However, I have my own theory regarding Glinda. She knew all along that all Dorothy had to do was click the heels of her ruby slippers together, say 'There's no place like home,' and she'd magically return to Kansas. Instead, she keeps her mouth shut and insists Dorothy go out and learn these lessons on her own. Let's face it. Glinda is not perfect. At times she's a bit smug and arrogant, especially with that giddy laugh of hers when the Wicked Witch lands in munchkinland. And she delivers one of the meanest lines in movie history: 'Maybe someone will drop a house on you!' And yet she knows, deep in her heart, it's important for Dorothy to grow up, go on a long journey, face challenges all by herself, and become an independent-thinking young adult. Exactly what my mom did for me."

Hope scratched her head and looked at me quizzically.

"Has-skull? She kind of dumped you at our house."

"Well, yes, but she knew that I was not growing up very fast at home. Yes, I had my acting lessons and my piano, but I had no friends. In fact, I spent most of my time holed up in the apartment, all alone. If I were going to succeed in this world, I'd be better off facing hurdles. In other words, like Dorothy, I had to grow up and discover who I truly am."

Hope bit her lower lip, as if she were holding back a burst of laughter.

Maybe I shouldn't have shared this with her, I thought. I never know when enough's enough.

"Does this make sense?" I asked.

"Not really." She reached over and grabbed the cookie on the table next to me. "If you're not going to eat your chocolate chip cookie, can I have it?"

I handed over my dessert—a Van de Kamp's cookie.

"This is my third chocolate chip. Don't tell Mom. I have a two-cookie limit."

"Your secret is safe with me."

"Good. Good. Good. I hope you're done ruining this movie for me."

She smiled and skipped off to her room. I sauntered down the hall and flopped onto my bed, wondering if maybe I was giving my mother too much credit, comparing her to Glinda. I also figured, in the future, I might be better off following my cousin's advice: No matter how tempting it is to share my innermost thoughts, I'm better off keeping them to myself.

31

HOLLYWOOD'S CALLING—JANUARY 8, 1967

The night before I started school again with my new nose, ears, and septum, the phone rang repeatedly. It rang and rang until I finally heard my uncle answer it, walk down the hallway, and knock on my door.

"It's for you."

"Oh my God. It's the Coastal Border Patrol, reporting some horrible tragedy! Yacht capsized. Mother's body washed onto shore. Whale sightings. She's dead. I know she's dead!"

"Stop with the drama! Answer the phone, for God's sake," my uncle implored. "It's not your mother. It's your father!"

I hadn't spoken to my father in nearly a year.

His first words on the phone were: "I've been regrettably late in getting back to you." Not an "I miss you. How's my son doing?" Not even a "hello" or "how are you."

I should not have been surprised. He deserted us when I was two, probably remarried several times since divorcing Mom, developed the reputation of being a ruthless and prolific film producer of bad movies that somehow made money.

"Why haven't you called me?" I asked. "Usually I hear from you at least on my birthday."

"Haskell, I've been sick with dysentery. We've had a horrible time in India. The whole cast and crew got ill, but I'm better now. In fact, I'm finally in town."

"You're in Los Angeles?"

"In the Valley, not far from you. I'm embarrassed by how long it's been since I've seen you."

I thought Delia's dead dog story was a good excuse for missing our date, but this tale of a whole cast coming down with dysentery had far-reaching consequences for many people, including my dad. Between the throwing up and the diarrhea, who would feel like making a phone call?

"You know we've been trying to cast a new film," he said.

"The articles in the *L.A. Times* say you've had some challenges."

"In the beginning, yes. We had a hurricane and few other natural disasters. The film is coming along fine. We have Alex North now writing the music. Mickey Rooney playing the boat captain. Films come and go, but this movie? We believe it will be a big hit with families, competing favorably with all the family-friendly films releasing next year." .

"I've read the script. I found it far-fetched and silly."

"It's been improved. Got some script doctors working on it."

"It's so derivative." Another word I learned from Mr. Varnish. In this case, it was a derivative of *Lord of the Flies, The Mysterious Island, Godzilla, King Kong,* and every jungle movie ever made.

"It has been completely revised. I'll send you the new script."

I asked if he'd met my friend Henry Stoneman, who had auditioned for Demetrius. My dad cleared his throat. "Henry gave a great read."

"Yeah?"

"Some of the executives, however, felt he wasn't quite what we were looking for."

"Physically, he's an athlete. I think he's going for a black belt."

"Doesn't matter if he has six black belts. We're seeking someone who doesn't fit in with the rest of the group."

As much as I thought I might be jealous if Henry won stardom, I knew how invested he was, how excited he got when he talked about his audition. I hoped he'd win this role.

"We decided we'd go in a different direction."

"He will be extremely disappointed."

"Getting rejected is never easy."

"Is it that he doesn't look Greek?"

"No. We're seeking a different kind of acting for this part. On the surface, Demetrius seems perfectly normal, but he has these terribly manic emotional breakdowns."

"Ah, huh."

"Your mother tells me you've played some emotional roles in Eva Hogan's method acting workshop?"

"They were exercises."

"I understand, but I called Eva. She played a Russian doctor in our *Rasputin* a few years ago, and she thought very highly of you."

"Really?"

"She praised you up and down. She said you were very believable, even in risky roles."

"Maybe not this one. Demetrius is a mentally disturbed thug. I don't do thugs. And I look nothing like a Greek son of a shipping tycoon, even after my surgery. You know I had plastic surgery."

"I'm sure you look fine."

"Fine or not fine, I have no idea how I'd play someone bent

on trading the lives of all fourteen boys on the ship for his own. Aren't there other roles available?"

"This is the one we're interested in casting right now, but I'll be honest with you. I'm merely making the phone call. I do not make the decision. The other producers and the director and the casting agent may decide to go in an entirely different direction at the last minute. I wanted to give you a chance, and it would give me an opportunity to see you again. Would you like that?"

I didn't want to sound too excited. "Sure."

Of course, I wanted to see my dad, but Demetrius felt way out of my comfort zone. "You know, I am a skinny kid. No one would take me seriously as someone who served on a high school wrestling team."

"He's no longer a wrestler. He's a pool shark."

"As in billiards?"

"Yes."

"You mean like Paul Newman in *The Hustler?*"

"Exactly. Demetrius is a champion pool player. Before the boys even get on the boat, we see this competitive side of him, a ruthless no-holds-barred pool shark."

"Where would he learn pool? I thought he was raised in Athens."

"Born in Athens, raised in England. The pub down the street has a pool table."

"I've never played pool."

"Whoever gets cast as Demetrius will be coached on how to play pool. We'll hire a billiards coach."

"Really? I'm not exactly coordinated. I usually don't pick sports up easily."

"With some practice, you'll appear convincing as a pool shark."

"I'm not sure I could pull this off, but I bet Henry could."

"As I said, Henry is no longer in the running. If you decide you want the screen test, I'll have a driver pick you up at your house in the morning."

"It's my first day back at school."

"Start the next day. Honestly, I wouldn't have called you at this ungodly hour if I didn't think it was worth your while."

"What other parts are available? Isn't there some comic oddball kid I can play?"

"No. Test for this part, and we'll see. I'll give you until the morning. Fair? If I don't hear from you, let's say, by seven, I'll assume you don't want the screen test."

I must have been dreaming. Was I on the phone? Was my dad on the phone with me? Did he really offer me the screen test for Demetrius, the main role in a major Hollywood film featuring a psychotic pool hustler?

What if he had said: I'm sorry for being such a terrible dad. I know how incredible you are. You're an amazing kid, and I long to spend time with you.

If he'd said that, I would have jumped at the idea. Instead, he sounded so business-like, so robotic and cold-hearted. I was nothing more than a component in a movie deal.

When I hung up the phone, I crawled back into bed and shook my head.

A pool shark? Probably easier to pull that off than a wrestler or a basketball star. Any idiot can take and shove a ball in a pocket, right?

I visualized myself entering a small pub on the east side of London, removing the pool stick cue, rubbing the end with cue chalk, and telling the guys, "I consider the hours I spend playing pool the most valuable hours of my day." If they asked me how I got interested in this game, I had the lines down pat. "I've been playing this game since I was a tiny tot. No one can beat me. I may not be your average pool hustler. I may not be Minnesota Fats or 'Professor' Harold Hill. But I'll tell you who I am. I am a winner, and I can beat anyone with the power of my cue!"

On the surface, I'm Mr. Cool. Mr. Perfect Pool Player. But underneath that slick veneer, I'm a killer, bent on winning at all costs.

"What's your name again?" they'd ask.

"They call me Titanic Demetrius."

I leapt onto my bed, puffed my chest out, rolled my hands into fists and raised them above my head. "I can beat anyone! Do you like to gamble on pool? Do you think I'm in any way, shape or form—a hustler? Anyone here up for the big challenge? Or are you all scaredy-cats? You may have heard of me, but you haven't seen me in action. So if you're willing to take a chance, step right up. Don't be afraid. Let's see if I'm the kid you've been hearing about. Put your five dollars down, take off your jackets, take the rings off your fingers, and let's see who's the champ around here."

Unfortunately, I paid no attention that my bedroom door was wide open and my uncle stood watching me, his chin jutting out like the prow of a battleship, his eyes staring at me in horror as if he had witnessed a ghost sighting.

"What's going on?" he asked.

"I got offered a screen test for a part in a major Hollywood movie, playing a psychopath. It's not exactly me, is it?"

Uncle Ted asked if I'd follow him outside. January in the San Fernando Valley felt like summer in Manhattan. A warm, pleasant, beautiful night. We sat on chaises longues and stared at the dark sky, partly lit by the moon.

After I explained my multitude of dilemmas—I'd never played pool, I wasn't insane, I didn't look Greek—my uncle put one hand on my shoulder and said, "You can't *not* do this."

"I don't have the acting chops. And on top of everything, this should have been Henry's role. Henry will hate me if I win it. He's my best friend. Best friends don't steal jobs from each other."

"You didn't steal it. He didn't get the job. Simple as that. If it were the reverse, and let's say you tried out and did not get the part, and Henry tried out for it and got the part, how would you feel?"

"I'd be upset."

"Would it end your friendship?"

"Probably not."

"It's life. We all compete with each other. I can't tell you how many jobs I got passed over in favor of a most unlikely candidate. Shortly out of the army, my best friend and I applied for a job with NBC. It was a great opportunity and with one opening. He got the job, and we're still fast friends. Good friendships withstand a certain amount of friction."

I could almost taste the fear on my tongue. I did not want to disappoint or anger Henry.

"I'm intrigued by the challenge."

"Good. I'm so glad to hear it."

"My other concern? I haven't had my acting lessons recently. I'm used to doing exercises every week. I'm rusty, and I'm not sure how I'd pull it off."

We sat for a few minutes, staring at the dark sky and watching what appeared to be a shooting star.

Uncle Ted turned sideways on the chaise longue and faced me. "Imagine sitting in the movie theater and watching your replacement on the big screen winning applause, accolades, maybe even an Oscar nomination. 'If only I had auditioned,' you'd say. 'Oh, I should have done things differently.' We get *should* on all the time. 'I *should* have taken my dad up on his offer. I *should* have done the screen test.' It's up to you, Haskell, but if I were you, I'd do it. I mean, what do you have to lose? You gotta go for it, even if you fail."

I went back to bed and tossed and turned. I could play this part and Henry, though disappointed at first, would support me. As my uncle said, that's what good friends do.

In the early morning, I called my dad, hopefully waking him out of a dead sleep. "I'll do it on condition you call Henry Stoneman, explain the circumstances, and offer him another part in the movie. Will you do that for me?" I asked.

"I can't offer him another part in this film."

"You're the producer. You can do anything."

"I'm an associate-associate-assistant producer with little power. Henry Stoneman is a talented, handsome kid who will get cast in other movies. Unfortunately, he will not be in this one."

"There are fifteen roles."

"I think I've made myself clear."

"I won't do the screen test if he's not at least offered another part."

"Haskell, I'll tell you what. I'll call him up and explain the circumstances. I'll let him know that although he did a good job, he wasn't what we're looking for. You, on the other hand, might be what we are looking for. Having said that, I cannot be certain *you'll* get the part. Our director met you last year when you auditioned for the Raisin Bran commercial, and he liked you. That's all very good, but it's a hard part to cast, and the scene you'll be doing is short but quite tense."

"The same scene Henry did?"

"Exactly. It takes place in a cabin, below the deck, during a terrible storm that will eventually destroy the ship and send the boys swimming to the monster-infested island. You'll be reading with Marley, the kid we just cast as Oggy, and I'm sure you'll both do a great job. My driver David will pick you up at nine. He'll hand you the pages. If you can memorize the lines, great."

I told him I'd show up tomorrow. I would read the part, and I'd do my best Demetrius. Deep down inside? I worried this would be yet another huge embarrassment.

32

CALL ME DEMETRIUS KAPADOPOLUS

Four hours later, I dragged myself into the bathroom, showered, pulled on some clothes, and waited outside for the driver. He arrived at nine on the dot, tipped his hat, opened the back passenger door, and said, "Welcome, Mr. Hodge. I hope today goes splendidly. I'm David." He handed me a copy of a small portion of the script, maybe three pages. "I believe we may hit some traffic, so you'll have plenty of time to study your lines."

He was right. Several accidents slowed our ride, and so by the time we arrived at the Universal Studios Lot, I had not only read the scene but memorized all my dialogue.

At the studio, the director of the film, Mr. Reginald Warwick—wearing an ascot and a brown tweed jacket—greeted me and asked me to follow him into a building labeled Stage Three. Inside the cavernous room, I saw cameramen, the script supervisor, and several others ambling about, including the actor who would play Oggy, a slightly overweight kid with freckles and red hair. "I'm Marley," he said shaking my hand, a big smile on his face. In this particular scene, though, we are not friends, so I figured the best way to get into character was to be aloof and rude.

"My name's Demetrius Kapadopolus."

"That's very funny," Marley said, bowing his head. "It's so nice to meet you, Deme."

"No one calls me Deme," I said in a firm hard voice. This came from my inner core. *Oh*, I could hear Miss Hogan say, *feel it in your corpuscles.* "It's Demetrius. And I could use a cup of water if you wouldn't mind. Maybe a plate of baklava?"

Now I was taking it too far.

Baklava was the only Greek food I could think of. Despite the laughs from Marley and some of the crew, I remained stoic. It was important to stay unpleasant and seemingly normal, though I completely avoided eye contact with the actor playing Oggy.

When my dad showed up, storming through the back door with arms outspread, I focused on not appearing surprised or delighted, even though I was grateful and relieved we could meet again. It had been a couple of years since I'd seen him, and as he swept me up in his arms and hugged me, I bit hard on the insides of my cheek, attempting to control my emotions.

"I am so glad you're here!" he said. I detected a strong cigar scent. "You look terrific. Wow! You've grown so tall!"

I hadn't seen good old Dad since he invited me to the film premiere of *Marnie*. His fingernails were polished. His cuffs were stitched with the initials: "TP." Tony Pawlikowski. His shoes were immaculately polished and his striped socks matched the color of his tie. Not a loose strand of brown hair on his head. When he unzipped his briefcase, I saw the papers meticulously organized with colored folders, the pens in a protective pouch, compartments neatly filled with rubber bands and paper clips. And when he opened up his calendar, it appeared color-coded.

My God, he's as compulsive as I am.

"So if you're ready, we're ready," he said.

Lights, camera, action!

● ● ●

I mounted the stairs and stood in the center of an empty stage. This was supposed to be a cabin on a ship—The Floating School— and my first physical action was to pretend I was rummaging through luggage and a chest of drawers, searching for something. I improvised since there was no furniture—not even a suitcase. I let out a deep sigh, unable to find what I was looking for, lifted my head back, and paused as I prepared for my first line.

"Did either of you guys take my compass?" I delivered this line knowing I would not get an answer. In the script, the roommates are supposedly asleep and, at this audition, no actors played the roommates.

I then pretended to walk into another room, without knocking. Marley (playing Oggy, of course) sat on a chair behind a desk. He was reading his compass and jotting down calculations. Without saying a word, I snatched the compass out of his hand.

"Hey, that's mine. What do you think you're doing?" he asked.

"I need a compass." I smiled at him and then studied the compass for a few moments, as if I were memorizing certain numbers.

"Demetrius, I was just finishing my homework."

"You want it? Try and get it back from me."

Here's where I moved closer. I remembered how Lucky had strolled up to me in the hallway after I had accused him of violating our agreement. He heaved his chest forward, in the most intimidating way, narrowing the gap between the two of us, nearly siphoning oxygen out of my breathing space. I wondered, though, if I should dangle the compass over his head or over his feet? The script merely said, " Dangle it." I decided I'd make Marley reach for it, and when the actor did indeed attempt to grab the compass, I dropped it on the floor.

Marley's eyes widened as he raised his eyebrows. And then, before he had time to retrieve his compass, I took the heel of my shoe and crushed the damned thing. If it was solid gold, it would not flatten like a piece of hard candy. The glass would merely break.

"Oh, my God!" he whimpered. Marley's eyes turned watery. Real tears slid down his cheeks. "That was my grandfather's. I can't believe what you just did!"

Now I nearly lost my cool.

I am an empathetic guy. I am the antithesis of this insensitive, heartless, and cruel creature. Certainly, if I start crying, the audition's over. Take a few deep breaths, Haskell, and stay in character.

Marley tightened his lips and glared at me. "I'm going to report this to Mr. Carlson, and you're going to get into big trouble."

"You know, I'll tell you a little secret, Oggy." I bent down so my lips nearly touched his right ear, and I lowered my voice. "You are not liked by anyone on this ship, and it wouldn't take much, in this great storm outside, to have a group of us pick you up and heave you overboard. I really don't think you'll be greatly missed, so if you want to speak to Carlson, be my guest. Do it. See what happens." This time, I didn't just smile. When I stood up, I let out a brief, malicious laugh.

Being evil can be a whole lot of fun.

Warwick now rose from his chair.

"All right. I'm going you stop you right there! That was something else, thank you, Haskell."

My hair was sticky from perspiration. Maybe I overdid it. I

was too overly dramatic, the exact opposite of what they asked for.

I figured Warwick would tell me if I overacted, but at first, he didn't say a word. My dad also locked his hands behind his neck and said nothing.

I was so bad, it had caused everyone to remain speechless.

Finally, I broke the silence. "I apologize. I am so sorry, everyone. I crushed the compass." I didn't realize it was a cheap prop. "If it was made of gold, this would not have happened. Also, I probably should have said those last words a little louder. What do you think?"

Warwick nodded his head as he turned and spoke quietly with several of the other men and women standing in the back of the room. Marley and I stared at each other, not saying a word. Do we stay or do we go?

"Haskell? Have a seat for a bit," Warwick said. "Don't go anywhere."

I ended up roaming back and forth across the stage, attempting to stay in character.

Finally, after an interminable half hour, Warwick returned from wherever he wandered off to and spoke. "It was perfect just the way you did it. We had criticized other actors for going too far. What we didn't realize was they hadn't gone far enough. I think we got what we were looking for. We have finally found our Demetrius. Meet Haskell Hodge, the new star of *Lost at Sea!*"

I could hardly believe it. "I got the part?"

"If you want it, it's yours," Warwick said, clasping his hands together.

There they were—my dad, the entire camera crew, even David the chauffeur standing in the back—all clapping, smiling.

I wanted to run the twelve miles home, I was so excited to share the news, and perhaps foolish enough to think Henry, of all people, would be happy for me.

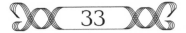

A SURPRISE VISITOR

Uncle Ted, Aunt Sheila, Hope, and I all ended up at The Queen's Arms that night, celebrating my success while sipping champagne. Mistress Marian poured the fizzy liquid into my aunt's and uncle's fluted glasses, making sure she angled her body so that Uncle could take a good peek inside her blouse. My aunt merely rolled her eyes and made a point of pouring a bit from her glass into cups for Hope and me. "We should all toast the big movie star. Haskell, I am *kvelling* with pride."

This was decidedly a different experience than the one we had at this same restaurant, in the same booth, four months earlier, when I had doused my cousin's head with ice water after she accused me of being the dorkiest kid on the planet.

This time Hope begged me all through dinner to make sure I invited her to the opening night of *Lost at Sea*, naming every star she was dying to meet—Paul, Ringo, John, George, The Three Stooges, Elvis, Shirley Temple, Judy Garland, even Topo Gigio—a puppet she adored on *The Ed Sullivan Show*. I doubted any of them would attend the premiere, so I suggested she lower her expectations. "You'll be lucky if Ann Sothern shows up."

Ann Sothern was the voice of the car in my favorite sitcom, *My Mother the Car*. This seemed to make little impression on Hope.

"I don't know who she is, and I don't care. The important thing is, Has-skull," Hope said, showing more enthusiasm than her mother, "that you'll take me with you. I know for sure what I'm going to wear, too. Something shiny, sparkly, glittery, and very short, above my knees."

The movie hadn't even been made yet, and Hope had already planned her wardrobe.

After our celebration, I thought I'd arrive home and go directly to bed. The alcohol made me drowsy, and it had been such a long, amazing, and surprisingly crazy day, I couldn't wait for sleep.

However, sitting on the steps in front of the house was Henry Stoneman. As Uncle Ted drove the car up the driveway into the garage, Henry stood up and waved.

"Hey, there!" he yelled. "Where you been?"

What would I tell him? I had hoped I could wait a day or two before we confronted each other. My stomach walloped me with sharp pains. Had my dad called him with the final casting news? If not, how would I break it to him?

Turned out I didn't have to say a word. Even before the Cadillac made it into the garage, Hope poked her head out her window and shouted, "Did you hear the news? Hodge Podge won the part, and he's taking me to the premiere. Soon he'll be a big movie star, maybe even get an Oscar for playing a terrible person who throws his girlfriend off a mountain."

The big smile on Henry's face faded.

I climbed out of the car and before he or I could say anything, I grabbed his arm and pulled him away from the garage, the Cadillac, and the entire family, reaching the sidewalk and then walking a few yards, out of earshot of everyone else.

"What's going on?" Henry asked. "I thought you'd be in school today. Delia was looking for you."

I shrugged and shuffled my feet, waiting until the thoughts in my head unscrambled.

We stood in front of a Tudor-style house with little concrete gnomes in the front garden and a riverbed with what appeared to be real goldfish.

"Did the studio call you and give you any updates?" I asked.

Henry shook his head. "Nope. What was Hope yakking about? Where were you today?"

I told him about the phone call I received from my dad. "He asked if I would audition for the role of Demetrius."

Henry gave me a puzzled stare. "You're kidding, right?"

This would be worse than I thought. I shut my eyes for a moment and opened them.

"All right. Well, here's what happened." Once again, I explained the late night phone call. I detailed almost the whole conversation, explaining how Dad basically begged me to do the audition.

"Got on his hands and knees, did he?" Henry asked, his voice sounding not just angry but belligerent. I wasn't sure being truthful had been the best tactic here.

"And so I went for the screen test today. For some reason, the casting people saw in me a different type of villain."

"How many types are there? He's Greek. You look less Greek than I do. You certainly don't have the physique of a wrestler, and let's face it, you're basically a nice guy, Haskell. You could never play this idiot."

"I don't know what to tell you. I was asked to go on this audition, and it went well."

His face went red. A massive crease appeared between his eyes.

"I had no opportunity to call you. I got the call late last night, and this morning a chauffeur picked me up. I did the screen test, along with many others. When I was done performing the monologue, Warwick said I got the part."

"Right then and there?"

"Yep."

Henry threw his arms in the air, turned and then did an about face. "It's pretty strange, because when I auditioned, they said it was down to me and one other kid. What happened?"

"The part changed. Writers! They're an odd bunch."

Henry removed his glasses and rubbed his face with one hand. "I still don't understand. In the original script, he was this tough kid who was into clinch fighting, throws, takedowns, and joint locks. That's all gone?"

"He's a pool hustler now."

"A pool hustler? Do you even play pool?"

"Yes, I'm a very good pool player."

"Since when?"

"Since I was a kid, growing up near a pool hall in New York City."

"I thought you grew up on the posh West Side. They have pool halls there?"

"Many." I was such a liar.

Henry shook his head. "It made sense he was a wrestler, which explains how he manages to lift the timber and save some of the boys when the boat capsizes, but to turn him into a pool hustler."

"As I said, I don't know why they made these changes."

"If you ask me, the script sounds like a disaster. I'm glad I'm not cast. It's a stinker in the making."

I let out a big sigh of relief. "You're probably right. I'll most likely regret this decision."

He kicked a pebble with the toe of his shoe. "Just to get this straight, did you read the same monologue I read? The one with Oggy?"

I nodded my head. "I think so."

"They kept that in. And he's still kind of crazy?"

"He is *completely* crazy."

"Well, he's not completely crazy."

"I played him as completely crazy. He threatens to murder Oggy."

"Yeah, but it's more of a tease."

I shook my head. "No, for whatever reason, he hates Oggy. He's jealous of the attention he gets because he's smart and very articulate. Honestly, he considers breaking Oggy's thick neck and throwing the body overboard."

"He doesn't worry about the consequences."

"Not when there's a big storm happening. He doesn't know they're about to crash into the rocks, but chances are, he'd get away with murder. Everyone would think he just fell off the ship."

"And that's the direction you took."

"Yeah."

"Well, there's only one direction, as far as I can see, and it's called nepotism."

"My dad had no say in the casting. It was all up to Warwick and the casting people."

"And you believe that?"

"I do. Apparently, whatever I did impressed them. I channeled my inner rage and became Demetrius. I was fierce, manic, insane. I even got a standing ovation."

"Weren't they all standing anyway?"

"I used everything I learned in Miss Hogan's class."

"Method acting, huh?"

"I channeled my inner demons. I thought about all the things Lucky ever said to me. I even imagined I was my cousin Hope having one of her super-duper meltdowns."

"Wow. You were a regular Marlon Brando. You with the nose job and the perfect ears and the contact lenses and the straightened oil hair. You were probably putting this whole 'look' together so you could win the role in the first place. I wouldn't be surprised if your dad engineered the whole plastic surgery, transforming you into his vision of Demetrius."

"My dad and I haven't spoken in almost a year. He knew nothing about the punch in the nose or my surgery."

"That's a lie and you know it."

"Henry, I'm being completely honest with you. I don't think I would have gotten the part had I not studied with Miss Hogan. I channeled all the hate and angst I experienced in and out of Encino High School."

"Oh, come on, Haskell. Just be honest. Daddy-oh is guilt-ridden. Haven't seen my sonny boy in so long. I'll give him this part. That will heal everything."

"I swear that's not what happened. I got this solely on my own."

Henry glared at me, then turned back around and started walking down the street.

"Henry, I wouldn't do anything to hurt you."

He waved, as if he were done with me.

"You have no idea what I went through trying to decide if I should even take this audition."

"I bet you worried about it for a whole five minutes," he shouted, his back facing me.

"I did worry. You know, I'd be happy for you if you got the part. Why can't you be happy for me?"

He finally turned around. He was maybe halfway down the block.

"Because, Monsieur Hodge, something feels wrong and unfair. It smells. And I am afraid I'll say something that I'll deeply regret, so I'm going to say nothing more except goodnight."

He stood there for a moment, took a few deep breaths, and turned toward me once again, putting one foot forward as if he changed his mind. Maybe I'll finish this conversation, he might have said to himself. But then—nah, not a good idea. He shook his head, turned, and headed down the street.

Waves of disappointment poured over me. Then, it started to rain. I bent my head back, opened my mouth, let the raindrops fall onto my tongue and pretended I was drowning.

I should have been ecstatic. I had won the role. I was the new Demetrius. I had a career in Hollywood ahead of me. Why, then, was I feeling so miserable?

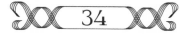

34

THE CLAUSE

The next morning and the morning after that, I decided I would not go back to school. I invented a number of excuses. I told my aunt I expected a morning call from the executive producer, afternoon calls from the script supervisor, and I even concocted the strange notion that I had to hang around the house all week in case I was needed in the studio to read lines with the other fourteen actors playing students.

The truth was I didn't want to go to school, and after a few days of this, when the phone didn't ring and no appointments seemed scheduled, my aunt knew I was stalling.

"You really need to go back to school. I don't know what's going on, but staying in your room moping is not going to solve anything."

By the evening of the third day at home, my aunt slid the latest copy of *Variety* under my door. She had circled in red an article about *Lost at Sea*. It mentioned the film would star an unknown, in his first feature film—Haskell Hodge. The writer focused, however, on the latest scoop about the film, claiming Reginald Warwick was out as director and the new French wave sensation, René Clément, was in, making his English-language film debut. The same article also recalled all the other fiscal disasters: the hurricane, the destruction of the boat, the hiring and firing of at least half a dozen writers, and the "kiss of death" for any motion picture these days—no bankable stars.

"I smell disaster!" my aunt announced. She poked her head into the crack of my door. "Can I come in?" I signaled for her to sit on the chair behind my desk. "You sure you want to do this? You're only as good as your last picture. New director? New writers? I betcha he'll recast the whole movie. And I think it says they are $560,000 in the hole. Ask Mr. Tony about this. I'm sure he has a thing or two to say."

On Thursday night, I finally got another phone call from good old Dad. The house had three phones: one in the kitchen, one in the den (not far from my bedroom), and one in my aunt and uncle's bedroom. I was in the den, but I could stretch the cord all the way down the hall into my room if I needed to. And tonight I demanded privacy.

I heard my aunt screaming at Hope to get dressed for her dance recital, and my uncle who was in the bathroom shaving, cautioned her, "Blood pressure, sweetheart. Don't want your arteries exploding like a hydrogen bomb!"

"Then you get in here and get her dressed. Why is this always my job?"

"If she doesn't want to go, Sheila, why force her?"

"Because we spent all this money on lessons. She's going. They depend on her!"

I pulled the phone cord as far as it would go and took the call on the floor of my bedroom.

My dad was calling from the Howard Johnson Hotel near Sepulveda Boulevard. "I thought I'd bring you up to date."

"Has the film been shelved?" I asked.

"No, what gave you that idea?"

I told him I had read the horrible article in *Variety*.

"Don't believe everything you read. Warwick pulled out of directing because he's juggling too many projects. He will still co-produce the film. René, his replacement, is a wonderful director. We're lucky to nab him. We've hired James Earl Jones to play the Cannibal King. He's one of the greatest actors of our time. Joseph LaShelle will do the cinematography. We nabbed Buck Arrico for costumes. André Previn will now write the music. And if I could throw your hat in the Oscar Derby, we got ourselves a great Demetrius! When can I pick you up and take my son to dinner? I'd like to get to know you better. It would also give me time to go over the contract so we can get it signed as soon as possible."

Four days after the audition, the night I was supposed to attend Hope's dance recital, Dad picked me up in his convertible Maserati and drove me down to Santa Monica. It was dusk, and we planned to park and visit Pee-oh-Pee, or POP, which stood for Pacific Ocean Park. Since they charged two-fifty for admission and access to all rides, the initials also meant Pay One Price.

"Did you want to go on some of the rides?" he asked. "I used to love this place when it was in its prime. I mean, Disneyland is probably prettier and certainly more sophisticated, but if you want to go on some fast, thrilling rides and smell the fresh salty sea air, this is the place."

I could see in the distance the Sea Serpent, a wooden Hi-Boy roller coaster soaring over the edge of a pier. I had read about the Ocean Skyway, the Diving Bells, and Davey Jones' Locker. I knew I couldn't go on any of these rides. "If they're anything like the thrill rides in Atlantic City, I'll be throwing up and getting dizzy," I told him. "But I'd love to just walk through the park, if possible."

It all seemed quite seedy, though. The buildings around the amusement area had been torn down leaving piles of brick and lumber, and many of the streets leading to the park were closed. It didn't look safe parking the Maserati in any of the empty lots, and my dad couldn't find a lot that had an attendant.

"No worries. We can go another time," I told him.

So instead, we drove down the Pacific Coast Highway toward Malibu. Dad told me stories about his women, his malaria, his typhus, his bout with syphilis, even his battle with alcoholism, cocaine, and other narcotics. "My life has been such a mess! It's all going to change now that you're in it."

By nine that night, we landed back in the Valley at his favorite haunt, the Fireside Inn. I had passed this restaurant dozens of times. It was not far from The Queen's Arms, but its architecture couldn't have been more of a contrast. This restaurant was once an old brick building used by the Spaniards in the eighteenth century to store grain and wheat. It was now a fancy nightclub and bar, famous for its piano players, red leather booths, and a bevy of single, attractive, middle-aged women. Put plainly, it was a pick-up place, and Tony's favorite haunt.

"This is where I met your mother some seventeen years ago. You know, Miriam was six years older than me. I met her when I was only twenty-four. She sat right there, sipping a Manhattan."

He pointed to a red leather stool near the oak bar.

"I loved her more than any other woman I had ever met. All these years, I haven't met her match. I come here hoping and searching. To be honest, I may never marry again because I will never find a woman as wonderful as your mom."

Speaking of bull, I had heard a completely different story.

Mom said she met him at the studio commissary where he was acting and finding small parts in B movies, some of the same movies my mom was in. They went on a whirlwind weekend trip to Las Vegas, spent most of it drunk, got married, and within the year, Mom asked for a divorce. "If it weren't that it produced you," she said, "I'd consider the marriage the biggest mistake of my life."

My dad had an entirely different memory. In fact, he hinted that it was my mom who wanted him back. "Miriam often said the year we spent together was the best twelve months of her life, and I agree. Too bad we couldn't work it out. I think your mom wanted a more settled existence. She was no longer finding work in Hollywood, and she missed New York. I didn't want to move back there with her. How could I? I had landed my first good producing job at Universal."

My mom said he couldn't control his temper or his alcohol or his dick.

Somewhere between these two versions of the story was the truth, and I wasn't probing further. I also knew something about moving from one coast to another.

"Haskell, I asked you here for a reason, so I'm going to get down to it. As part of the acting community, you will sign a contract. You're aware of that?"

I told him I was.

"This is one of the reasons I wanted to spend some time with you, so I could explain the contract before you sign it."

"Fine," I told him.

"This contract details your salary and a number of other financial responsibilities the studio has. If there are sequels, the contract requires your participation. Nothing out of the ordinary."

"Sounds good."

"Oh, one more thing. The morals clause. Were you aware you'd be signing one?"

I shook my head. "My mom always signs contracts for me."

"Well, I talked to her, and she said if you agree to all the stipulations, she'll sign off on it as well. Let's go over it together, shall we?"

He removed a four-page document from his briefcase and set it on the table.

"I'm going to read you a few sentences from it. It says you will 'uphold a certain behavioral standard so as not to bring disrepute, contempt, or scandal to the other individuals or party and their interests,' meaning me and the studio. It also says, 'This contract attempts to preserve a public and private image of such a party.' In essence, the studio is lending its good name and reputation to you, and the studio wants it protected. 'The party does not want any irreverent or amoral behavior spoiling or damaging its image.' Everybody signs this. Not everyone, as I said, understands the repercussions."

"I'm not sure I know what you're talking about."

Morals clause? Why would he possibly be worried about that? I was only sixteen years old. I never had sex with anyone, at least not yet. I hung onto my morals whether I wanted to or not.

"Let me just give one example. Many years ago, in the 1920s, Fatty Arbuckle, one of the biggest names in silent film comedy and a rotund guy—hence the nickname—was accused of murdering a young woman. Some said that in an attempt to seduce her, he lay on her and squashed her to death. He claims she had a stomachache, left his room, went into her own room, and eventually died in a hospital of a ruptured bladder. In any case, Arbuckle was accused of the crime and went through three notorious trials. In the third trial, he was acquitted. He was a big star, as big as they come, yet with his reputation ruined, he would never recover from the bad publicity."

"I'm not planning on squishing anyone to death," I told him.

"I know you're not. You're a good kid. I only use this example because it was the case that changed Hollywood. Ever since, we've had this morals clause. Let me give you one other example. One famous actor, I'm not going to mention his name, enjoys the company of other men. At first he'd take his boyfriend with him to various clubs and parties, pretending he was his 'best friend,' but word got out. They were lovers. Gossip travels, and before he knew it, Hedda Hopper, the powerful gossip columnist, threatened to write up the whole story, accusing him of sodomy. You know what that is?"

"I have a pretty good idea."

"The studios didn't want trouble. They paid off gossip columnists and gave the actor an option. Either he marries and creates the pretense at least of living a 'normal' life, as they called it, or they would fire him, and he would never work in this town again. Which one do you think he chose?"

I shrugged. What would I do? Job or boyfriend?

"Well, of course, he chose his career over love. He dumped his male lover, or so he said, and married his secretary. They have three children, live happily in Beverly Hills. Whatever he does on the side, he keeps very private, because he makes hundreds of thousands of dollars a year starring in major motion pictures. I'm telling you a cautionary tale. If there is something people shouldn't know about you, don't let them find it out. Understood?"

"It's clear, yes."

"And you may also be aware that one of Disney's biggest stars most recently was found having sex with a boy in a swimming pool, and he was fired immediately. His career is dust."

"I'm getting the picture."

"Great. Glad to hear it."

"I think I've heard enough."

I was fuming. Obviously, he was giving me these examples because my mother must have mentioned the party I attended where I was kissed by a boy. She may have even gone as far as sharing my concerns about my sexual orientation. My mother and her big, fat mouth.

"So, can I ask you something? What brought this up?" I asked.

"I'm giving you the same speech I'll give each and every boy who is going to spend months out of the country where the rules are very different. Watch yourself."

"I always do."

"Good. We bring a bunch of good-looking American teenage boys to Buenos Aires, things can happen. Sex. Prostitutes. Venereal Disease. Drugs. Alcohol. We're asking that you follow certain rules of behavior. Otherwise, you take the risk of being thrown off the movie."

"I'm about the last person you have to worry about."

"I'm glad to hear that."

"Thank you for this evening. I promise you, I'll behave."

"I'm sure you will follow all the rules."

My problem wasn't the rules. It was that the first dinner we'd had together in years, he chose to focus on a few examples of the studio's intolerance for queers.

What choice did I have? I'd believe him. Maybe this was the same speech he would deliver to all the other actors. And yet it was also the perfect opportunity for me to tell him about my complicated sexual identity. Goddammit, I was a two on the

Kinsey Scale, not a six or a five, and I hadn't ever had sex with a guy. All I may have done was lusted after Henry Stoneman, who hated me. Lust was not a crime. You couldn't arrest someone for thinking lustfully, could you? So I kissed a guy once in a bathroom. Big deal.

I didn't open up, although I began to wonder, what was *his* problem? He'd been a bachelor since divorcing my mom. He had a history of picking up women, and with his history of venereal disease, there must have been many of them. What kind of morals clause was he breaking every night?

My dad paid the bill. "Let's go for a ride," he said, "and we can talk." I hated that phrase. We can talk. My mom used the same technique when she wanted to dump some bad news on me. When you get home from school, we can talk.

We didn't talk, though. We sat for the longest time in complete silence. He took an exit and pulled over. It was dark. No street lights. Just a big cement wall up against the freeway.

Here it goes. He's about to dump some bad news on me.

"Tony?" I had no interest in calling him Dad. "Drop me off at home. It's been a great night. Thank you. But I could use some sleep."

"One minute. I don't know if you know this, but before you were born, your mother and I couldn't agree on a name for you. I liked Oscar. She wanted to name you after her father."

"His name was Solomon."

"Exactly, so you'd be Sol Hodge, which I thought was terrible. We were in our apartment in Burbank. Your mother's water broke. We knew that night or the next morning our baby would be born. The doctor said there was no hurry getting down to the hospital—labor could last hours—but he suggested we leave right away. And as I was driving down the 101, on the way to the hospital, we threw out some other names. If it was a girl, your mother said, 'How about Barbara?' Which I thought was very plain and ordinary. I suggested Laramie. She suggested Betty. We went back and forth. But your mother and I were not in sync regarding a name, so we figured we'd wait until you were born. The name would come.

"We were driving on the same freeway we were just on when your mother noticed smoke coming out of the engine. I kept driving, but soon we could hear a grinding noise coming from under the hood. I had no choice. I had to get off the freeway. I pulled off onto a road—this road we're on right now. Your mother panicked. 'Oh my God, what if I have the baby right here, right now!' And sure enough, she began having not just cramps but real contractions. It was happening faster than we expected. I figured I better get some help, so I ran out of the car, knocked on the door of that house, right over there." He pointed to a dark tan, one-story house with a shake roof. "I knocked on the door and this lovely lady seemed more than happy to help us. She brought out a bowl of hot water and some towels."

"Was she going to deliver the baby herself?"

"I don't know. She called the hospital, and they sent an ambulance over. Fortunately, it arrived just in time."

"What does that mean?"

"You were delivered in the ambulance."

"Mom said I was born at Valley Hospital."

"You were born right here, on this spot. As soon as you were born, your mother nestled you in her arms, looked up at the sign above the freeway, which said Haskell Avenue, and shouted, 'What a perfect name! Let's call our son Haskell.'"

"I was named after a freeway off-ramp?"

"Not too many kids can admit that, can they? You're very special."

And Dad was a very special writer with an inventive sense of originality and wit. This tale nearly rivaled the ridiculousness of *Lost at Sea*. He was about to restart the engine when I put my hand on the steering wheel and stopped him.

"Dad, why did you make up that story?"

"It's the truth."

"All of it?"

"Most of it, yes."

"How can this be true when my mom said she named me after my grandfather, Harris Hodgeberg."

"I don't know what to tell you. As far as I can recollect, that is how we came up with the name."

I wasn't going to make a big deal of it. My dad chuckled. He seemed excited as he slapped my knee lightly and then leaned over and put one arm around my shoulders. "I'm not sure your mom would like me telling you this story, but it's the truth. It really is. Want me to knock on that woman's door and you can ask her?"

I shook my head. "No, she probably doesn't live there anymore."

"I wouldn't count on it. Come on. Let's go knock on her door. I bet she'd get a kick out of seeing the little baby all grown up."

"No, that's all right."

If Dad was being honest, now I wanted to be a hundred per cent honest with him. Not that it mattered much, but tonight I was deeply bothered by his whole lecture on the morals clause. I was almost certain Mom told him about the kiss at the party, and I had the feeling his lecture was a warning: Be careful.

Hide my true identity. Don't do something that could ruin my career before it even got started.

I thought I should say something, but my heart was beating too fast for me to speak coherently.

"Dad?"

"Oh, Haskell. I love it when you call me that."

The words finally fell from my mouth. "I kissed a guy once. That was all it was. I might be gay. I think that's the word they're using these days. But I'm only sixteen. I'm reluctant to label myself. I'm not certain of anything. I'm more confused than ever, and I'm upset because it's not like I'm going to board the boat and start kissing every guy on the ship. Still, I feel compelled to tell you this. Sometimes I'm in total agony. I have these desires that I can't control."

My dad gripped the wheel tighter. Was he angry? Dammit, should I have kept this to myself?

We sat for the longest time, not saying a word. I could feel tears stream down my cheek. Why did I speak up? Now he's probably angry at me.

As we headed into traffic, he said: "Let me be blunt."

Oh no.

"I knew about this story."

"My mom told you?"

"No. Your mother never said a word."

"Scout's honor?"

"I was never a scout, but yes, I swear this is true. The boy you kissed? Tom Shapiro works for me. He attends USC, and he's in our apprentice program. When he saw your screen test, he recognized you. It's a small world."

If this were true, the world couldn't get any smaller.

"His story is slightly different from the one you just told me."

"What did he tell you?"

"It doesn't matter."

"Nothing else happened."

"It doesn't matter. This is an important lesson. There are no secrets in Hollywood."

"I told you the absolute truth. He tried pulling my zipper down. I escaped as fast I could."

"I don't care if you're queer or straight. The only thing I care about is your safety, your health, and your future. Being gay in this business, as Tom well knows, is the absolute shits."

I wanted to close my eyes and let the silence swallow me whole. Why did I go to that party? Who would think one party would haunt me?

"You're a wonderful kid, Haskell. I can see this really bothers you. It worries me that you may not be able to brave what's ahead. If you're queer, son, you can make it just fine, but it's not going to be easy."

If the boulder housed on my chest could grow, it had reached massive proportions.

"And maybe it's my fault," he laughed. "Maybe, had I been around, taken you camping, coached you in football—"

"Made a man of me."

"Exactly!"

I shook my head. "I don't think it works that way."

I felt flushed. I could also feel my head growing hot, as if I were coming down with a fever.

"I've been fighting this my whole life, and I'm realizing I can't do anything about it. I have to accept who I am, and it's painful. Frightening. My mom's best friend was queer, and he was brutally killed. I would lie in bed at night and pray for my urges to go away. That didn't work. I dated Delia hoping she'd make me straight. That didn't work. What am I going to do?"

"So, if I may give you a piece of advice?" His tone sounded awfully earnest. "If you want a career in Hollywood, you have to stifle your impulses. For the public, you're one person and one person only. A big handsome movie star who makes love to women. In private, you may be someone else. Not everyone, however, is good at juggling two identities. I know some movie stars who stay in the closet and somehow keep their sexuality hidden from the public. It's difficult, and they do it out of necessity."

"You went over this with me."

"I don't want your career to take a nose dive before it even gets started."

Was this supposed to make me feel any better? It was so unfair and uncomfortable. And contrary to what Madame Scheherazade warned me about: "Your only obligation in your lifetime is to be true to yourself." Why would she say something like that to me if she hadn't suspected I would endure these challenges?

"I'm giving you heartfelt advice. You're an actor. You can probably pull this off better than anyone. You want to be an actor, right? That's your dream?"

"I think so."

"Then you'll be just fine. Keep your eye on the goal. I know you can do it. You're a kid. You've got your whole life ahead of you. I mean, you never know. You may outgrow this, as many men do, and settle down with a nice wife in a nice house with a few nice children. At least for the present moment, you're safe. It's not like you're in the throes of some great love affair, right?"

No love affairs. No boyfriend. No girlfriend. He was right. Why was I stressing out? These feelings could dissipate over time, crumble into dust or merely collapse, like a rickety old roller coaster crashing into the raging ocean.

35

THE NEW OBJECT OF MY DESIRE

"Oh my God! You're going to be famous. I heard the news, and I couldn't be happier for you!"

At school the next day, in the middle of the hallway, Delia embraced me as if I were her long-lost puppy, Yves, back from the dead.

"Oh, it's so good to see you. I have a ticket for you." She handed me a red piece of paper. "You're coming to my opening night, right?"

I hadn't intended on going.

"The play is at eight. I will reserve a seat for you. You look wonderful. No wonder you got the part. You're so groovy. Wait until the girls see you! Oh, Trudy will be all over you. You'll come, right?"

I told her I'd think about it.

"Don't think about it. Be there." She bent over and whispered in my ear. "I'm told I've nailed it. Really. With your help and the acting coach's help, I am Lady Macbeth."

"Well, then I can't wait."

My first day back at school went perfectly. Teachers were happy to have me back. Kids complimented me on how well I looked, though many of them admitted they saw little difference. At one point, I saw Henry and waved at him. He did not wave back. We were stuck in Study Hall together, but we sat at separate tables, on opposite sides of the library. He sat next to Wendy Rosen, this girl I knew from French, and neither of them made any effort to say hello. In fact, they whispered to each other, occasionally glancing in my direction, and giggled.

I wondered what they were talking about. Maybe he was making fun of me. I was tempted to walk over and make yet another stab at an apology. But what was the point? If he was that hurt and wanted to sit with this girl and make fun of me behind my back, let him.

After school, I told my aunt how wonderful everything went and mentioned I had been given a ticket to opening night of *Macbeth*. It was this Thursday.

My aunt insisted I go. "You've been stuck in the house for over a month. It's the last week of January. Go and enjoy yourself. Have fun!"

Fun? I wasn't watching *Guys and Dolls*. This was *Macbeth*, one of the bloodiest of Shakespeare's plays. Well, not quite as gory as *Titus Andronicus*, but gory nevertheless.

Taking my aunt's advice, I attended Delia's opening night, bringing a dozen long-stemmed red roses with me. I expected not to enjoy this *Macbeth*. I figured this high school production would drag along for three hours and convert one of the bard's shortest tragedies into the longest night of my life.

This was not the case, at all.

First of all, the sets—particularly the rocks and a forest representing Duncan's camp at Forres—were realistic and spooky. Even the witches—all six of them, by the way—hovered over what appeared to be large steel cauldrons with real smoke.

Most spectacularly, Macbeth's castles at Inverness and Dunsinane were intricately constructed with high walls stained from soot, featuring a medieval fireplace with fake flames you'd swear would singe Lady Macbeth's long flowing gown.

Although I expected Delia would give an embarrassingly awful performance, she had obviously done her homework. When she calls on the evil spirits to remove all that makes her soft and feminine so that she can convince her husband to commit murder, she acted the scene with real conviction, as if she had swallowed some potion that turned her into a sorceress of darkness.

I waited for her outside the stage door on the warm January night—still in the mid-70s, I suspected—holding the withered flowers, practicing the compliments I'd deliver.

You were truly the best Lady Macbeth I've ever seen.

That was going too far. She was good, just not that good. Even Delia would not believe me.

I was overwhelmed. It was an amazing performance in so many ways.

Try again.

It was a performance filled with unusual nuances. You captured the dark forces so convincingly. I loved your Scottish accent.

Too phony. Why can't I just say something nice without going overboard with praise?

Suck it in, Haskell. Tell her you loved her as Lady Macbeth. Make her feel good. Delia spotted me the moment she exited the stage door. "Your performance?" I beat my fist against my chest. "It was such an improvement. You were outstanding!" I shouldn't overdo it. "I take it all back. Sometimes in life we make terrible mistakes. I was wrong about you. Your performance was winning, alive, and delightfully, Scottish-ly wicked! Too bad Judith Anderson wasn't here to see you." Will I go to hell for this?

I hoped people were as kind to me after my movie comes out.

I handed her the dozen roses. She grabbed them and held them against her full, plump bosom. She was wearing the low-cut velvet queen's dress, a big beauty mark on her left breast, the silver crown still in her wispy hair.

"Oh my God. You're not just saying this, are you?" she asked.

"No, of course not."

"I did get a standing ovation, didn't I?"

"You got a major standing ovation!" I told her.

"But only half the audience stood. Not even."

"A lot of older people came to see their grandchildren perform on stage. The back of the theater was cluttered with walkers and wheelchairs. Plenty of people stood, and plenty of people sat, depending on their health conditions. Don't take it personally."

I didn't know what I was talking about.

She leaned in and touched the tip of my nose. "Where are your glasses? Did you have glasses on when I saw you at school the other day?"

"No, I wear contact lenses now. A birthday present from my mom. She sent us a check, and I bought the lenses with the money."

"I like your nose too. It's so smooth." She reached out and touched it.

"The doctor even repaired the inside of it, so I don't sound like a train whistle when I'm sleeping."

"I do miss the curls." She reached over and lifted one of my greasy strands of straight hair. Maybe I used too much goo.

"I was trying for the mop-head look."

"I will offer no further comment on your hair. However, you look fine, my friend. Tomorrow night, after the performance, we're all meeting at Farrell's Ice Cream Parlour. Join us."

"I'll try."

"Don't try. Come. I'll know a genuine celebrity. Please join us, won't you? The girls will be there eager to see you. Wait until they all see what a handsome wolf you are. Except, you're you. You can't take the you out of you." She did what my mother's Aunt Sylvia often did—pinched both my cheeks. "You have no idea how glad I am you appreciated my performance. Thank you."

"Don't you mean, 'Ankthay ouyay'?"

She kissed me yet again, this time on the lips. "I'll see you tomorrow night."

Was Delia now interested in dating me? Would this develop into a relationship where I might invite her to the prom? Would I even be in town for the prom? And if the Studio were to send publicity to cover the prom, wouldn't Delia get a kick out of having her picture in the newspapers? If all this went as it seemed to be going, it would be just so perfect, and Dad would be very pleased.

● ● ●

Friday afternoon, after school, I spent a good hour trying to decide what to wear that night and ended up in black jeans, a plain black T-shirt, and a pair of black and white Keds. My uncle dropped me off smack in front of Farrell's. It had red, white, and blue awnings. The waiters were dressed in white pants with American flag shirts, white socks, and shiny black shoes. Several of them greeted me as I got out of the car.

"Welcome to Farrell's. We're so glad you could make it!"

I smiled and stuck my head back into the car. "Bye, Uncle. I'll call you later."

"Have a great time!" He stuffed some dollar bills into my shirt pocket.

The crowd was so thick I had to angle my body sideways and stick my arms in front of me to make my way through the room.

"You're here, finally!" Delia yelled from across the room. "You know Nate, right?"

He was standing smack in front of me wearing a big cowboy hat, Macbeth T-shirt, and jeans. He greeted me with a handshake, and said, "I'm glad you're here. I was looking forward to it."

At that very moment, a herd of waiters marched through the crowd, singing "Happy happy birthday!" over and over again to a tune I'd never heard.

It was not my birthday. Whose birthday was it?

The waiters in their bow ties and waitresses in their red, white, and blue-striped skirts continued chanting the birthday tune as they carried out a mountainous sundae. It had dozens of scoops of various ice creams, hot fudge, nuts, cherries, and whipped cream. They set the monstrosity—called The Zoo—on a long wooden table and told us, "Dig in, everybody!" They sang again in four-part harmony the same lyrics: "Happy birthday! Happy, happy birthday!" over and over.

Someone from the school finally yelled, "This is not anyone's birthday party! We're celebrating the opening of *Macbeth*, you idiots!"

Some kids were smoking as they ate ice cream. Many still wore the outfits they'd worn earlier as part of their performance. The six girlfriends of Delia who played witches still wore make-up. A couple of them had on their wigs and putty noses.

"Oh Haskell, you look terrific," one of them said.

"What did you think, handsome? We were witchy enough for you?"

I could barely hear them. The room was not designed for so many people. It was definitely a fire hazard.

I needed air. It was too soon to call my uncle, and yet, the noise level was deafening. The smoke irritated my sinuses. It seemed I was one of only a few people not in the play. Why was I even there? This was a cast party. I did *not* belong.

I squeezed through the crowd and made my way down a hallway into a quiet, empty room. I sat down on a chair, stretched my legs out, and ate the rest of my ice cream.

A few minutes later I heard footsteps and a voice say, "Haskell? Mind if I join you?"

It was Nate. He and I had rarely spoken to each other one on one. During lunch, he would tell us a few things about the set he was constructing, and on my first days in town, he had coached me on the rules of touch football. That was it.

"I don't know about you, but the smoke? Horrible!" he said, squeezing the end of his nose with two fingers. "Why does everyone smoke? It's so irritating. You don't smoke, do you?"

"No, I hate the stuff," I told him.

Though we were away from the commotion of fifty kids chatting away in the confines of a small dining area, now we were in the flight path of waiters scampering in and out of the kitchen. Nate motioned for me to follow him. "There's a room on the other side. I don't think there's anyone in it. Let's check it out." I followed him. We moved into yet another empty dining hall. Tables, chairs, no people. Who would think an ice cream shop would be this expansive? We each grabbed a chair, resting our elbows on a small rectangular table.

"I've been here many times," Nate said. "When I was a kid, my mom held birthday parties for me here."

"Well, the ice cream's good."

"Yeah, I love the caramel fudge ice cream with real fudge, nuts, and cherries."

He was a fellow ice cream lover.

"Nate . . ." I decided to ask a question that had been bothering me for a while. "Why did you let Lucky push me against the wall on my first day at school?"

He stared down at his shoes, looking ashamed.

"And weren't you in the hallway when Lucky started up again calling me names and we had that face off?"

He didn't answer me at first, so I stood up. I was about to leave when he gently grabbed my arm. "I'm sorry I treated you the way I did. I was on the swim team. I was under pressure. I hated the way Lucky treated you, but I was too scared to say anything. I am really sorry."

"Why would you ever be friends with Lucky?"

"A number of reasons. He's the swim captain. He's also my cousin."

"Wait a moment. Lucky Miller is your cousin?"

"Yeah. The thing is, when we were younger, it was kind of cool to have him as a cousin. All the girls liked him."

"I don't think *all* the girls like him."

"Well, he became different this last year. He had to attend summer school, make up for a few classes he flunked, so he kind of took his frustrations out on others. A few years ago, though, he was a lot more fun."

I couldn't imagine ever having fun with Lucky.

"We both went to Valley Beth Shalom, and we ended up ditching Hebrew school together half the time."

"I would never ditch Hebrew school. What if you got caught?"

"We never got caught, believe it or not."

"Also, you and Winston always kowtow to the Swim Master."

"Not always. I do, at times, challenge him. For example, he thought I was crazy when I decided to take dance lessons. With the prom not far off, I didn't want to be the worst dancer at Encino High, so I enrolled in the Arthur Murray Dance Studio."

"You mean you learned ballroom dancing?"

"A little of that, but also fast dances. I've learned the Twist, the Watusi, the Swim, the Hully Gully, and the Giraffe. Lucky teased me a lot, but I kinda got the last laugh. Two weeks ago, we were both attending our cousin Laurie's Bat Mitzvah. Lucky and I sat at the same table. Girls asked us to dance. Both of us got onto the dance floor. And Lucky was not terrible. It doesn't take a whole lot of skill to move your arms while you swivel your hips a few times. But I was the most amazing dancer on the dance floor. Every girl wanted to dance with me. I mean, at one point, the entire room of guests surrounded the dance floor and applauded me, while poor Lucky stood against a wall, arms across his chest. When we sat down, he whispered in my ear, 'You dance like a homo.'"

"Why would he say that?"

"Because he was jealous. All the girls wanted to dance with me, not him, even though Lucky is much better looking."

I didn't think so.

"And I guess, lately, he is upset because he's flunking two classes, and he has to graduate. He can't retake twelfth grade. He registered for the draft a year ago, and if he flunks out, he'll be drafted."

"I thought he quit school."

"Yep."

"And landed the role of Tarzan."

"Nope. Series was cancelled. He was pretty upset. My aunt told me he's living somewhere in Fresno with our grandparents and going to night school, hoping it will keep him safe from the draft."

I was glad he didn't get Tarzan, but I suppose there was a tiny part of me that felt sorry for him.

"I asked Delia if she would make sure you were invited 'cause, well, I wanted to apologize."

He was probably interested in me because I landed a role in a motion picture. My father was a producer. I now had connections. He wanted my connections. Any moment, I expected a little speech about his passion for Hollywood, his desire to "break into" the movies.

He reached over and squeezed my shoulder. "I'm excited for you. What a role you got!"

"It hasn't started filming yet. A lot can happen between now and then."

"I guess. By the way, you liked the sets on *Macbeth*?"

"I did. Yes."

"What did you like best? Your opinion matters."

"I liked the fluidity. How the walls moved and collapsed. How you went from the castle to the landscape scene, and then the cave with the witches. It always bothers me when you watch a play and have to wait for the prop guys to move the sets. You did it seamlessly."

"Everything on tracks. I designed a model of it first and made sure it all worked in miniature before we constructed it for the play. In fact, I have a dozen models at home for different plays. Most of them I just did for fun. I did a set of the 1964 production of *Medea*. You played one of the children, right? With Judith Anderson?"

"You're following my career?"

"A bit, yeah. I found the blueprints in a book about stage design, and I built it on a piece of plywood. All my models are stacked one on top of another in our garage."

I must have lost my mind. I don't know what I was thinking. All my animosity toward him melted, as I said: "I'd love to see those models some time."

And he said, "How about tonight?"

"Tonight?"

"Why not? I could show you the miniatures. Why don't you come over after the party?"

"You want me to come over to your house tonight?" I asked again, examining my watch. It was already ten. "Kind of late, isn't it?"

"It's a Friday night. Can't you sleep in tomorrow?"

I shrugged. "Not at my aunt's house. She turns on *Exercise with Jack LaLanne* every morning at nine a.m. I'd have to call my uncle and tell him not to pick me up at Farrell's but at your house. I mean, it's complicated."

"We'll have a sleepover. I have an extra bedroom. My parents are at a retreat. My brother's in Texas. Spend the night. I could show you all my miniatures and, if you want, we could watch Johnny Carson together."

I let this simmer in my brain for a bit. Nate and I had much more in common than any other kid I'd ever met. Maybe more than Henry Stoneman, who now hated my guts. I sat back down on the chair for a few seconds, thinking about this strange invitation, and I came to the conclusion, this was not a good idea. "I think we should do this another time."

We both stood up, though neither of us made any move toward the exit, leading into the main banquet room.

"That's fine," he said. "If you can't make it tonight, I understand. But just so you know, it would be great if you did come over."

We both stood inches apart, facing each other. It felt very strange. I wanted him to touch me, maybe put one hand on my shoulder, and yet I was relieved when he didn't.

"Haskell, I want you to know that all these months I felt badly I didn't stand up for you."

"As my mother would say, it's water under the bridge."

"Yes, I love that expression, and now that I think of it, I'd especially enjoy watching one of your mother's movies with you on the Late Late Show."

"Maybe we'll do that sometime."

I couldn't believe we were talking about my mother.

"If you came over tonight, we could stay up until one or two in the morning. I think *Love in Athens* is on."

He got the title correct. I couldn't deny it. This guy seemed to like me. I couldn't be precise on this. He and I had more in common than a love for theater and movies. Maybe I was reading into it, but I figured if I slept over, it might involve more than just sleep. I wasn't sure I could control my impulses. It did not feel safe and comfortable. I had signed a Morals Clause. I'm back at school, and I don't want kids talking about us behind our backs. I couldn't risk this evening turning into something that might, down the road, haunt me.

"I can't sleep over tonight," I finally told him.

"Well, if you change your mind, call me." He wrote down his phone number on a scrap of paper and handed it to me. "Haskell, no one's going to know." He lowered his voice to a whisper. I barely could hear him. "Believe me, we'd have a great time together."

Are you nuts?, a voice in my head asked as I walked into the main banquet hall. You like him. He likes you. What are you waiting for?

I felt an uncanny excitement building up inside me. As I paced the restaurant, I tried thinking this through.

I wanted to be alone with Nate, a nice boy whom I had forgiven. How could I turn that down?

I feared, however, that whatever we did, we'd get caught. His parents could surprise him and come home early. His brother could show up unexpectedly. Someone could see us going off together, and we'd both get blackballed by the rest of the kids in the high school. And, of course, the studios had their spies. If someone from Universal found out, my career would be over before it ever started.

Then again, I'm just sleeping over at a kid's house. Boys do this all the time.

I wandered through the restaurant searching for a pay phone. When I found one, I called my uncle and asked if it would be all right if I slept over at a friend's house. "He's a set designer, and he wants to show off his sets!"

My uncle said that was fine. "I'll pick you up in the morning. Call me when you're ready."

Just like that.

When I told Nate I had changed my mind—I'd sleep over— his face beamed.

I spent fifteen minutes in the large dining room with the Drama Club members, scooping from the gargantuan platter of melted mushy ice cream.

After a while, Nate tugged at my arm. "You ready to go yet?"

I was very ready.

I followed him into the parking lot.

Nate drove his mom's brand-new Firebird, and though the signs said thirty-five miles an hour, he kept up with traffic going fifty. In minutes, we pulled onto the driveway of this modern glass-style house in the hills of Encino, not far from where Delia lived. He pressed a button, the garage door opened, and he parked on the right side of the three-car garage.

It was the only area of the garage available for a car since the rest of it was devoted to large pieces of plywood on wood benches. Each piece of flat plywood was approximately four feet long by three feet wide, and each one contained a miniature set. He must have constructed at least half a dozen. He pointed out the exterior house from *A Streetcar Named Desire*. "I won second prize for this one at the High School Set Design Conference last year." His first prize blue ribbon was for the inside of the two-story home in *The Little Foxes*. He had even constructed a replica of the gunboat from *The Sand Pebbles*, a midwestern-style living room for *Who's Afraid of Virginia Woolf?*, and, of course, the wild forest of Birnam Wood for *Macbeth*. No question he was very talented. Someday he'd land a job in Hollywood doing set design.

"Ready for a tour of the house?" He showed me the bedroom where I'd be sleeping, and gave me a quick tour of the modern, marble-floored home with sliding glass doors leading to a beautiful kidney-shaped pool, a waterfall cascading down lava rocks into a Jacuzzi.

"Anytime you want to go to sleep, just let me know. I'll put a towel in the room for you."

He let me borrow a pair of his pajamas and a new tooth-brush. I met him back in the living room, both of us still dressed in our jeans and T-shirts.

I joined him on the couch in the living room, and we ended

up enjoying the last half hour of *The Tonight Show*. The Rolling Stones were the musical guests and, as a sexy, near-shirtless Mick Jagger sang, "(I Can't Get No) Satisfaction," hopping and skipping across the stage, Nate rose off the couch and began dancing on the rug.

"Join me, Haskell!"

He had great moves. "I would embarrass myself if I got up and danced with you."

"Embarrass yourself, then! I'm the only one here."

He handed me a beer. We drank, we danced, and at some point, he swung his arms around my neck. I closed my eyes and drew closer to him.

"Wait one second."

He turned off the TV and pulled an album out of his record collection.

"I just bought this. It's the most magnificent rock and roll song of all time. Tell me if you know this."

He carefully removed the album from its cover, wiped the album with a soft cloth—I thought I was the only one who did this—and set it carefully on the turntable.

"This, my friend, is the future."

He played "Light My Fire" by The Doors. I had never heard it before, and the repetition of the same title phrase, over and over again, put me in an odd state of mind. At first, I concentrated too much on the ridiculous rhyme scheme: "liar" with "higher," "mire," with "pyre." But then I realized this was a song about leaving inhibitions behind. I had to stop thinking so much, and yet as the song went on, I could no longer dance. I stood still, mesmerized by the extended organ solo. Feeling aroused, I closed my eyes and drifted into a space outside of Nate's living room. I was on a beach, dancing in circles, spreading my hands out above my head, reaching for the moon and the stars.

"Haskell, I'm going to confess something." Nate's voice quavered as he put his hands around my waist. "I've never told anyone this, but you know when I was at that Bat Mitzvah party, dancing all those dances I had learned?"

"Yeah." I opened my eyes, finally, and stared into his. Nate had turquoise eyes, a small nose, and almost-perfect skin. He wore his straight brown hair long so it almost reached below his ears.

"And I said I had all those girls after me?"

"Yeah?" I knew where this was going just by the inflection and tone of his voice. Also, I could feel his warm breath on my face. He must have chewed on some spearmint gum.

"This distant cousin of mine was at the party. His name is Jon, spelled J-O-N. And he's the one I wanted to dance with."

"You wanted to do the Funky Chicken with your distant cousin named Jon?" I asked.

We both laughed.

"Are you cool with that, Haskell?"

The organ solo continued almost relentlessly.

Nate leaned in, our noses an inch apart. On an impulse, with my heart beating, I nervously kissed him.

He kissed me back gently at first and then intensely.

I could feel my heart pounding as if it would leap from my body and do a little jig in the middle of the living room. I felt both excited and fearful at the same time. Was this really happening to me?

He removed his T-shirt and slid his jeans off. All he had on were his boxer shorts.

I was almost too embarrassed to do that, too, but I gave in to the moment, and when he saw my white jockeys with the Li'l

Abner comic strip, he smiled. He didn't laugh.

"Let's go in the bedroom," he said.

I couldn't get the thought out of my head. I am not the only homo in the San Fernando Valley! I couldn't say I was surprised. Well, maybe I was surprised how my fear turned into desire for this beautiful young man.

"I guess we're not going to stay up and watch my mom's movie on the Late Late show, are we?" I mumbled.

He held my hand as we wandered down the hallway. Once inside his bedroom, we pulled down our shorts, and now stood naked, facing each other on the plush green shag carpeting. I didn't care any longer if he was the one who laughed when Lucky called me a homo or did nothing after I got shoved onto the cement floor. This was a moment I had dreamed about. We hungrily kissed and groped each other as I thought how could anything that felt this good be considered wrong?

36

A DISTURBING INCIDENT IN HOLLYWOOD

I think I'm in love. Nate was all I could think about for the next few days. We agreed we'd bypass each other at school, to avoid suspicion. Designed our routes to our classes so we walked down separate hallways. If I'd see him pass, we'd say nothing. At lunch, we usually ate with Delia and friends, rarely by ourselves, for we didn't want anyone having the slightest clue we had some sort of "special" relationship.

After school, however, he would sometimes borrow his mother's car so we could escape and be alone together. Most often we'd venture out of Encino—either deep into the Valley, like Northridge or Chatsworth, or as far as south as Venice. That way we figured we wouldn't bump into anyone who knew us.

I didn't really fear anyone from the studios spying on us. *Lost at Sea* wouldn't start filming until June, and it seemed highly unlikely I'd be the object of paparazzi. I was hardly a celebrity.

One afternoon, right after the school bell, Nate told me he didn't have the use of his mother's car so we both headed toward the bus stop. We were on separate buses, so we waited in different lines. Both buses were pulling into their respective parking space when I happened to raise my eyes and spot Henry climbing into the driver's side of a new Volkswagen. He leaned over, rolled down the passenger window, and waved.

"Hey!" he shouted.

Was he talking to me? Was the wave a signal I should join him?

"Come on! What's taking you so long?"

Maybe he landed a part in another movie and decided to let bygones be bygones. My heart was beating too fast. I couldn't speak. I was grateful the animosity between the two of us had subsided. I jumped out of the line and headed toward the Volkswagen when I heard Henry shout, "Annabelle, get a move on!"

Annabelle? This girl, who stood directly behind me, nearly on the heels of my shoes, her books all piled up in her arms, scooted forward and scurried toward the Volkswagen. Henry got out of the car and opened the door for her, and she slipped into the front seat, smiling away.

The Stonemans must have bought their son this new car, and he was obviously picking up a girl and taking her home. Or taking her out for a snack? He wrapped his arm around her and whispered something into her ear, which made her smile and turn toward me.

What did he say? That's Haskell Hodge. He's such a loser. See that kid over there? He's the one who stole my part.

I showed no emotion. I remained stoic, impassive, numb. Someone might even interpret the expression as cold-hearted.

"Hey, Haskell? You taking the bus?" The driver knew me by name and was kind enough to say something. I boarded the bus and sat there, every emotion bruised and trampled. I hated

Henry Stoneman, and yet I knew full well how irrational this was. He was hurt. It would take a while for him to recover. But why couldn't he be a good sport?

As soon as I got home that afternoon, I called Nate, and I told him about what happened and how Henry deliberately pulled this stunt in the parking lot just to infuriate me.

"I'd let it go. It's not worth the aggravation. We going out tonight?"

"I'd like that."

"Good. I'll meet you at our usual spot. Six tonight?"

As usual, I'd walk down to the boulevard, pass the Encino Theatre, and dash into an alley.

Nate would be waiting for me.

Tonight, though, it was raining, and I couldn't find an overhang to stand under. When he finally showed up, I was wet, cold, and angry. I hated the fact that Nate and I could not be as transparent as, for example, Henry and Annabelle.

"I can't stand sneaking around," I told him, as I removed my soaking wet jacket and placed it on the floor of the back seat.

"Well, it's more your idea than mine." He handed me some paper towels. "Wipe your face off. Take a few deep breaths." He turned on the radio—Petula Clark, singing "This Is My Song." "This will cheer you up. It's written by Charlie Chaplin, of all people. Wait until you hear this. What a beautiful old-fashioned melody, and it's on KFWB!"

Nate loved pop music more than I did. I appreciated his enthusiasm. When the cheerful song was over, he asked me where we were venturing to.

"What would really cheer me up?" I asked. "A double feature in Westchester. Two Don Knotts films: *The Ghost and Mr. Chicken* and *The Incredible Mr. Limpet*."

Nate rolled his eyes.

"You know I can't stand those kinds of movies. They're silly and childish."

I had to think of something else. I pulled the movie section out of my jacket pocket. It was soaking wet and smelled musty, but I still could read most of the listings.

"What are we seeing, Hask?"

"A SNEAK Preview of a new film at the Vogue. All it says is that it's an exciting new dramatic film, takes place in depression-era America. I'm hoping it won't be too sad."

Nate and I enjoyed previews. These were films brought out months before they would be released to the public. Most of the time we had no idea what film we were about to see until the curtain parted and the credits came on. Recently, we had viewed some good ones, including *Up the Down Staircase*, about an inner city school with truly incompetent teachers. It was one of the funniest movies we had seen all year. We had also endured a few turkeys including a Frank Sinatra snore-inducer entitled *Sergeants 3* and the dumb *Santa Claus Conquers the Martians*.

Nate parked on Vine Street in a lot with an attendant and a steep parking charge of two-fifty. Each of us chipped in half.

Before we climbed out of the car, Nate looked both ways—out through the front and back windows—making certain no one was watching. Then, he leaned over and kissed me.

Sometimes, as on this particular night, we sat in the car and talked. "Tell me why you're letting this upset you so much."

"We can discuss it after the movie. Hopefully, I'll be in a better mood."

The movie at the Vogue turned out to be a gangster film entitled *Bonnie and Clyde*. Through most of it, we rooted for

Faye Dunaway and Warren Beatty, these gorgeous actors playing the famous depression-era bank robbers. We enjoyed some off-beat comic scenes and a manic performance by Estelle Parsons that brought big laughs in the nearly sold-out theater. Of course, it seemed inevitable Bonnie and Clyde would get caught, and yet, we were not expecting such a violent ending. I figured they'd eventually get arrested. What did I know? I hadn't read the history of this couple. I had never studied their murder spree in school, and this was, after all, a Hollywood movie starring beautiful movie stars. Even *Birdman of Alcatraz* had sort of a happy ending.

So, regarding the tragic demise of Bonnie and Clyde. Bonnie Parker takes one bite of her sandwich while her handsome outlaw boyfriend Clyde cruises his stolen car into a trap. It's quiet, peaceful, and then a hundred or so bullets hit them in less than twenty seconds. The film goes into slow motion, and as their bodies bounce into the air, the two stars stare into each other's eyes and finally collapse onto the seats, their bodies riddled by bullets. It's gruesome and sad and terribly grim. It made me cry.

"Why didn't the police just arrest them?" Nate asked, as we walked out of the film. "I was rooting for them. Weren't you?"

I couldn't speak. I was afraid I'd break down sobbing right there in the lobby. Faye Dunaway dies? Several representatives from the film's studio—maybe the brothers Warner themselves—asked if we'd fill out little evaluation cards. They handed out these tiny pencils, and I managed to give the film four out of five stars, but Nate rated the film with two stars. He told one of the Warner Brothers representatives standing outside the exit doors, "No one will see this movie. It's a complete and utter downer."

As we strolled onto the sidewalk, Nate continued his rant. "Why couldn't they give it a happy ending? Hollywood does that all the time."

"It's based on a true story. It had to end badly," I told him. "Otherwise, it wouldn't have been faithful to its history."

"I'm sure they ignored a lot of facts. This is one fact they could have changed. Bonnie and Clyde miraculously survive the massacre and end up living in Mexico."

"As much as I would have liked that, it would violate historical accuracy."

"You know Hollywood changes endings all the time, Haskell. In Dickens' novel, *Oliver Twist*, Fagin gets hanged as a thief, but in the new musical version that they're about to film, I hear he skips off into the sunset, singing, 'Cheerio, I'll be back soon!' Even if Bonnie and Clyde die, why in such a horrible manner? They better change the ending, or this film will tank at the box office."

Nate reached for my hand and squeezed it. I didn't stop him. There we were, on Hollywood Boulevard, leaving the Vogue Theatre, hand in hand, forgetful of what people might think. Or did we do it on purpose, regardless of how people might judge us? I don't know. "I'm so glad I have you," he said, as we strolled back to the car. "You can be a voice of reason."

"Hey, you queers! Aren't you going to kiss each other? Kissee kissee kissee?" The voices were just a few feet behind us. "Hey, faggots, slow down!"

We were not slowing down. We ran as fast as we could. I felt a hand on my shoulder, and it wasn't Nate's. I turned and did a back kick, knocking this animal with long red hair flat on his back, his mouth agape. He lifted himself off the pavement and reached for my leg. Nate ran as fast as he could with several guys chasing him, and here I was on the ground with this ugly leather-jacketed goon grasping a hold of my ankle. As I twisted myself free, my shoe fell off. I ran with one shoe on. Fortunately, Nate had parked his car right off the boulevard. As soon as we each zigzagged into the lot, the attendant, a black man about my Uncle Ted's age, put his hand up and made the ruffians stop. I thought at first they were going to hit the attendant, but he was a big beefy guy, holding both his huge fists in the air, ready to smack the daylights out of them. "Should I call the police on you boys?" he shouted. "You better haul ass or you'll be spending the night in jail."

We managed to climb into the car. Nate did a U-turn and headed in the opposite direction of the ruffians. We saw them running across the lot, up the side street, cutting us off at the pass.

There were four of them against two of us. Of course, they were outside the car and we were inside. Each of them had beards and long hair, some longer than others. Several had their jackets unbuttoned, showing off their tattooed, hairy chests.

None of them had weapons, as far as we could see.

"Nate? What are we going to do?" I asked.

"I have to gun it. Brace yourself."

"You can't run them over. That's murder."

"Haskell, they're going to hop on this car and drag us out into the street. Do you want to get beaten to death?"

"No, but aim the car so you go around them."

"How am I going to do that?"

"Drive on the sidewalk!"

I didn't see any other possible escape route. They blocked our entrance onto the street, but if Nate stepped on the accelerator and we jammed forward, would they get out of the way in time?

They walked gradually toward us, and Nate, crazy Nate, rolled down his window.

"Don't roll down the window!" I screamed. "Are you nuts?"

Nate smiled.

"Hey guys?" he shouted. "Get out of my way or you'll get flattened."

"You think you can hurt us, fag? You want to run us over? Run us over!"

They ambled closer, now just a few feet from the front fender, and Nate shoved his foot down on the accelerator, turned his wheel as far to the right as possible, zoomed onto the sidewalk and then onto the street. I heard a clunk against the car, and I think one of the guys either jumped onto the back fender or Nate's car did indeed roll over someone's foot. We heard screaming. I closed my eyes. I thought for sure Nate crushed one of the idiots, but when I opened my eyes, I could see through the rearview mirror all four hoodlums chasing after us, yelling an assortment of obscenities. Not a policeman in sight, and there was a red light ahead.

"Nate, you can't stop for the light!"

I knew if Nate stopped, we were goners. They'd find a rock or two and throw it at our back window or jump onto the car, this time on the back fender.

I covered my eyes with both hands but could see in between my fingers as Nate raced through the intersection, ignoring the red light, narrowly missing a truck.

"You faggots are detestable abominations!" We heard one of them scream. "You'll rot in hell!"

We each took some deep breaths as we finally made it onto the Hollywood freeway.

"You okay?" Nate asked.

"I lost a shoe," I told him. "Half of my brand-new pair of Keds."

"We'll get you a pair of tennis shoes this weekend. We'll go to the Topanga Mall, make a day of it. There's a Pickwick Book Store and a Wallichs Music City. You've been there, right?"

"No. I don't even know what that is."

"We can sit in sound-proof booths and listen to albums. Any album you want. How's that sound?" Nate patted my arm. "You ready for some ice cream?"

I loved the way Nate snapped out of this gruesome mishap. He rarely ever grew depressed, and most of the time he had this cheerful disposition, even after we almost got ourselves murdered.

"I'm shoeless," I told him. "I can't go into an ice cream shop without my shoe. And I'm tired, and I'm scared." I lost it. I had held it in for the most part until now. I began crying uncontrollably.

"It's okay," he kept saying. "Everything will be all right. They have no idea what they're saying. They grew up hearing these terrible things from their parents."

"I only wish we could have thrown a can of paint over them like they do in *West Side Story*."

"Where are we going to get a can of paint? You can be so silly." He put on the widest smile. "We'll figure it out. We really will."

"It only shows you—there's no safe place for us."

"Well, we're safe now, in my car, aren't we?"

He stopped the car and pulled over to the side of the road. We were somewhere in Studio City, about twenty minutes from Encino.

"Don't pull over."

"Haskell, we had a rough patch. It will be fine. You're going to make that movie and make lots of money and take me on a Tahiti vacation, and then we'll both go off to NYU together. How's that?"

"I thought you wanted to go to Cal Arts."

"If you get into NYU, I'll try to get in there as well so we can be together."

"That's not very smart."

"It will be perfect."

"I heard two guys can't even rent an apartment together. If the landlord has any idea we're a couple, he or she won't rent to us. We'd have to get a two-bedroom."

"So, we'll get two bedrooms."

"I looked it up. I read articles about homosexuals in New York. It's terrible. Police make arrests all the time. We can't be seen in bars together. We can't kiss in public. People get arrested for even being suspected homos. If I'm discovered, I'll never get another job in Hollywood, and you will never get a job designing sets or working anywhere. The police harass anyone even suspected of being homosexual."

"Where did you read this garbage? New York is probably much safer for us than here in Los Angeles."

"My mom's friend Reynaldo was talking friendly-like to a handsome dude in a gay bar, and he turned out to be a cop."

"You told me this story."

"I told you he was murdered in his jail cell?"

"Yes. That's terrible. A horrible story. No one's saying we shouldn't be careful."

"Nate, I don't know about you, but I'm already frustrated and tired of all the hiding and pretending. I'm not sure how much longer I can stomach it."

"What's your point? You want to break up? You going to date Delia? Are we calling it quits?"

Nate started the engine, pulled back into traffic, and we drove the rest of the way home in silence. Eventually, he violated our rule. He stopped smack in front of my house on Noeline Avenue.

"Nate, please don't stop here. What if the neighbors see?"

"Get out. Stop worrying about it."

"I don't want anyone seeing me get out of your car."

"It's too late. I'm here. No one's up watching us."

"If my aunt got up for some reason and saw you dropping me off? I don't want her to think I lied. I told her I walked to the Encino Theatre."

"You walked. I drove you home."

"Humor me. Please, Nate, drive down a few blocks."

Nate did as I asked and rounded the corner onto Libbit Avenue. He pulled onto the empty lot near a boarded-up gas station.

"This hide and seek is lame," he said.

"You're telling me."

"It will get better."

"I don't think so."

"In September, we'll go to college together and everything will be much easier than here."

I opened the door and stood on the sidewalk. Nate rolled down his window and signaled for me to walk toward him, which I did, reluctantly.

"Hask, promise me one more thing? No matter what we face, no matter how difficult things may be, whatever challenges are ahead of us—and, of course, we know we'll face plenty of challenges—know you'll always have me. I'm not going anywhere, and I think we make a pretty good team."

"I'm a mess. Why would you want to be with me?"

"You're my wonderful mess."

I rolled my eyes. "Goodnight, Nate."

"I'll call you tomorrow! Haskell?" I heard him yell. "Come on, turn around one more time, and let me have a look at you!" I did not turn around. I walked, then jogged back up the street, without acknowledging him.

37

MY MOTHER OFFERS WORDS OF WISDOM

The next morning, I heard the phone ring and ring and ring. It was a Saturday, and I figured Uncle was playing golf. My aunt must have taken Hope out for her dance lesson. It was almost eleven. The two of them should have been home by now.

I finally strolled into the kitchen, still wearing pajamas, and picked up the phone.

It was my mother.

"Oh, honey, I am having the best time. Bob's working. I'm in Florence, the most beautiful city in the entire world. How are things with you?"

"I'm fine."

"So good to hear it. I bought you a lovely jewelry box."

"I don't own any jewelry."

"You have a watch, right? You have some cufflinks, don't you?" She went on and on, sounding so animated and lively. I kept quiet. The last few phone calls, she hadn't sounded so chirpy. This trip excited her. I figured, let her share the joys and wonders of Europe while I'm here suffering from the death of Bonnie and Clyde and struggling with homophobic slurs uttered by leather-jacketed cretins. "Someday you're going to have to visit the David. Oh my God, Haskell. He is exquisite." She paused, finally. "Why are you so quiet?"

"You woke me up."

"Isn't it after eleven, for God's sake? What's going on? Tell me everything. I don't care how much this call costs. I'm all ears."

"I am a little down. That's all."

"Talk to me."

"I haven't had my Sanka yet."

"Speak up. What's going on?"

"Well, I'm worried about the shoot in a foreign country with fourteen boys I don't know. Plus, I get seasick. Working on a boat could be a problem."

I was making this up, of course.

"Silly, the boat's in dry dock most of the time." I knew this. "In fact, Tony said half the film will be done on the backlots at Universal. They're only filming a few scenes on an island off the coast of Buenos Aires. You'll be back from there in thirty days."

"I thought we were filming interiors there as well."

"No, darling. You'll be in L.A. I'm almost sure of it. You heard Warwick decided to let René Clément direct the film?"

"I did."

"Did you see *Pardon Me, I'm French*? It's wonderful. He's such a talent. Totally unconventional. New Wave."

"I heard he doesn't speak a word of English."

"That won't stop him. It will be just fine."

The garage door opened. That meant my aunt and Hope were home, so I stretched the phone cord until it was long enough for me to duck inside the front hall closet and sit cross-legged on the floor. I wanted privacy. If I were experiencing a nervous breakdown, what better place than here among the raincoats, winter parkas, a half-dozen umbrellas, and my aunt's floor-length mink coat.

"I'm not getting off this line until you tell me what's going on. I hear sorrow in your voice."

"I had a rough night."

"Well, we've all had rough nights. I'm sure the worst is over."

"I think the worst is not over. I think in some way I'm facing a gloomy and disturbing future."

After I said those words, I regretted them. Why pounce on my mother? This was a long distance phone call. Very expensive. It wasn't the time for me to bare my soul and complain wildly about injustice and prejudice.

"I heard from your Aunt Sheila that you've had some very nice things happen to you. You had a sleepover. You went to a drama party. You're making all sorts of new buddies. I'm so proud of you. You're doing well in school. And you landed this amazing part in a major Hollywood movie. It sounds to me like the world is your oyster. Aren't you glad I ripped you from your world in New York and gave you your wings?"

"I'm glad."

"Good. I never ever, ever got into a major film like the one you're about to do. My films had zero budget. Mr. Warner wouldn't even film *Love in Athens* in Athens! We filmed in Burbank and Thousand Oaks, of all places. This movie? It has a wonderful budget. What opportunities you have ahead! I'm so happy for you. You might want to practice your Spanish, no?"

"That's not a bad idea. I don't know any Spanish. And if you want to know the truth? I feel completely unprepared for what's ahead of me."

I should not take this out on my mother.

"Mom, I'm getting off the phone. This is costing you a fortune."

"Let me worry about that. You sound very perturbed. Tell me what's going on?"

I could tell her I was upset about the ending of *Bonnie and Clyde*, but then I'd be giving the ending away. I even thought I'd blame it on Henry and his burst of actor's envy. I might even whine about the Morals Clause I had signed.

Oh, what the hell. I'd spit it out.

"Mom?"

"What is it, darling?"

"I think I may be in love."

"Wonderful. I'm delighted to hear that. Who is the lucky girl?"

"It's a boy, mom."

Hardly a pause. "His name?"

"Nate, and I held hands with him tonight in public. We nearly got killed by a gang of hoodlums."

"Well, that's not good, is it? Though there's nothing horrible about holding a hand."

"This group of hoodlums started yelling horrible things at us. 'Die faggots, die.' I've been called a lot of names, but they were quoting from the Bible and shouting awful things."

I heard only silence on the other end.

"Haskell? There's a lot of stupidity in this world."

"I don't know what I'm going to do. I think about what Reynaldo went through, and I worry about what I may be facing, day after day. And even more importantly, if the studio found out, they'd fire me. I'd never work in Hollywood again. It seems so unfair. If we love each other—Nate and me—why can't people accept that? What's the big deal?"

"People can be cruel for the oddest reasons."

"I'm sure Aunt Sheila would be angry if she found out I'm a homo. I've lied to her now numerous times. Uncle Ted will also be disappointed. I'm not sure what Hope would think, but she'd tell everybody. That's for sure."

"Who cares what they think?" she finally said. "Really, who cares? You love him. First love? It's a wonderful feeling, isn't it?"

I cleared my throat. "Mom, let's talk later."

I hugged my knees and rocked back and forth. Unable to control these spurts of crying, I finally muffled them with my hands.

"First of all, you have this wonderful future ahead of you. You won this part because of your uniqueness and talent. Whoever you are sexually fits neatly into that package and no one will take that away from you. You're not going to be the only gay actor working in Hollywood. Let me tell you that. I know dozens. Dozens, and they do fine. It takes some work. Some crafting of situations, but you'll figure it out."

"I'm tired of this hiding and pretending."

"Well, it's good you recognize that. Get some more sleep. You'll feel better."

"I don't know if I want to live a secret life. I know this sounds weird, but there was something so liberating when I grabbed Nate's hand as we walked out of the movie theater. I want to be with him and not feel paranoid every single day. I want to feel joy when I touch him, not fear."

"Give it time. Things will get better."

"I doubt it. I realized today that Nate and I are like in a different universe, totally unaccepted by the rest of the world."

"Don't say that. You have to be discreet, that's all."

"Henry didn't have to be discreet. He drove up to school today, a big smile on his face, and this girl climbed into his car, and he hugged and kissed her there in the parking lot. And you know what? No one cared. No one gave it a second glance. If Nate did that to me, we'd be committing a crime."

"One thing to remember is that the world isn't always fair and doesn't always make sense. In spite of this, you must keep your spirits up. You can't let all this get to you. Certain things we have no control over, so you know what you have to do, right? You decide how you want to live your life. You make it work within the boundaries of what's acceptable in this society of ours. So what if you can't show affection in public? You'll work around it. When Bob and I check into a hotel, we pretend we're married. Simple as that. And when I'm around his children, I don't dare even pat his arm or touch his hand. There are certain rules we all have to follow. You won't be the only male movie star with a boyfriend. You'll have lots of company, and you'll watch and see how others navigate the world. It won't be easy. You know that. But you're young, and the world will eventually change as you grow older."

"It won't change."

"Of course, it will. The world always changes. Believe me, being the only woman in a real estate agency in 1950 is very different from being one of many in 1966. When I started out making movies in 1940, everything was very different from the gritty films they make today. The world will change and before you know it, it will adjust to the idea of two men or two women loving each other. I guarantee you, over time, people will learn the power of acceptance. What's there not to accept?"

I closed my eyes, took some deep breaths, and tried soaking in these words of encouragement.

"Know this for sure—I love you, darling. I'm throwing you a kiss. Throw me one back."

I made a kissing sound with my lips.

"Oh!" She gave this slight noise, almost as if it were a hiccup. "I can't believe how late I am. We have reservations at Anton's, and I hear the *Tagliatelle Funghi Porcini e Tartufo* is divine."

Tartufo? I'd have to look that word up.

She hung up. I dropped the phone onto the floor and hugged my knees tighter against my chin. At this moment, I realized how much I missed talking with my mom. It just wasn't the same thing when I shared stories with my aunt or my uncle. My mom was the real thing, especially when she was fully present, listening with both ears.

What scared me the most was falling in love with someone and keeping him and my feelings to myself. How would I come out and be true to who I am? Would there ever be a time when it would be safe for people like Nate and me to hold hands?

Lots of questions ran through my head. I nearly fell asleep until I heard a knock on the door.

"Haskell Rascal? We've been looking all over the house for you. Are you in there?"

I opened the door slightly, and Hope stood pressing her hands against her cheeks, mouth wide open, eyes nearly popping out of their sockets.

"What are you doing in the closet, Haskell Rascal? Oh my God. Mom! Dad! Something's wrong with Haskell. Hurry! He's on the floor, glaring at me like he's sick or something." And with that, my cousin screamed at the top of her lungs, waking me out of my gloomy reverie. I figured I couldn't sit here all day feeling sorry for myself. I had to face my future, even if it scared the hell out of me.

Acknowledgments

Writing a book is harder than I thought. Every once in a while I wish I had chosen something else to do. But writing a novel is a dream that simply would not go away, and I had a wonderful, loving partner who was always there for me. None of this would have been possible without Gordon. His extensive detailed comments as well as his difficult questions were instrumental in helping shape the book's direction. I could not have completed this novel without him.

I also want to thank Lorna Partington Walsh for her wry, witty comments and edits on the many early drafts.

In the summer of 2018, I attended The Writer's Hotel Conference in New York, and I had an inspiring mentor, Sapphire, who truly believed in Haskell and gave me great hope and encouragement. Also, Scott Wolven, and Shanna McNair were instrumental in shaping early versions of the story. I am so appreciative.

Thanks also to my wonderful friends whom I have known since my college days at Rutgers: Linda Roemer, Howard Grimwood, and Joseph Boles. Each of them gave me critical feedback that helped make this book better, as did Shoshanna Brower, fellow trainer and good friend, whose notes on the final version of this book became especially helpful.

I'm not sure if I would have completed this project without the feedback of my weekly writing workshop, 9 Bridges at the Zweet Cafe. Special thanks to the entire group, especially Geneva, Jill, Gobind, Paul, Tish, and Bill.

Thanks to everyone on the Acorn team who helped make this novel come to life. I'm so grateful for Molly Lewis, who did the final edits of this book, as well as the geniuses behind Acorn Publishing—Holly and Jessica. I'm also especially grateful for Debra Kennedy, who formatted and proofread the manuscript.

Finally, I'd like to thank my family for their constant encouragement and support.

Made in USA - Kendallville, IN
1094960_9781947392663
04 29 2020 1141